PRINCE CHARMING, INC.

JAMIE BRAZIL

SOUL MATE PUBLISHING

New York

PRINCE CHARMING, INC.
Copyright©2011
JAMIE BRAZIL

Cover Design by Rae Monet, Inc.

This book is a work of fiction. The names, characters, places, and incidents are the products of the author's imagination or are used fictitiously. Any resemblance to actual events, business establishments, locales, or persons, living or dead, is entirely coincidental.

Published in the United States of America by
Soul Mate Publishing
P.O. Box 24
Macedon, New York, 14502

ISBN: 978-1-61935-095-3
eBook ISBN: 978-1-61935-002-1

www.SoulMatePublishing.com
The publisher does not have any control over and does not
assume any responsibility for author or third-party Web sites
or their content.

In memory of Mark "Kit" Kittleson,

adventurer,

chicken fried steak connoisseur,

and self-styled Buddhist.

Acknowledgements

Special thanks to Debby Gilbert for taking a leap into fiction during what may be publishing's most historically-important era.

To my family, for always being there, always reading the latest draft.

To Frank Haak, best critique partner ever from the first cold read to the final edit.

To Amanda Westmont for her honesty. Yes, the humorous internalizations worked better as dialogue.

To Romance Writers of America and especially the Rose City Romance Writers for showing me the way when I was lost.

Chapter 1

"Yes!" Elyse Tobin yelled toward the locked bathroom door as her best friend rattled the knob from the other side. "Yes, I'm *still* in here."

Stuck. Completely and utterly stuck.

"Well you better hurry up because they're about to toss the bouquet," Jackie complained.

Great. The bouquet toss was the whole reason she'd been trying to leave the reception early. After six walks down the aisle in a supporting role, she did her best to avoid this ridiculous wedding tradition. Catching a bunch of flowers was risky at best. Taking a chance at getting hitched? No way. Tobin women were proud feminists who, for generations, had shunned the need for men.

Well, not entirely. Men were good for some things, like procreating more Tobins. Though so far, pushing the ripe old age of thirty, Elyse hadn't gotten around to expanding the Tobin gene pool. Yet.

And if she didn't soon, she'd be the last Tobin.

In the meantime, she chose to remain single. With a stash of street clothes hidden in the bathroom, she was always the first to leave, long gone before flowers went airborne. Just not today.

Not after the bridesmaid's dress from hell had attacked.

This whole mess had started innocently enough with a stuck zipper. So why not turn the gown inside out and pull it off over her head? Grabbing the hem, she'd slithered her way out. Almost.

The wire bodice dug into her chest.

The zipper chewed into her scalp.

And the multiple layers of salmon-pink crinolines wadded around her head, blinded her.

Deep within the layers of gown, Elyse winced with pain. She weighed whether or not to ask Jackie for help. Should she tear the dress off and possibly scalp herself? Or chance the humiliation if anyone were to see her like this?

"Elyse!" The doorknob rattled again. "Is everything okay?"

"I could use a little help." Unable to see a damn thing, she wobbled toward Jackie's voice. Good plan, if she hadn't tripped over her purse. Crashing to the marble floor, she sat there stunned. The cold chill of the tile numbed her butt cheeks through her underwear.

She moaned, frustration mounting.

"Are you alone in there?" Jackie quizzed.

"Of course!"

"Hey, don't bite my head off. Nick was staring at you through the whole wedding. I just thought . . ."

"You thought wrong." Elyse felt her face redden. How could Jackie think that? She'd made the *Nick* mistake once. Every woman did at some point.

Three years ago, in a weak moment, she'd slept with San Francisco's most notorious playboy who'd seduced his way through the upper crust of the Bay Area's female elite. Sure, one hot, sweaty night of unbridled lovemaking had been the greatest experience of her life. Sex with him had been so powerful, so all-consuming, Elyse knew this mistake could never be repeated.

Ever.

Nick had changed her life.

Okay, maybe he'd just changed her career.

Still, there was no denying Nick's effect on most women. Luckily, raised in the tradition of Tobin self-reliance, Elyse dismissed any fairy-tale notions of forever.

She'd banished Nick and all his charms from her kingdom.

Still, he had the worst habit of turning up in all the same places she frequented, despite her best efforts to avoid him like the plague.

"He's really not the big, bad wolf you make him out to be," Jackie insisted.

"I never said he was a wolf." He wasn't. He was a dog. A dog crossed with Satan wearing a tux. Elyse scooted across the floor.

"Just finish whatever you're doing and get out here. There's some stiff competition for the bouquet. Kinsey Adams already elbowed her way to the front of the pack."

"Do you still keep those little folding scissors in your purse?" Fighting through the layers of tulle over her head, Elyse struggled to her feet and groped for the doorknob.

"Once a Girl Scout, always a Girl Scout," Jackie said through the door, then asked, "What do you need scissors for?"

"I just need them, okay?" Elyse sighed as her imagination raced. If she didn't get help soon, she'd probably die from the exhaustion of trying to get out of this thing, the cleaning staff would stumble across her lifeless couture-swaddled body, and she'd become a cautionary tale. The crazy socialite who died trying to shimmy out of a form-fitting dress.

Not that she cared about fashion. She wasn't even a real socialite.

She was a matchmaker. More than that, actually. Head Mistress, so to speak, of an unofficial school for Prince Charmings. She turned out perfect grooms for wealthy, high-maintenance brides. Her business was a little unconventional, but it made for a terrific life.

Elyse loved weddings. The guests and family arriving in a line of white limousines. The orchestra playing as the bride marched to the waiting groom under an outdoor arbor of climbing white roses. The crisp lines of perfectly-prepared food and the heady scent of the flowers.

Pure magic.

It was also nice that the bridesmaid dress came with a sizable check. A gift for her services.

The only thing she loathed about the whole project was the bouquet toss. A useless superstition.

"Found them," Jackie chirped. "Should I slide the scissors under the door?"

"No." Through the folds of dress, Elyse felt the doorknob. Jackie, her very first client, was just on the other side. Soon she'd be free and no one the wiser.

Though if anyone saw her in her bra and panties with her dress wadded around her head, they'd have an eyeful. Not that she minded her body, she was slender enough and of average height. Her legs were a touch on the short and stubby side. Blame her mother's eastern European genetics for that. And maybe there was a hint of *muffin top* threatening her otherwise narrow torso. Nothing that couldn't be solved with sit-ups. Or avoiding the cheesecake at La Sals. On second thought, she'd rather buy a new wardrobe than skip the cheesecake.

The cake was that good.

Back to business.

Elyse wanted out of the dress.

Her hand seized the doorknob and flipped the lock. "I just need your help."

Jackie, an auburn-haired bridesmaid, pushed the door open. "Oh my . . ."

Behind Jackie, there was a flood of sounds. Feet hurrying across tile floor. Women chatting excitedly. *The bride's coming, I want the bouquet, It's mine this time.* Elyse's stomach lurched. Through the tunnel vision of the dress bundled around her head, she saw the outline of twenty women, and one very close, tuxedo-clad man.

Nick.

Parting the crinolines, Nick excavated the layers of fabric and came face to face with her. "Elyse, is that you in there?"

She inhaled his expensive scent. Spicy, with citrus, and a hint of something else. Toothpaste. Cinnamon toothpaste. Their eyes met, and he smiled two rows of perfect gleaming teeth.

She glowered back at him.

Jackie pushed past Nick in the doorway. "I didn't mention that Nick just walked up, did I?"

Elyse slammed the door in his face.

She wanted to scream. "You let everyone see me like this?"

"Just Nick."

Nick Salvatore. Swarthy good looks, impeccably tailored suits, manicured nails and a lean, karate-toned body that made women swoon. Unfortunately, Nick was also self-aware. He knew he had the whole package. Manners, charm, and a suspect personal agenda. He was a bad boy, a man of many accomplishments, and an attentive lover all rolled into one. Nick was the ideal.

"Don't worry," he called through the door. "I'm sure no one else knows it's you."

"Go away, Nick," Elyse shouted, then turned toward Jackie for help.

"What are you doing wearing your bridesmaid gown as a hat?" Jackie asked as she prodded and pulled at the dress.

"Ow. Stop it," Elyse protested. "It has my hair." She could feel Jackie tugging the dress this way and that until they came face to face.

Jackie held up her little scissors. "I'll have you out of here in two snips, if you'll line up for the bouquet toss."

"That's blackmail," Elyse objected.

"It's a wonderful tradition."

"It's a death sentence."

Jackie scissored her little blades in the air. "No bouquet. No freedom."

Elyse shook the folds of her straightjacket. "Help me or I'll shred this thing."

"It's couture!" There was horror in Jackie's voice, then snipping sounds. "I can't believe you'd threaten an innocent dress."

"I'm desperate."

"Your hair should be okay."

Elyse twisted inside the dress. It didn't hurt, but she was still stuck. "Help me pull it off."

"Are you sure there's nothing I can do?" Nick questioned through the door.

"What don't you understand about *go away*?" Elyse shouted.

"Don't pay any attention to her," Jackie said. "She's just having one of her moods."

"My moods?"

"You have several moods with Nick." Jackie smiled, and whispered, "Most of them angry."

"He pisses me off." It was true. He was a womanizing lothario, yet he was wonderful in every other way. Unless, of course, you didn't want him, then the man was just annoying.

"They're going to toss the bouquet any minute now." Nick knocked urgently. "Shall I save a spot up front for you?"

"She'll be right out, Nick." Jackie wrapped two fistfuls of fabric in her hands.

"On three?" Elyse asked.

"Sure," Jackie said, and yelled, "Three!"

The zipper burst open as Jackie pulled and Elyse reared backwards. The dress and bodice gave up and tore off, inside out. Elyse fell back and landed on the toilet with a solid thump. Minus a clump of hair, but free.

After a stunned moment, she donned the sweater and

jeans she'd stashed earlier.

"He's sweet on you," Jackie spoke in a hushed voice. "Why can't you just accept it? Give in."

"I will not. I don't want to see Nick. I don't want to catch a bouquet. And I absolutely don't want a husband."

"Fine," Jackie replied. "You can move in here. It's nice. Maybe you could put a little sofa next to the toilet."

"You are so mean."

"He's waiting for you."

Defeated, Elyse knew she'd lost her chance to slip out unnoticed. She'd have to face the music. Nick, bouquets, all of it. "You win. Let's get this over with."

"It'll be fine." Jackie linked arms with Elyse and swung open the door. "You might even have a good time."

Elyse took one step into the foyer and faced Nick. Damn, he looked good. Just being near him made her feel all hot and bothered. She cringed, hating herself for wanting him. Their one night together was never to be repeated. Taking a deep breath, she pushed forward.

"Move aside," she commanded.

Nick stepped aside. A dozen feet behind him, a crowd of young women faced the opposite direction, waving their arms. It took her a moment to understand what was going on. It was one moment too long.

Elyse stepped straight into the flight path of the bouquet toss.

The floral missile, flung backwards from the bride standing in the front door of the mansion, sailed just above the fingers of the unmarried crowd. As floral arrangements go, this one was very nice. The scent of white roses and freesias filled the air as the bouquet smacked Elyse square in the face.

She staggered back a step as Jackie lunged forward and grabbed the flowers. "Elyse got the bouquet!" she called victoriously.

Silently, Nick slid up next to her. "Congratulations, Elyse," he said in a voice that reminded her of the snake in the Garden of Eden. "I hope I'm there for your big day."

"Don't hold your breath," she warned as a tingle ricocheted through her body before landing between her legs. The man was dangerously sexy. Avoiding him was her only hope of not landing in his bed. Again.

Watching Elyse Tobin storm out the entrance, Nick Salvatore knew two things for certain. One was that he wanted another night with her. The second wasn't important enough to remember.

Keeping tabs on her as she paced through the parking lot, he smiled. She wasn't hard to miss. With her bright orange, ostrich-leather Hermes carryall slung over her shoulder and the salmon pink gown wadded up under her arm, crinolines trailing behind her, she made quite the spectacle.

Passionate, independent, opinionated, Elyse wasn't anything like her high society friends and clients. No, there was a fire in her. Three years ago, in a frenzied night of lovemaking, her intense heat had ignited his curiosity. True to her roots and defiantly unconventional, she'd captured his heart and imagination, too.

The trouble was, she wanted nothing more to do with him, and Nick had no idea why. He didn't even know what it was about Elyse that made him react in a way that he never reacted. She flummoxed him.

It made no sense at all.

"Nick, have you seen Elyse?" Jackie rushed up to him, still holding the bouquet.

He nodded, shifting his eyes to the lot.

She still hadn't found her car, a little black Prius with tinted windows adrift in a sea of little black Prius cars with tinted windows. Eco-de-rigueur, anyone under thirty-years-old in their set drove the same gas sipper.

"Thanks!" Jackie raced out to catch her ride home. "Elyse, wait for me."

Ambling between the small vehicles, Nick came up behind them as they tried to peer through the dark windows. "Lose something?"

Elyse flashed a glare at him. "My car."

"Use the alarm," he suggested.

"I think I've already drawn enough attention to myself for one day," she said as she glanced back toward the house where the bride and groom waved to the crowd and climbed into a limousine.

"Just trying to help."

She moved away from him, peered in another car, then keyed the lock. "I got it, Jackie!"

Nick pondered her as she jumped into her compact Toyota with Jackie and they drove away.

He'd been with lean, sleek models and more than his share of actresses. While they were stunning to look at, there was always something missing. He didn't know what it was. But he knew that Elyse had it.

He knew it the night she gave in to his wiles, and her own desires. Ever since, he'd been drawn to her like a moth to a bug zapper. He laughed to himself. No one here had any idea where he was really from. No one cared. He liked that about San Francisco. Gay, redneck, artist, billionaire, everyone was welcome. Though to stay in the upper crust, you either had to be of service, or one of them.

He and Elyse were more alike than even she knew.

That's what had nailed him. For three years he'd waited for another chance. He was getting tired of waiting.

Still, he couldn't help but love her. He was smitten.

Elyse glanced over at Jackie riding in the passenger seat. She held the wedding bouquet and a pink envelope in the lap of her bridesmaid dress. "I love the bouquet toss," Jackie said wistfully.

"Not me!" Elyse disagreed.

She could feel Jackie studying her. "You'll come around."

"Don't hold your breath."

Jackie was from another world. One of privilege. Privilege from birth. Her Nob Hill condo had been a gift for her twenty-first birthday. Jackie was a Stanford-educated, classic Anglo-Saxon beauty that never had to worry about anything . . . except finding someone to truly love her.

"Why do you always go this way?" Jackie complained. "They built a freeway for a reason."

Elyse piloted the Prius through the old section of San Francisco. To most people, it was a tedious drive through bland commercial buildings. To Elyse, it was a tour of history.

"There's nothing to look at on the freeway," Elyse repeated for the hundredth time. She loved Jackie like a sister, but she'd never understand the importance of overlooked architecture. "These buildings are wonderful."

"They're old," Jackie sighed.

"They're classic. Look at that one!" Elyse pointed to a four-story concrete brick building. "It's perfect."

"It's a wreck," Jackie countered. "It's crumbling."

Old buildings fascinated Elyse. Her favorites were the ones that had survived the Great Earthquake of 1906. They may have been shaken, but they were still standing. They were survivors. "It's got beautiful iron work."

"Moldy green iron work."

Jackie was like a lot of San Francisco's upper class, they wanted everything shiny and new. Elyse didn't have anything against shiny and new, but there was room for the old and austere, too. "Look at the cornices. And the base."

"It's a waste of real estate."

"See any cracks?" Elyse asked.

"No."

"We live in earthquake central. That's a solid foundation. Why don't people see this? Men and buildings are the same thing. You didn't complain when I found Donnie for you."

"You cleaned him up first," Jackie replied. "And I didn't have to drive through old sections of town to get him."

"I think you'd drive to the ends of the Earth for him." She knew it was true. Jackie and Donnie were coming up on their third anniversary. Elyse was proud of the match and close to both of them.

"So how far would you go for Nick?" Jackie asked, giving in.

Elyse shot her a nasty look. "To get away from him?"

"You always said Nick was *the base* for all your Prince Charmings."

"Maybe." Elyse shrugged. She'd built all her grooms on the Nick Salvatore ideal. "It's the structure that counts."

"So what is he?"

It took Elyse a second. What was Nick? First off, he was a mistake. One she'd never make again. But if he was a building, he'd be modern. Steel and glass. Strong and transparent at the same time. "Let's put it this way, if Donnie is a solid four-story courthouse, Nick is a brand new nightclub."

"Nightclubs are fun," Jackie said, encouragingly.

"For a night. You don't settle down with one." Elyse turned the Prius up a steep hill, and the gas engine kicked in. Three years ago when Jackie was at the end of her romantic rope, she'd confessed all her longings and desires to Elyse. All she wanted was a good, solid man that she could trust to be home on time. She wanted loyalty and routine.

Jackie waved the pink envelope and put down the bouquet. "Is this the last one?"

"The last groom? I wish." Six marriages down, Elyse closed in on her goal, but wasn't quite there yet. Maybe one or two more marriages, and she'd have enough money to start thinking about her own happily ever after. Tobin-style.

Like her mother, and her grandmother, and her great-grandmother before that, she wanted it all. The home, the man, the children, she just didn't want to get married and be subjected to male domination.

Ripping open the envelope, Jackie stared at a cashier's check. "Your prices have gone up. A hundred thousand for one husband? Donnie only set me back ten grand."

"You were my starter bride. No warranties on him."

She needed the money for this groom. Badly. It was a cliché, but her house was a money pit. Since she'd graduated with an associate degree in web design, every penny she made went into her home. "That check will barely cover the renovations to the fourth floor plumbing I had done."

"You have to keep the pipes clean," Jackie said slyly. "Speaking of Andrew, any plans for Mr. Good Wrench?"

"Down, girl. You're a married woman." Elyse grinned. Jackie and Donnie were her first couple. It had come about by sheer accident. Jackie was the only person who was nice to her at a hoity-toity charity event. They were both there stag. They talked. They drank. They complained about the lack of good men in San Francisco.

Two things happened that night. She and Jackie became friends. And she met Nick.

On first glance, she wasn't even sure he was straight. When he'd introduced himself, he seemed over-polished. His clothes were immaculate. From all her experiences, *real heterosexual men* weren't supposed to be overly groomed or too comfortable at social functions. Nick was. Nick was like a fish in the ocean . . . his ocean.

He'd also admired her Hermes purse way too much. She'd never known any man to give a damn about accessories, at least any man that might have an interest in sleeping with her. She decided there were only two options for Nick, gay or gigolo. After a couple gin and tonics, either seemed entertaining, and she decided to find out.

She did.

Six times over the course of that fateful night in a suite at the Regency Hotel. The man had been a stallion in bed. She'd let go that night. The emotion from her mother's then-recent death, the end of a long-time relationship, the responsibilities of home ownership, her disappointment in her career options, all came flooding out of her like a river overflowing its banks. A dam of emotion, lust and craving, pent up for years, burst.

Through it all, Nick had been the perfect gentleman. He listened when she needed to talk and made love to her after each wave crested. The greatest night of her life had felt like ten years of therapy rolled into one long session of incredible sex.

"You're thinking about Nick!" Jackie shouted.

"What? No!" She hated it that Jackie read her so well.

"You had that wistful look again."

"There are no stars in my eyes." There weren't. Not for Nick.

Elyse thought about the day after that incredible night . . . when she found Donnie. There may not have been stars in her eyes, but there were tears. From paint thinner fumes.

It was her habit to haunt the antique district every other weekend. That's why she'd slipped out of the hotel suite and away from a sleeping Nick to walk the aisles of Granny's Antique Alley. There was no way she'd allow a man like Nick get under her skin. Sure, his skills as a lover were beyond compare. Top that off with looks and charm. But to let herself think for one minute that a man like Nick might become the lover in her bed, the father of her children, pure foolishness.

Yet it was so easy to fantasize about just that.

She reminded herself over and over that men like him didn't choose strong, independent women like her.

As she had paced through the vendors' spaces cramped with Partridge Family lunchboxes, military paraphernalia and turn-of-the-century kerosene lamps, she wondered why there weren't more men who had a moral base, but the mannerisms of a Nick Salvatore.

Why were the good men so inattentive, and the bad men such a draw?

She thought she was going to faint from the stench of the 19th century paint lacquers. A strange little man had a dozen cans open. This was Donnie. He was a fine art restorer for the San Francisco Heritage Society on a mission to find linseed oil from the late 1800s. He wasn't much to look at. His eyeglasses seemed permanently askew. His fly, open. His shirt, wrinkled and untucked. But there was something about him.

A spark.

The man was obsessed, and that meant there was passion inside him.

That's when Elyse decided to experiment. Could someone with passion be redirected? Was it possible to take a man who was the walking-talking-breathing definition of *hopeless eternal bachelor* and train him as a loving and committed partner?

As the Prius rolled up to Jackie's Nob Hill condo, the answer stood on the sidewalk walking their dog, a Papillion. Donnie was a perfect man. He was dressed simply, but nice. A sport coat, chinos, and comfy French shoes. Lasik eye surgery got rid of the glasses once and for all. Exterior work was easy. The inside of Donnie had taken longer.

Elyse hadn't expected the long process. Changing

a man was like turning an ocean liner around. In the beginning, it was easy to get their attention with a hint of romantic possibility, but it took a lot more to steer the ship into uncharted waters. Little by little, date by date, she'd become his best friend, confidant, and a guiding hand. Bad habits were rooted out and good ones practiced. In the end, months later, Elyse introduced her man-creation to a lonely, hopeful, and well-moneyed woman.

Jackie jumped out of the car and planted a big kiss on Donnie's lips. He lit up. If Donnie were a dog, he'd be wagging his tail.

"How was the wedding?" he asked.

"Another success." Jackie petted the Papillion. "Hello, Poppy."

"Hi, Donnie," Elyse called from the Prius without getting out. "Looking good."

"I picked this out myself," he said, holding open the jacket.

"It's perfect."

She could see in his face that Donnie was proud of what he had become under her tutelage. She had given him a wife and home. Now, he had more in his life than he could have dreamt of. Elyse waved and sped away, leaving Jackie and Donnie in each other's arms.

Hauling in a deep, cleansing breath as she steered for home, Elyse felt satisfied. She patted the pink envelope on the passenger seat. Not everyone could do what she did. Rebuilding regular, everyday men had become her specialty. She was proud of her business.

At the same time, she knew it couldn't go on forever.

It was a short drive over the Golden Gate Bridge. The setting sun cast a pinkish glow on the hills of Sausalito. The modern glass-and-steel mansions, nestled among the

Victorians, reflected the warm light back to the bay. It was always a welcome sight to Elyse.

House after house clung to the steep grade of Ivy Loop. Though many had barely a walkway between structures, the street felt important. In all of the Bay Area, Ivy Loop was the only block-long cluster of original Queen Anne heritage homes that held their integrity and remained faithful to their architecture. There were no add-on bay windows, no slick steel shutters, no candy-color paint jobs, no obnoxious satellite dishes or solar panels.

To discover Ivy Loop was to step back in time. The houses looked exactly like they did over a hundred years ago, right down to copper rainspouts, wraparound porches, bracketed eaves, hooded moldings, and wrought iron cresting. Even the carriage houses that once kept horse and buggy dry stayed true to their original narrow dimensions, denying access to SUVs.

Elyse was a purist when it came to Queen Anne architecture, a die-hard history zealot whose heart had been stolen by the craftsmanship of another era.

Pulling to the curb in front of an imposing masterpiece, she peered up the thirty-two stone steps that led to her front door. She was home. This was her history, her family, her house.

Technically speaking, it wasn't entirely her house. Though it had been passed down from generation to generation, the bank still owned a good portion of 358 Ivy Loop. The four-story marvel had never been free and clear. Since her great- grandmother broke ground in the late 1800s, there had always been a mortgage payment due.

Inside, Elyse took a deep breath, inhaling the woody scent. The walls of the entry and adjoining formal parlor were linked with ornate woodwork, its glossy patina a testament to more than a century of regular polishing. Oriental rugs overlapped and angled across the expanse of oak flooring. Brass light fixtures hung from molded ceiling medallions. A built-in bookcase commanded the far wall, its shelves heavy under the weight of generations of knowledge. Couches and chairs, left over from the prohibition era, sat dutifully overstuffed. Doilies covered sun-bleached and worn armrests. But it was the hand-carved mantle, all fourteen majestic feet of it that centered the room.

The mantle always raised Elyse's spirits. Unlike the huge stack of bills that piled up inside the mail slot and on the bench opposite the front door. More than a foot deep, it had been awhile since she'd gotten around to bills and creditors.

When payments were late, the utility companies always called. Which was when she'd settle up her tab before they turned out the lights, refused to pick up her garbage, or shut off the water. They had her phone number.

She poked a toe at the pile to make sure there wasn't anything interesting. There wasn't. Besides, the only envelope of importance was the one she was holding in her hand. $100,000 was just enough to get her over the next hump. She'd deposit it Monday morning.

"Hello!" Elyse shouted to no one in particular. She thought Andrew might be lurking in the basement, but she never knew. That was the price of employing a mystery plumber.

While this latest financial "gift" helped, most of her money had to go toward the loan. She was working toward her goal. Paying off the house had been her great-grandmother's dream, and she was going to make it come true once and for all.

Great-Grandma Tobin had fallen in love with the view from this hillside while she and her young lover picked wild huckleberries. That was over a hundred years ago. She had to have it. Possess it. She borrowed money from every relative she had and bought a little square of land on the steep desolate hillside. Ivy Loop had no name then, and was just a dirt wagon track. That didn't stop Great-Grandma Tobin from hooking horse to trailer and hauling the stone, concrete and lumber up the hill. She broke ground in the late 1890s.

It had been the first house of what was now a crowded community.

Elyse cherished the history of her home. Four generations of Tobin women had worked, each in their time, to keep the house. It was a challenge to say the least. Renovations, mortgages, land developers. Men had come and gone, but the determination of the Tobin women kept the family home in place.

That was Elyse's goal. The completion of the dream. No mortgage. No debt. And the house in perfect condition. Once she had that, she'd think about making a perfect Prince Charming for herself.

Of course, if he decided to stay around, he'd have to change his name to Tobin. Any children would bear her surname. They would be the next generation to cherish the Queen Anne and its history.

"You know, there's a reason people invented PVC," Andrew called up from the basement. His voice was followed by the *thump thump thump* of heavy footsteps on the stairs. The door to the basement creaked open, and he stepped up from the stairway holding a ten-foot length of iron sewer pipe. The muscles in his arms were taut from the weight, but there was no shake to his hands. "Cheap and easy is okay with me."

Elyse tipped her head. Did he make a joke? A sexual joke? It caught her by surprise. Andrew was a master plumber, but he wasn't known for his wit. "My Great-Grandma Tobin said, *flimsy is as flimsy does*."

"And your great-grandfather probably died laying pipe

for her."

What? Was that another joke? "I haven't noticed you giving back any of the checks I write."

"Speaking of checks . . ."

She flinched. Money was the last thing she wanted to talk about. "So, what are we up to anyway?"

"We can put off my labor for a while," he said with a half-smile. "I know you're good for it. But I'll need four thousand for material."

Elyse couldn't imagine how he'd gone through the last few thousand. "Are you plumbing this place with gold?"

"It's all on the invoices. Copper in and iron out. As you ordered. I could have had the whole job done a year ago for a tenth the cost if you went with PVC."

"Sorry," Elyse apologized. "It has to be authentic. One hundred percent."

"No one will ever see the pipes."

"But I'd know." It was important to make the house exactly as it was originally built. She was going to finish her great-grandmother's dream and have it paid for. Every inch of the house would be exactly as it was designed, with the tiny exception of the fourth floor bath.

Andrew shook his head. "You're going to take another bath, aren't you?"

"It's my bath."

"Well, until it's all paid for, they're my drains. Stay in your tub for an hour, I don't care. But do not pull the plug. You do, your basement gets soaked."

"Okay."

"Don't forget."

"I won't forget."

"It's a reaction. People don't think. They just get out of the tub and pull the plug."

"I won't pull the plug," Elyse huffed.

Elyse loved her fourth floor bathroom. True to the word, it was a room defined by the bath.

On a platform raised up twelve inches, on its own dais, the turn of the century hammered copper tub gleamed. It could hold enough water to irrigate Wisconsin in a drought year and still soak two people comfortably. Not that there had ever been two people in it. Elyse ran her hands over the curved, textured edges. It took two water heaters far below in the basement, working together, to force a hundred gallons of steaming calm up four floors. Twisting her shoulder-length hair into a knot, she slid into the bath.

The scent of lilacs produced an instant euphoria. She inhaled deeply. It had taken her years to perfect this special aromatherapy bath. Like most people, she started with commercial bubbles and foams. Then one day, on a particularly prolific lilac year, so prolific that she had to prune the bushes back waist-high before they took over the entire postage stamp backyard, she was faced with a pile of yard debris that would take months to process through the every-other-week garden recycling container. Then inspiration struck.

Overwhelmed by the perfume-like fragrance of the flowers, she dropped some into a bath to add a hint of their bouquet. It also gave her aromatic spa bits of wood, blooms that tried to adhere to her skin, and insects that paddled along the surface of the water. The ultimate lilac bath became a quest. Drying the flowers made it easy to sift out the bugs and debris. An old cotton pillowcase, two handfuls of dried blooms inside, kept the water litter free and gave it the scent of spring, of hope.

In a mere two years, she became so proficient at harvesting the lilacs at their peak, processing them, then dividing the blossoms into individual Ziploc bags to be stored in a separate basement freezer, that she now had a lifetime supply of lilac packs at the ready.

Andrew had been quick to point out that she was nuts. More specifically, he'd said, "Who the hell buys a frost-free, Sub-Zero freezer for their bathtub habit?"

Men, they didn't understand. Especially Andrew. Perhaps the only man who'd possibly have an inkling of aroma-therapeutic bathing was Nick. Though he'd never be allowed to see the inside of her sanctuary.

The hot water splashed over her shoulders. She needed the complete calm of the perfect bath. She didn't want to think about bills or the house or the mortgage or where she was going to find another wealthy client that needed a husband.

Peering over the edge of the tub, outside the window, the bay and the skyline glowed in the distance. Elyse closed her eyes and let the subtle waft of flowers envelop her, determined to let the water soak away every ounce of stress, each moment of doubt, despair, or longing, and any other wayward emotion that had been left hidden in a dark corner of her mind.

It was a wonderful two minutes before the phone beside the tub rang. As much as she loved the bathroom and all that it stood for, she was having second thoughts about her decision to install the phone. It was irritating. Especially when she needed peace. The phone rang again and again. She considered not answering, but on the eighth ring she picked up.

"Hello," she said, annoyed.

Madeline Whittlesworth-Rothburg had a high, excited voice like a Shih-Tzu on amphetamines. To follow her train of thought was like a ride at Six Flags. If only she could stay on the tracks that long. Elyse had developed a Zen method of distilling Madeline's frantic ramblings into a condensed strand of rational thought. She would clear her mind and let the sentences wash through.

A friend in turmoil; rain in the Hamptons; coffee tonight

at Wedgeworth's; disparaging household staff; seven-thirty works for Jackie; was that a cat in the dahlias; a flower heiress in need; did cat urine kill aphids?

Elyse hated the dahlia garden, but "flower heiress in need" intrigued her. *In need* was code for a woman who had given up on traditional means of husband hunting and had, at long last, been informed of Elyse's Prince Charming service.

Madeline was great for business, but a bit eccentric to say the least. The woman had her gardener plant the dahlias because she loved to announce the word "Daaah-lia" like an English aristocrat. The garden was actually filled with chrysanthemums. No one had the heart, or the nerve, to break the news to her. "I'll see you at Wedgeworth's at seven-thirty," Elyse replied.

She smiled broadly and hung up the phone. There weren't many more old-money, unattached women in town. But maybe this flower heiress could be her ticket to a new group of unsatisfied, lonely female millionaires that roamed outside the confines of Nob Hill? To finish her house, she only needed a couple more clients with their grocery lists of seemingly elusive male qualities. Lists she'd gladly fill.

Elyse glanced at a black and white cat clock on the wall. The eyes tick-tocked back and forth as the tail swung. It was the only cat that would ever be in her home. A single woman, no matter how satisfied with her bachelorette life, had to be careful of her image. No one took a woman with cats seriously. Though she guessed that sometimes cats just happened.

The clock read six fifty-five.

Elyse jumped from the tub, grabbed a towel, pulled the plug, and yanked open a drawer filled with makeup. And somewhere in the distance, from far underground...possibly four...there came a howl of drenched anger.

Chapter 2

At 7:45, Elyse stood at the top of the marbled steps next to the marbled pillars that led to the marbled entrance of the very-marbled Wedgeworth's, San Francisco's most famed institution of haute cuisine. Of course, she was the first to arrive, being only fifteen minutes late. It was the pecking order. Jackie would arrive between 7:50 and 7:55, with Madeline making her entrance at 8:00. The schedule was simply the way it was in Bay Area society.

Waiting on the stairs with the salty night air gusting up from the ocean, Elyse checked the time as Madeline's Bentley rolled to a stop. She was the only one of her crowd who refused to give in and drive a gas-sipping planet saver. Then again, she was Madeline, and no one dared say a word.

This was wrong. Entirely wrong. Not the car, the time.

It was barely 7:50. Elyse bounded down the stairs two at a time and stepped up to the car. The passenger door opened, and a brunette woman in her 30s, overly serious, unfolded herself from within. Was this the flower heiress and the solution to her financial problems?

On the driver's side, Madeline continued a stream of speech as she handed over the keys to the valet who spirited the car away. "So bridge, as a card game per se, is far too complicated, much like the interpersonal relationships within an organization, such as the Amnesiacs Booster Club."

"I so agree," the brunette exhaled her words.

Madeline took a couple quick breaths as they walked toward Elyse. "They always forget to come to meetings, you'd think that with four suits and everything in numbered sequence that bridge would be simple, men, it's harder to find a good man than a trump in a deck of cards."

"Good evening," Elyse called.

Madeline waved and herded them to the entrance. "Speaking of men, we all wouldn't be happily married if it weren't for our little matchmaker, Elyse."

Elyse thrust out her right hand. "It's a pleasure to meet you."

"Yes, a pleasure." The woman folded her hands to her chest.

"Kisses!" Madeline demanded.

Leaning forward, Elyse and Madeline exchanged air kisses. "Thank you for calling me."

"Who else would I call?" Madeline winked. "Saban and I were just talking about you. Only good things, of course."

Madeline, at 40, was a matriarch in San Francisco society and a self-help author. Born old, along with her money, she'd never had children and wore wafts of her signature perfume. She helmed the boards of every major philanthropic endeavor in the Bay Area, and had entertained the governor at her estate. Eight times. A fact she allowed no one to forget.

To be in Madeline's favor was a coveted position reserved for those who had achieved, in her opinion, their higher calling. Elyse's higher calling, husband-making, had cemented her in a permanent *friend and confidant* standing.

"I am so glad you could pull yourself away to meet with us tonight." Madeline tilted her head and smiled knowingly at Elyse.

Elyse knew she didn't have a choice. Anything less than an audience with the President would be turned down to attend a Madeline summons. "Happy to be here."

"This," Madeline announced gesturing to the woman beside her, "is my new best friend, Saban Vandernacht, flower heiress."

Relieved she was real and not just someone Madeline had invented so she had even more to talk about, Elyse studied her. Small nose and chin. A forest of dark hair. A little hefty in the middle with spindly legs. But not hopeless. If she could find this woman a husband, her hundred grand fee equaled a free and clear mortgage. Well, almost.

She still had Andrew to settle up with and other random bills. But now was not the time to consider her personal finances and looming payments.

Saban stood tall. Tall and scowling. She scanned Elyse suspiciously. "So you're a matchmaker?"

"Matchmaker," Madeline squealed. "You have so much to learn. Where's Jackie?"

On cue, Jackie screeched her Prius to a stop in front of the valets. She jogged to Elyse, Madeline, and Saban. "I'm not late, am I?" There was concern in her voice.

"Not at all," Madeline soothed. "We're early."

"Madeline and I are both married, thanks to Elyse," Jackie enthused. She thrust out her left hand toward Saban and flashed a four-karat sparkler with its complementing wedding band. "You are going to be so happy."

Elyse noted Saban's reaction. She seemed to be mentally tabulating the cost-per-karat and unable to peel her eyes off the diamond. An obvious and covetous appraisal. A knot of anxiety twisted in Elyse's stomach. Who was this woman?

"For a hundred thousand dollars?" Saban sneered. "I better be so happy I can't walk for a month."

"Isn't she a wit," Madeline trilled. "And Sabby just loves *dahhhlias*. Her family has millions of *dahhhlias*."

"Tulips," Saban grumbled.

Madeline ignored Saban, trilled *dahhhlias* one more time, linked arms with Elyse and Saban and strode into the hallowed halls of Wedgeworth's.

For most of the people in California, Wedgeworth's signaled a level of grandeur accessible only to the upper crust. Stark white tablecloths set on the diagonal to show off the dark walnut table beneath. The chairs were austere, Louis XIV reproductions with the added comfort of well-padded seats. The servants, a word that would only be appropriate here since they willingly took the attitude of Masterpiece Theater characters, were extremely attentive. The customers were those who had clearly risen above the masses and gained a level of sophistication only dreamt of by the middle-class. Wedgeworth's was the American dream.

Just not Elyse's.

"Is it brighter in here than usual?" Jackie asked.

Madeline squinted at the crystal chandeliers. "Did you dust those?" she asked the host who escorted them to Madeline's permanently reserved table.

"Daily, Mrs. Whittlesworth-Rothburg," he answered with a tone of reserved respect. He pulled out Madeline's chair. She always sat in the same place, to the inch.

Elyse knew why. Madeline had table placement down to a science. Critical to see and be seen, yet not be too obvious about it, the table was situated an acceptable distance from the entrance so as not to advertise one's presence. The primary seat holder, Madeline, required a peek-a-boo view of the other patrons through strategically placed potted foliage. Foliage, for those in the know, that also afforded the lower climbers on the rungs of the social ladder, a glimpse back. But not a full gawk.

"I love this table," Elyse said, validating Madeline.

"It took us forever to choose it," Madeline replied in a mock whisper as the ladies took their seats. "It has the perfect placement. Far enough from the kitchen and not too close to the bar. The distance from the entrance to the ladies' room is exactly halfway."

Jackie leaned forward into the conversation, "I'm certain

that the social fate of more people have been determined at this table than in the state capitol."

"Well, of course, dear," Madeline oozed. "That's the point of having oodles of money and your own table at Wedgeworth's."

A waiter appeared. "It's a pleasure to see you again," he said with a soft, polite voice. "We have missed you the last few evenings."

"Busy, busy," Madeline replied. "Now that I'm married, I can only get out four or five times a week. Though I can always get out for a wedding. Absolute heaven today. Another win for the home team. And now Elyse is up next. You can't deny the power of the bouquet."

"It's just a tradition, not fate." Elyse felt a lump rise in her throat. Was she really going to bring this up now? In front of a prospective client?

"You will be so much happier. Marriage is your destiny."

"But I am happy now," she argued. Tucking a strand of hair behind her ear, her fingers grazed a small, sheared patch where the bridesmaid gown from hell had claimed a lock. The spot still smarted. "I'm happy that I have a talent for bringing great people together. Like you and Cyril."

Madeline loved being married, though finding her a mate had proven almost impossible. Eventually, Elyse had found him, and it was through Madeline's wedded bliss that, although lacking in funds, she'd been assured a spot in society.

"What would madams enjoy this evening?" the waiter asked.

Madeline didn't bother to unfold her reading glasses and instead waved them at the menu in front of her. "Decaf lattes and a sorbet. A tropical fruit. Then something chocolate. Cake. Yes, cake. Is Chef Patterson in the kitchen tonight?"

"Yes."

"I've been thinking of Spain. Marvelous foods. Wasn't

Columbus Spanish? That's probably how we got paella over here. They must grow olives, too. I love tapenade. Have Patterson make us some tapenade with toast points. Isn't that fun to say? *Tapenade!*"

In over a hundred visits to Wedgeworth's during the last three years, Elyse had never seen Madeline order from the menu. Instead, Elyse sat back and food was delivered to her without saying a word. The poor culinary staff was sent scrambling with every Madeline visit. A drought in Africa would inspire an order for a dried fruit tort. An Aquarius horoscope, a water sign, might result in a demand for poached scallops. The chef, always alert, had never disappointed. Elyse felt lucky that all she had to provide were husbands.

"That will be all," Madeline added, dismissing the waiter.

"So you're looking for a husband?" Jackie asked Saban as the waiter hurried away.

"Is she ever!" Madeline interrupted. "She was at the Children's Hospital Bachelor Benefit Auction waving her paddle at anything male. Isn't that an odd word? Benefit. Maybe it was a man named *Ben* who thought it was a good *fit* to organize fundraisers. It's probably Greek, though. God I love Sardinia in the spring. What's the Greek word for paddle?"

"You were trying to buy a man?" Jackie said with more than a bit of disbelief.

"She was bidding like a maniac," Madeline continued. "Especially for that pediatrician. A week at a Cook Islands getaway with him. Twenty thousand. Thirty. I trumped her at forty!"

Elyse turned to Madeline. "You bought a pediatrician?"

"God no." Madeline rolled her eyes for effect. "I'm quite happy with Cyril. I passed the doctor along to my niece, Tristan."

"I can't even buy a man," Saban confessed.

Jackie shook her head. "You can't buy love. Even for forty thousand dollars, you're just renting it for the week. Have you read any of Madeline's books?"

"Not yet."

Jackie nudged Madeline. "I think an intervention is necessary."

"Oh, I love a good intervention," Madeline replied, enthusiastically. "That's my next book!"

Saban shook her head. "All I need is a man."

Madeline patted her hand. "We'll get you a man and signed copies of all my books."

Jackie patted Saban's other hand. "Now confess all your inner doubts to Elyse so we can get started."

Saban scrunched up her face and forced a tear out of one eye. "I'm rich and alone, and I thought that bidding on a young doctor for charity might be a nice way to meet someone."

Madeline chuckled. "Baby doctors are not what you need. I know. The fundraiser was my idea. I love being on the board."

Jackie waved her diamond-heavy hand at Madeline. "Dear, you are the board."

"Yes, of course, and we have wonderful lunches every month," Madeline prattled on. "Last month we had venison. Why doesn't the meat of an animal sound like the animal? Deer, venison. Cow, beef. Sheep, mutton."

"There's chicken," Elyse added, only to be ignored.

"So after the auction, I heard sobbing in the ladies' room. In the stall next to mine was Sabby, poor thing. Of course, all I could see were her red Jimmy Choos. You can't turn away someone in Jimmy Choos."

"Jimmy Choos are nice," Elyse agreed as she watched Saban glance down at her slip-on patent-leather mules. At this moment Elyse was as conspicuous as the Queen of England at a garage sale. The shoes led to a scurrilous evaluation of her dollar-store stockings. Saban's eyes then trailed up to Elyse's simple black suit.

The jacket and matching skirt were from Wal-Mart. Elyse didn't care. She loved their "George" line. Easy clothes. Timeless styles. All in wrinkle-free polyester blends with good solid buttons sewn on tight. While Elyse liked to think of herself as understated, she could almost see the tickertape letters spelling out Saban's judgment: T-A-C-K-Y.

Elyse remained calm. She knew it was an undisputed fact that if you had one fashion-saving-grace, all else was forgiven. It was a societal predisposition, a code of honor, even among enemies. Great shoes relieved any transgression. What sin wasn't absolved in the presence of Blahniks? For others, the colorful drape of a Missoni scarf whisked the eye away from a Gap blouse. For Elyse, her social savior was her handbag.

Casually slung over the back of her chair, the shiny clasp of her Hermes handbag shone like a beacon of success. Despite the fact that it was the $25 rummage sale find of a lifetime, the very glint of the polished zippers, buckles, and telltale lock reflected well on her status. However, judging Saban's snide lip quiver in its direction, she realized Saban had already dismissed the bag as a knockoff.

Good accessories never lie. Elyse smirked, reached back for her purse and drew it to her lap. Like a Japanese Garden that takes hundreds of years to perfect, balancing color, sound and scent, Hermes had perfected its ultimate carryall bag. The luster of its shell denoted an unmistakable feminine strength. A flick of the hardware produced a quiet *thunk*, elegant and solid. Saban responded, narrowing her eyes and daring Elyse to prove her unspoken suspicion wrong.

She did.

Opening a Hermes bag was one of life's simple, yet deeply satisfying pleasures. Like sex, only better. A woman could surrender herself dozens of times a day, taking full gratification that the petal-soft inner folds were actually the foundation of something much greater than a purse. Men may come and go, but a Hermes was a guaranteed lifetime commitment.

Elyse opened her bag conspicuously wide, dispelling Saban's thoughts of a well-made forgery. The interior, as posh as the exterior, was revealed. But it was more than that that set the real thing apart from the fakes. Hermes bags held a heady, intoxicating scent. While cheap leather always smelled of leather, the subtle fragrance of a Hermes bore the unmistakable aroma of handmade French quality.

Saban listed toward Elyse, her nostrils flared accordingly.

Approvingly.

Elyse breathed a small sigh of relief. It was not only a test for Elyse, it was a test for Saban. Would she recognize the icon? She did. Saban belonged. Up until that moment, Elyse had been unsure. Perhaps she'd read the eye-popping covet of Jackie's ring all wrong. Maybe Saban was simply jealous that Jackie was married. While Saban had Madeline's approval, which was hard to come by in the first place, the flower heiress at her core still seemed, well, base.

Elyse set the purse down and turned to Saban. "You've given up on online dating, you're tired of attending social functions alone, all your friends are married, and you want me to fix that."

"So, you find men?" She sneered.

Madeline and Jackie turned on Saban like a pair of famished jackals on a cornered gazelle. "Dah-ling," Madeline bayed, "she resurrects men from their musty little ashes and remolds them into husbands."

Elyse stifled a laugh.

Jackie joined in for her share of the kill. "You've got horse trainers for horses."

"Dog trainers for dogs." Madeline leaned in close with Jackie.

Together, they chimed in unison, "Elyse is our own little man trainer."

Studies and statistics might claim that women of a certain age and income bracket have a better chance of being hit by lightning than getting married, but Elyse knew better. The odds were as fixable as the men themselves. Elyse was a godsend to women who had trudged past their thirtieth birthdays in a state of romantic defeat. Women like Saban.

It was nearly ten o'clock, the plates had been cleared from the table, and the four women sipped the last of their decaf lattes.

Elyse put down her cup, perturbed. "I'm not a magician. Finding the basic material of a single, straight man with morals in this city is not easy." Neither was striking a deal with Saban. "Then I have to recondition them."

Despite testimonials from both Jackie and Madeline, Saban didn't get the timeline at all. "I want a husband now," she whined.

"Be patient," Madeline said, comforting. "Elyse found partners for me and Jackie. Look at us now. We're happy."

"And you're desperate, Saban," Jackie added.

Saban pursed her lips, unhappy.

Most clients were just grateful to have Elyse on their side. Saban was different. Suspicious. If it hadn't been for her current financial situation, Elyse would have left over an hour ago. Instead, she forced a smile. "It's taken years to develop my method."

"I don't have years. My ovaries are frickin' time bombs."

Madeline laughed. "You see why I love her? *Time bombs!*"

Elyse cringed inwardly. She wasn't exactly a spring chicken herself. How many years did she have left before her monthly cycles slowed? Her reproductive years had sped by as she earned a useless college degree, then accidentally wound up being the matchmaking wunderkind to women who could afford to buy a mate. Though all wasn't lost. Not yet. Even though her thirtieth birthday loomed, lots of women got pregnant for the first time at that age. And if pregnancy was out of the question, she'd adopt.

But not before she was able to provide a secure and stable home for the next generation. She wanted a house full of life, of children. Which was why she was determined to pay off the mortgage, build an ideal man for herself, and then make sure every bedroom in her four-story Queen Anne was occupied by a Tobin.

Suddenly, she felt sympathy for Saban and her limited possibilities.

"It doesn't take years," Elyse soothed.

"I want a husband and the sooner the better." Saban put both elbows on the table. "I don't care how much it costs. You make husbands. Make me one."

Could she? Finding men was similar to finding great rummage at a tag sale. Usually it was simple, but the results weren't guaranteed.

For Elyse, finding treasure in a church basement was part intuition, part good sense, and always being a good judge of character. If you run with the stampede of buyers to the jewelry table, you won't get much. The smart move is wandering the aisles of tables and digging where the throngs of dealers aren't.

She'd found her Hermes purse that way. Giving it a little pat, Elyse's fingertips thrilled to the touch of luxurious Ostrich straps. It was her prized possession on the social battlefield of Wedgeworth's. The bag confirmed her place in society. She'd found the handbag rummaging through other people's cast-offs, a hobby that paid her way through college.

With a colonial chair here and a dresser there, bought for a couple dollars then flipped to an antique store for a hundred, maybe two, Elyse knew how to spot gems under a bad coat of paint.

Men were exactly the same. Most men developed a bad coat of paint over the years. Clothes, food habits, work obsessions, fanatic sports, and hobbies. Though not all men were gems underneath. Once she found a decent base to work with, she took time to carefully strip, polish, and place him where he would be appreciated.

Locating the right man for Madeline had been Elyse's most difficult assignment. Madeline was a relationship counselor, author by trade and philanthropist by birth. Which was to say that her main purpose in life was to spread her family's money around. The books and counseling were a sideline, something aimed at making her look somewhat useful and career-oriented.

So where could Elyse find a man who could perform the mental multi-tasking necessary to translate Madeline's thoughts?

The perfect man had to possess an extraordinarily high IQ to keep up with her, yet not have the common sense to run. Elyse took to the UC Berkeley campus and trolled the hallways for the right overachiever.

Having no luck at all, she retreated to the student union. It was there, over a cup of coffee that tasted like week-old chicory grounds strained through a gym sock, that she struck pay dirt. While nursing the suspect black liquid, a man in his mid-forties approached. He read while he walked, so deeply engrossed in his pages that he bumped through the crowd like a pinball. Focused and multitasking at the same time. He had potential.

As luck would have it, Professor Cyril Rothburg was a cryptographer, deciphering the codes and messages of ancient and extinct civilizations. It couldn't have been a better match. Making sense of Madeline's ramblings would be a cinch compared to Anasazi hieroglyphics.

"So," Saban demanded. "How long do I have to wait?"

Desperation was even less attractive on the rich. Elyse thought it was because it was quite a drop for them. They have careers, staff, money, events, and stylish people to lunch and gossip with. How could they be desperate?

"It depends on how selective you are," she answered.

"I'm not picky. I just want someone I can take to a fundraiser and not be embarrassed, then when we get home, he has to have manly skills to, like, unclog the sink before we get busy in the boudoir, if you know what I mean."

Elyse grinned. "You want a gentleman plumber."

"Can you fix one up?"

Elyse thought about Andrew's lean, sinewy muscles. How fast could she make him into a gentleman? Maybe this job was going to be a lot easier than she thought. The right men always fell into her lap.

With that thought, a man did just that.

Nick Salvatore flopped into Elyse's lap, face first. He lay there a moment. Elyse stared down at his mop of dark hair. What she would never admit to anyone was that she also found herself suddenly aroused.

"Your timing could be better, Nick." She kneed him in the chest.

He looked up, then at the table behind them. Elyse followed his gaze. A man was seated at the table with two well-attired women. He looked away innocently and slid his foot back under his chair.

"Excuse me, I seem to have misplaced my balance as

well as a good portion of my dignity," Nick said, standing up.

"I don't think balance and dignity were behind someone tripping you," Elyse replied.

"Ah yes. This may be a case of petty revenge." Nick straightened the lapels on his tuxedo. No faux pas was so big that a man in a tuxedo couldn't gloss over it.

"Hello, stranger," Saban swooned.

"Good evening, Elyse, Jackie, Madeline." Nick nodded to Saban. "I don't believe we've had the pleasure."

"Believe me, I'd remember if we had." Saban had the hungry look of a woman on a diet at a buffet.

That was Nick, chocolate to the starving. Elyse felt the draw, too. She wasn't immune, but she could still fight it.

Though no one in Wedgeworth's would dare stare, the sidelong glances were multiplying quickly. Madeline noticed. This was her sacred ground, and Nick had just sullied it. "I'm afraid this is a private affair, Nick."

She tried not to, but Elyse couldn't help the smirk that turned up the corners of her mouth. *Affair* was the right word to use when Nick was involved.

"Sorry to have intruded," he apologized.

"I don't think you're intruding at all," Saban blustered.

First the wedding, now Wedgeworth's. Elyse thought there should be a federal law that limited one's exposure to Nick within a 24-hour period. Usually she saw him no more than once a month, but lately, Nick sightings had picked up. So had her aversion to him.

Madeline leaned over the table toward Nick so that the other tables couldn't hear. "This is not the time or place to cause a scene. Call me later."

"Call me anytime," Saban echoed.

Elyse heard *the tone* in Saban's voice. It wasn't a good sign. To the uninitiated, the tone was nothing more than a woman's voice dropping an octave and drawing out a word.

Elyse knew exactly what it meant. Interest. And not in a *let's-be-friends* way. There was lust in it. Desire. She had to take control of this situation before her new customer followed the enemy home. "Thank you for dropping in, Nick. You may go."

Madeline nodded. Elyse had handled the situation admirably.

Nick angled an eyebrow at her. "At least let me treat you to dessert to make up for any embarrassment."

Elyse couldn't believe it. This man never gave up.

She watched Madeline evaluate the room. Everyone was actually staring now. Madeline spoke softly, but with strength. "We do not wish your desserts nor your company at this time."

"We don't?" Saban howled. "I do."

Nick bowed and took a step back. "I understand and obey."

Madeline had established her dominance once again, though she flashed him a discreet *call me* hand sign.

With his square jaw and soulful brown eyes, his fearless attitude and a rippled six-pack stomach—not that she'd seen his abs in three years, though Elyse assumed he still kept himself in shape—Nick was a walking, talking, Prince Charming dream. There was only one chink in his otherwise perfect armor. Nick Salvatore was a gigolo.

Elyse hated him for that.

He swaggered like Robin Hood, preyed on the rich, and gave to himself. Referring to Nick as a leech demeaned bloodsuckers. Unfortunately, he was also the model that she rebuilt her potential husbands on. His style, interests, and manners were as polished as a bronze statue. He had it all.

"Good night ladies," he said and walked toward the lounge.

All four of them couldn't help watching his buttocks as he left. They swayed back and forth like two muscular muskrats doing a slow Tango in an Armani sack.

Jackie elbowed Elyse. "You have got to wrap that up and put it under your tree for Christmas."

Saban gawked. "I'd pay a hundred grand for that in a heartbeat."

Elyse shook her head. "And he'd blow through twice that in one night."

"Does he have an hourly rate?"

"I'm sure he does," Elyse answered with bitterness in her voice. "But wouldn't you rather have something long-term?"

"I'd settle for twenty minutes in the bathroom."

Madeline swatted Saban's hand. "Ladies don't do that kind of thing."

"Who said I'm a lady?"

Elyse couldn't agree more, but she didn't want to blow a hundred thousand dollar fee either. "I'll build you a man that you can have every night. You won't even think about someone like Nick Salvatore."

Jackie choked. "I have a great man, and I still think about Nick."

Madeline held a hand to her heart. "That is simply not proper. Thank god there aren't thought police. Can you imagine them driving around in your head. No, we are happily married women. What happens in our dreams stay in our dreams."

"You slut!" Saban snorted.

Madeline whispered, "The vagina wants what the vagina wants."

Jackie and Saban sputtered with laughter. Elyse was appalled.

Couldn't they see what Nick was really about? Sure, he seemed to be an attentive male with depth, interests, and skills. He could dance, golf, skate, fish, cook. He was comfortable on any sports court, but could also appreciate ballet. These weren't passing fancies, either. He was highly proficient at everything. He could ski a triple black diamond run, cook a Cordon Bleu meal, and top the evening off with a conversation on Descartes philosophy or Paraguayan economics.

Elyse detested everything about him. He was everything a man should be, without having the honor of a real man.

Nick was dangerous.

Nick was a loaded gun in the hands of a monkey, a horny monkey.

Worse yet, Nick was inventive and curious. He always knew a new viognier wine, found a previously unknown restaurant tucked away in a Chinatown back alley, or discovered a budding artist having a premiere in Napa. To be with Nick was to have an adventure. To live.

Secretly, Elyse had a little jealousy toward all the women who so willingly gave in to the Nick experience. As she had even done once. With the exception of faithfulness, Nick was everything a man should be.

It was also apparent to Elyse that men didn't like him any better than she did. Nick was great company, which was why he had been able to sleep with almost every woman in this rarified social set. Other than envy, men loathed him because he was a necessary evil. Nick was *the fling*.

Every man in the room knew that if his wife, fiancée, or mistress hadn't wound up in Nick's bed, they would at some point. Nick was inevitable. Death, taxes, and Nick. He was the undisputed master of comfort sex. Elyse knew first hand. He made women feel beautiful, wanted, desired.

Temporarily.

Elyse waved a hand in front of Saban to get her attention off Nick's buttocks. She had to put an end to this. Once and for all. For Saban. For herself. For all the women everywhere who'd delayed meaningful gratification in their lives and instead chosen the enemy.

Chosen Nick.

Nick certainly wasn't the only *Nick* in the world. But Nick Salvatore of San Francisco, the man who'd seduced his way through throngs of his worshipful female fans, had stolen their youth, their dreams, and everything that was supposed to represent a loving, stable relationship.

The man was despicable. Thank God she hadn't lingered in his bed long enough to join his fan club.

Elyse locked eyes with Saban. "I'll deliver a man that makes Nick Salvatore look like chopped liver."

Saban took a last furtive glance at Nick's retreating rump. "Who says I don't like chopped liver?"

In Wedgeworth's lounge, Nick slid onto the leather barstool next to a cool blonde and waved the bartender over. "I'll have whatever she's having."

The blonde sized him up, head to toe. "What if I'm having you, Lover-boy?"

"I'm afraid I'm not on the menu anymore." He hadn't been for three years.

She took a long sip of her drink and left a red smudge of lipstick on the rim of the martini glass. "Me, either."

Nick placed an affectionate hand on her arm. "That, and you're a lesbian, Vicky."

"Rub it in." She stroked a tired hand over her face. "Just in case I ever change teams, can I keep your number on speed-dial?"

"I'd be nothing without you." Nick grinned.

"Damn straight."

"I am." From where he sat, he had the smallest peek-a-boo view of Elyse in the restaurant.

Vicky shook her head. "Are you still puppy-dog-pining for that woman?"

He was.

Flicking her long hair over one shoulder, Vicky leveled a calculating look at him. "So what was the ruckus in there?"

"Reincarnation is a bitch." He felt bad about the incident in the dining room.

"What?"

"My past life sometimes catches up to me." Nick was the first to admit that he deserved to be tripped for his adulterous transgressions. Maybe shot, hung, castrated, tarred and feathered, and keelhauled, too. For several years, he had been a very bad boy.

"How's New York?" he asked, changing the subject. Since they were both born-and-bred New Yorkers, there was almost always a story there.

"Harrowing."

"So everything's the same?"

The bartender slid a martini in front of Nick.

"Your ex ran her business into the ground," Vicky announced.

Normally such news would have cheered him up. "It's nice to believe that bad things happen to bad people. Karma. Then again, if karma really works, I'm in deep trouble."

Being a former lothario didn't change the fact that he'd slept with lots of women. Wives, girlfriends, sisters and mothers, he was well-versed in the art of the seduction. It wasn't all his fault, though. Sure, he'd been the predator in the beginning, but after word got out that he was a proficient Casanova, women often approached him. It would have been rude to turn them away, right?

That was all in the past. He'd reformed. Now he was a dyed-in-the-Italian-wool, born-again monogamist.

Vicky was having none of it. "Cheer up and get laid, you big pussy. This isn't the Nick I know. He's fearless. I need fearless. I need books. Have you written the cheesecake story yet?"

Nick frowned. Why was she always pushing for the

cheesecake story? "I told you, that's private."

"It's romantic." She rolled her eyes toward the dining room and Elyse. "I can't believe you're inventing a thousand cheesecakes to win the heart of the woman you love."

"It hasn't worked."

"Give it time." Vicky returned her attention to her martini. "Worst-case scenario, she'll hit three-hundred pounds and you can roll her home."

"It's always so uplifting to talk to you."

"I'm your agent. I just tell it like it is. Do you have a title?"

Nick took a gulp of his martini, stalling. "No."

Vicky punched him in the shoulder. "You're lying. I can tell when you're lying. What is it?"

Nick liked Vicky. Or Victoria Barnsdale, as she was known professionally. She was one of the best literary agents in the business. She repped some of the hottest writers in the Bay Area. With Vicky's help, he had his own restaurant and a dozen cookbook titles. His most popular were the Sex Food Series . . . *Bread, Bed & Breakfast*, *Sushi Seductions*, and *Cook-up a Hook-up*.

That was part of his past, too.

Lately, he'd been writing children's cookbooks. He wanted children. They'd had a lot of success with *One, Two, Three . . . Let's Eat Peas* and *A, B, C . . . We Love Broccoli*. At the heart of the books were recipes to make vegetables palatable as well as entertaining for kids. Nick longed to be a great father. Vicky said the books were selling like hotcakes, which then became *Billy Bakes Hotcakes*, another bestseller.

"Don't make me beat the title out of you," Vicky threatened.

Had he really spent the last three years concocting and perfecting cheesecakes in a crazy attempt to lure Elyse back into his arms? He hung his head and whispered, "*True Confections of a Reformed Lothario.*"

"Ka-ching!" Vicky's face lit the room. "This is going to sell a million copies! We're going to be rich."

"We're already rich."

"We're going to be richer!"

Nick didn't care. When he'd first come to San Francisco, broke and broken-hearted, all he had were his name, his good looks, and a set of chef's knives. The only work he could find was bussing tables. But that's where he had met Madeline. With a word here and an introduction there, she turned his life around.

Now he had all the money in the world, and he didn't care. Money didn't buy happiness. It didn't buy love. Having everything meant nothing without the woman he loved.

Vicky wagged a finger at him. "You have got to close this deal or it's going to take you down, Nick."

"I'm trying."

"If anyone can nail her, it's you. You said she remodels men-for-resale?"

"Yeah."

"Based on you, right?"

"That's the rumor," Nick conceded.

There was a gleam in Vicky's eye. "Does she have an agent?"

"She doesn't have a book."

"She doesn't need one. All I need is the title. *Elyse Tobin: Man Factory*. I could sell the shit out of that."

Chapter 3

Elyse's house stood proud, even in the dark. Only the basement windows showed any life. They gave the stone steps a welcoming glow that spread over several small shrubs and the white railing and banister encasing the front porch. Hanging over that banister was a damp pair of faded 501s and a tattered work shirt.

Andrew was still on the job.

What had she been thinking when she said she'd deliver a husband ASAP? A good match took half a year. Her fastest rebuild was four months. Standing at the gate to her yard, she took a moment to inhale deeply. The fragrant smell of her mother's prized Daphne bush always calmed her.

She could do it. For her mother and all the other Tobin women. She was on a mission.

Elyse found Andrew in *the belly of the beast*. That's what she called the basement. It made sense. The guts of the house were here. The furnace, water heaters, washer and dryer, telephone and TV cables, small pipes bringing water in and large ones draining it away. Everything that brought the house to life began here.

Andrew, in his leather work boots and white jockey shorts, strained a wrench on one of the iron intestines.

"You're still here." Elyse descended the steps to the cold concrete floor.

"Yeah. Thanks for the shower earlier," he replied without even a glance over his shoulder.

"You said everyone hops out of the tub and pulls the plug without thinking."

"I was hoping you weren't everyone." Andrew gripped the wrench with both hands and tightened a pipe coupling. With a look of satisfaction, he patted the pipe affectionately, like petting a dog.

Elyse felt her stomach twist. Andrew was certainly in good shape. Every part of his body was toned. From the look of his jockey shorts, he'd be more than ample in filling Saban's requirements for the boudoir. But she knew she couldn't just take a man in work boots, drop him into a suit, and call the job done. She needed time with him. She needed to polish and refine him.

Andrew scratched his ass.

A lot of time.

Was an intensive possible? Could she do it in weeks, not months? If she had access to Andrew everyday, maybe. "So how's it going? Another month or two for this job?"

"Not quite." Andrew spread his arms wide toward the maze of pipes. "I was just about to bust out the party hats and streamers. It's done."

"Done?"

"Yeah, done. Finished. Com-plee-ta-mento."

"It can't be done."

"I'm a plumber. I know plumbing. It's done."

As thrilled as she was that the job was finally completed, she wasn't. She needed a gentleman plumber. She needed Andrew. Elyse scanned her memory for plumbing terms. "What about the GPF ratios?"

"Gallons per flush?" he asked, puzzled. "A-okay."

A-okay? Yikes. Saban would never stand for that. Vocabulary lessons would be part of his curriculum. "Pressure regulators?"

"Perfecto."

"I don't think we have enough cleanouts on the sewer."

He folded his arms across his chest. "There's nothing left to repair or replace in this house. She's solid. Unless you stuff a sweater in your toilet and flush, you won't be seeing me again for at least a decade."

Elyse pictured her wardrobe. She could live without the ivory cable knit she wore on brisk spring mornings, but stuffing clothes in toilets wasn't the answer. "What about the faucets on my tub," she blurted, relieved to have recalled something that still needed attention.

"They need replacing."

"Good."

"But vintage taps from the 1890s might take years to find. I'll keep my ears open and give you a call if I hear of something."

Damn. Why did she have to be such a purist about fixtures? Her copper tub was an antique. A rare one at that. Andrew found it at a metal recycler in Oakland, but its original faucet and handles had been lost long ago. He'd found dozens of proper-age fixtures for the other bathrooms at flea markets and junkyards—toilets and tanks and basins and faucets. Everything except the hardware for the tub. A pair of faucets wasn't going to keep him here for a month, though. She needed a plan.

"Would you like a cup of tea? Let's have tea!" Before he could answer, she dashed up the stairs.

Elyse understood tea. She loved tea. Her kitchen was tea-sipping central. The room was country simple. White enamel and light natural woods. Chickens and farm animals on towels and accents. Even her china was a country pattern.

As she measured the tea into a ceramic pot shaped like a rooster, Andrew entered. He wore his shirt, but carried his pants.

"They're still wet," he explained.

She set the table with the pot, her best bone china cups, and the canister of tea. "You can put them in the dryer."

"Makes them too tight." He glanced down at his briefs. "Do you mind?"

"It's fine." Of course it wasn't fine. A *gentleman* plumber would never wander about the house in tighty-whiteys.

"If you say so."

The kettle on the stove whistled. Elyse poured the boiling water into the teapot as Andrew took a seat and pulled the tablecloth toward himself to cover his legs and underwear.

"Cream or sugar?" she asked.

"Both," he nodded.

"Sugar's there." She waved to the edge of the table, then went to the fridge and reached for the creamer that was tucked behind a bottle of expensive French champagne.

Reminding her daily of her mission, the two-hundred-dollar bottle of bubbly had sat there for years, waiting for a celebration. Elyse promised herself she'd pop it open the moment the house was paid off once and for all and she held the deed in her hands.

"Bet you're glad to see the last of me," Andrew said softly.

"No, we're like family." To tell the truth, she hadn't thought about him. He was a great plumber. Very dedicated. His world was pipes and faucets. She just hadn't considered him beyond that.

"I don't drink much tea," he confessed.

"I think you'll like this." She tapped the canister on the table, then took her special strainer and poured. She loved her strainer as much as she loved tea. The strainer was just a tiny little nothing you'd hardly notice. The wire mesh was extremely fine and it was just the size of the cups. It had a small steel loop handle and it always worked perfectly. Never a stray leaf or twig.

He stirred in the sugar and cream, then picked up the cup by its dainty porcelain handle. "Smells good. Like a flower or something."

"That's the jasmine." She filled her own cup and

appraised him. There was humility here. Funny that she'd never taken a good look at him. He was one of those solid buildings she drove past every day and never saw until something drastic changed. Thank God he was still here, in all his underwear glory, seated before a cup of Mariage Freres Jasmine tea.

Andrew picked up the can. "It says this tea is from Ceylon."

"Yes."

"Didn't they change the name of that country, like, thirty years ago?"

"You're a history buff?" Elyse asked, excited. Maybe Andrew was more than just pipes.

"Nah. A buddy had a band. They thought Ceylon was a cool name, but then with the whole change thing, Sri Lanka didn't sound as good."

"Oh." Elyse was somewhat deflated, but not entirely. "You like music?"

"Actually, they sucked."

Maybe he was more work than she could handle. It was time to change the conversation. "The only place I can find this tea is Bergdorf's." Was he interested in tea? Or shopping? If he had any husband potential at all, she needed to find his charms. There must be something.

Saban was counting on her to deliver. Elyse needed the money. If Andrew turned out to be Saban's ideal mate, and Elyse played her cards right, he might be the last man she'd rebuild and sell.

She stopped herself from going further. There was no point in projecting her hopes and dreams for herself on him. Either he'd work out or not. Her heart pounded steady and loud. She desperately wanted Andrew to be the last one.

He was her ticket back to leading her own life, giving up the husband factory, and beginning again with a solid base to work from, her family home.

"Bergdorf's is that spendy department store downtown . . ." Andrew studied the can again. "So this is French tea that the company buys from Sri Lanka . . ."

"The jasmine comes from Formosa."

"That's Taiwan, right?"

"Right."

"Don't they have an up-to-date map of the world in France?"

"I guess not."

Andrew nodded. "So they get this tea from all over, put it in a fancy can, and sell it at a la-dee-da department store and clean up?"

Elyse had never thought of it that way. "You think it's an incredible waste."

Andrew grinned. "I think it's friggin' brilliant. That's marketing genius."

Friggin? Elyse cringed. Who would make up a word like that? Probably a hockey player whose wife threatened to leave him over his crass language. If Andrew were to be the gentleman plumber, the first thing she needed to do was fix his vocabulary. "I'm glad you like the tea."

Andrew took a gulp. "I understand if you're short this month."

"I'm not short." She heard her words and immediately regretted the lie. She had a hundred thousand dollars, but she also had that much again in debt. She was most certainly short.

"I been working for you, off and on, for two years. Three times you've come up short. Last August you had me in for a glass of wine, white, nice and cold. The year before that, in September, you gave me one of those microbrew ales. Now I'm sitting here drinking a cup of French tea. Tell you the truth, I'd just as soon have the beer."

Two things scared Elyse. First, that she was so predictable. Second, that she'd underestimated Andrew. He was very perceptive to see a pattern that stretched over the span of years. She had always assumed that man, living in his natural state without feminine influence, lived meal to meal and remembered little.

"I did like that wine, though," Andrew continued. "You said it was a Pinot Gris from Oregon. I think the label had a duck on it."

Had she read him all wrong? What if Andrew was working class gay?

Elyse had a gay uncle. A mid-western closet variety. He lived in Tulsa with a partner named Jules. They never admitted to a relationship, but were together to the very end. She knew they were gay the minute they pulled up the linoleum in the kitchen in favor of tile and installed dimmer switches in every room in the house. She took a good look at Andrew, trying to sense him.

He didn't give off a gay vibe, but he didn't give a heterosexual vibe either. Andrew was practically vibeless. In the two years he'd been working on the house, he'd never hit on her. Not once. What kind of man has that kind of control if he isn't gay?

If he were ambivalent to women, that would flush this project straight down the toilet. No woman wants a man who can take her or leave her. Girls don't read thousands of romance novels to dream of a wishy-washy lover who sweeps onto their balcony, proclaims undying *like* for them, then discusses the origins of French tea.

Elyse had to find out, and fast. Either Andrew was going to be Saban's husband in training or she was going to have to locate a replacement. Pronto. "Are you gay?"

Andrew looked as if someone had snuck up and hit him across the back of the head with a two by four. "No."

"Committed relationship?"

"None of your friggin' business."

There was that word again. "There's no shame in being

celibate."

"Why are you badgering me?"

"I'm curious," Elyse shrugged. "Two years, and you've never mentioned a girlfriend, a boyfriend, or a pet."

"We never talk unless it's about my money or your plumbing. That's pretty much all the relationship we have."

"So it's a communication problem."

"I don't have a problem."

"You're sure you're not gay?"

"I like women, though I don't have one at the moment. I have a dog. Black lab. His name is Riley. My folks dog sit him while I work. They're retired. My dad was a carpenter. My mom was a CPA. My great-grandparents came to the United States through Ellis Island, and they changed our name from Younstadt to Young. That's why I'm Andrew Young. I got good grades in school, had my first crush on a girl named Becky when I was ten, drank too much beer in college, which was the only thing I liked about college. I have my own one-man company, and I'm very happy, thank you very much. Now you know everything about me!"

His face was a bright shade of red.

Elyse liked it when men got worked up. It may have been part of her job, but it was the best part. She'd punched his buttons, flipped his switches, and poked him with a stick. Finally, the real Andrew was coming through. Loud and clear.

"You didn't mention the part where you like men."

"I don't like men," he sputtered.

Good. She had him off balance.

"Prove it," she said with all the taunting in her voice that she could muster.

He took the bait. Andrew stood, angled around the table to her, gripped her shoulders with his pipe-strong plumber hands, and drew her to her feet. His head tipped down. Hers up.

This was a complete change of tactics for her. She'd never gone this close to a full romance before. How would she make the transition from her to Saban if he imprinted on her like a baby duck? What were the consequences?

She closed her eyes and stilled her mind as their lips met. It was a great kiss. His hands were strong, but he didn't force himself on her. The kiss was soft and gentle, then his arms wrapped around her and their tongues danced lightly. A shiver ran down Elyse's spine.

When training a husband for someone else, she had to be close, but keep a professional distance. This was not a professional distance. She felt him rise through his jockey shorts against her. Obviously no problems in that area.

Elyse stepped back. "You are definitely not gay."

"You want more proof?"

She did. Badly. But that would cause far too much trouble later. She had to keep her mind on the money. On the house. "Let's take this slowly."

Andrew reached over, took his jeans off the chair and pulled them on. "You're the boss."

Elyse couldn't be happier. She *was* the boss, and Andrew had passed her first test with flying colors. He had a good base of work ethics and manly morals. Above average looks. Passable kissing technique and was quick to rise to attention. He had enough going for him that it was hard for her to stay objective.

Money, house, money, house, she reminded herself. This gentleman plumber was for Saban.

Someday she'd train a man for herself. One for keeps. One just like Nick Salvatore, only a much better version. Faithful and true. A man she'd be happy to spend the rest of her life with.

At 7 a.m. Nick waited with a cup of coffee in Bert's Bagels.

"Hey!" Andrew called loudly as he swung open the café door. "Thanks for coming."

Nick pushed the chair opposite him out with his foot. "Anything for the team."

Andrew sat. "This isn't about our basketball league."

"I didn't think it was."

Nick and Andrew played charity basketball for Bishop Hegeland's church team. Andrew was a great power forward. Nick was adequate as a guard, but his forte was charming the female donors, mainly past conquests with deep pocketbooks. So far the funds raised had sponsored a youth center and vaccinated thousands of children in third world countries.

Andrew looked around, embarrassed. "I think I'm in over my head."

"I warned you." Nick had. He was also the one who told Andrew about Elyse and her matchmaker projects.

"I just didn't know what else to do," Andrew confessed. "Online dating was a disaster. It takes me a week to sign a birthday card without screwing it up. My only option is to sell my house and buy a mail order bride from Russia. I really want to get married."

Nick sipped his coffee. "On the other hand, you got paid for two years while you waited your turn. Not bad."

"Almost paid," Andrew corrected him.

"She's running behind again?" It was well known among Sausalito residents that generations of Tobins had barely made ends meet. Like a family tradition, their financial style was legendary for thrift. "Her last delivery was this past weekend. She'll catch up."

"It's not the money." Andrew shook his head. "I just don't know if I can go through with it. It seems dishonest."

"It's not dishonest. It's a game." Nick knew. He didn't like games, but he'd played a lot of them. "That's why she's not telling you anything."

"Nothing," he complained. "I'm stumbling around in the dark here."

"Just play along. See where it goes. You might learn something. Call me if you get into trouble."

To tell the truth, Nick liked knowing what Elyse was up to. It wasn't stalking. Between his business, working on his next cookbook, and the Bishop's charities, he didn't have time. If Elyse wanted her space, she could have it. Still, he liked being informed. Sooner or later he'd have his chance to prove to her that he wasn't the playboy she thought and they could pick up where they'd left off three years ago.

"I feel like I'm in high school again." Andrew slumped back into his chair.

"Except this time you're the teacher's pet." Strangely, he felt jealous.

Ding-Dong.

Elyse had a love/hate relationship with her doorbell. Mounted on the wall in the entry hall were two brass tubes three inches wide and almost a foot long, though one was a little shorter than the other. They sounded like mini-church bells when someone pushed the button on the front porch. It was an announcement. A statement. Someone had come to see her. But seven in the morning was far too early.

In a fluffy robe and slippers, she parted the foyer curtains and looked outside.

The someone was Saban.

"I just had to talk," Saban said as she entered and clicked across the wood floor in her Jimmy Choos.

Elyse noticed them right away. They were the same pair she'd worn last night. A strange choice of footwear for a

Monday morning, unless the tulip heiress had never made it home. "Please tell me you didn't track down Nick Salvatore last night."

Saban sparked up. "Why? Do you have his number?"

"No," she lied. Every female in the Bay Area had Nick's number. Including her. She kept it hidden away, stuffed between musty pages, forgotten.

In the parlor, Saban surveyed the room in her usual furtive manner. That was a problem with the rich, Elyse thought, they were always so judgmental.

"How quaint," Saban stated flatly and lowered her posterior to the floral-print sofa. The cushion contoured to her bottom as she settled. She patted the next cushion over for Elyse to join her. "I hope you don't mind. I just couldn't wait to get started. Where's your catalogue?"

"Catalogue?"

"I want to pick out my man."

"I can see that you don't understand how this works."

Saban smiled, though it looked more like a sneer. "I don't understand at all, but I think it's marvelous. Who has time to weed through all those horrible men out there? When our forefathers asked for the teaming, yearning wretches and all that, well, they certainly got them, didn't they? Now *we're* stuck with the huddled masses. Do you have someone in mind?"

"Aren't you an immigrant? I thought you were Dutch?"

"Second generation Dutch American." Saban's eyes darted to the ceiling. "On my father's side. But let's not waste any time on family. I'm here to procure a husband."

"I'm in my bathrobe," Elyse said and nodded to the door. "As you may have guessed, I'm not open for business right now."

"Oh Elyse, I'm sorry." Saban's voice dripped with a faux guilt that had not a smattering of truth in it.

Elyse had heard it before. The rich weren't particularly

sorry for anything, least of all inconveniencing someone they paid for services. Elyse chalked it up to the cost of doing business. "This really isn't a good time."

"For a hundred thousand dollars, I don't care. I want to see photos. I have to know that he's good-looking."

"Trust me, he's very good-looking."

"So you've found him! And so quickly."

Elyse winced, immediately regretting the words. She couldn't backtrack, so she hedged. "I'm not sure he's trainable. Not yet, anyway."

"Who is he? What does he do? Where is he? I must see him." Saban jumped up from the couch, her frenetic energy threatening a full-scale strip search of the room if she wasn't appeased. "How will I know if he's good-looking the way I think good-looking should be? I had a blind date last year. Gigi Thorp set it up. Do you know Gigi? Lovely woman. Her brother. Brilliant man. No chin. His lower lip seemed to fade straight down and start his neck. Hideous. Gigi, to this day, swears that he's good-looking."

"I know good-looking. Trust me." Elyse opened the front door. "I think you need to go."

"I can't go now. If you've found my husband, I need details. Immediately."

"I'm sorry."

"Well, I'm desperate. You want the money, don't you?"

She did. Elyse let the front door slam shut and resigned herself to this temporary visitor. "You don't seem to grasp what I do. So let me tell you what I don't do. I don't rebuild men for a spec market, or keep catalogues of eligible prospects, or a stable of studs."

Saban's enthusiasm sprung a leak, and her face crumpled. "So what do I get for a hundred thousand dollar fee?"

"It's not a fee. It's a gift."

Saban winked. "A gift. Right."

"I'm sure you don't want people to think that you went out and bought a husband?"

"Heavens no. I'd be the laughing stock at the Sonoma Country Club."

The wealthy never wanted to admit that they had to pay for men. That a rich woman had to shell out her trust fund dollars to have a man reconstructed and re-cultured, often with blue-collar roots, wasn't something to be broadcast about.

"I have a discreet service," Elyse said softly.

"Hush-hush."

"Exactly."

"So now that we've covered that, I made a list of the things I want you to build into him." Saban flipped open a leather clutch and took out a tiny piece of pink, frail paper two inches wide. She unfolded it, then again and again. Longer and longer. It grew to be over a foot long with tiny scribbles of sparkled gold ink. "Handsome, kind, funny, loving, smart, tall, athletic, spontaneous, a well-proportioned member. Minimum eight inches."

Elyse raised an eyebrow.

Saban continued. "All the better if he can give a good massage, a pilot's license would be nice, likes to mow lawns, outdoorsy, he absolutely must be able to make a good martini, and I want him to protect and serve."

"Protect and serve?" Elyse asked.

"I got that off a police car door. It has a ring to it. Official like."

"I think you need to be a little more realistic."

"I know what I want. You provide it. That is, if you want your *gift*."

"Are you threatening me?"

"I did my homework, you do your job."

Elyse took a deep breath to calm herself. How badly did she need the money? She could always take out another mortgage. That's what every generation of Tobin women did. That was why Great-Grandma Tobin dubbed the house *The Monster* in 1930 when it started eating bank accounts.

In the Tobin house, repairs took precedence over all else. Elyse was the only kid in her school that *wanted* braces. The small gap between her two front teeth, on an otherwise perfect smile, had always annoyed her. But orthodontic dreams had been put on hold when an invasion of carpenter ants laid waste to the sagging roof.

In like fashion, a junior high ski trip to Big Bear had been replaced by electricians ripping through kitchen walls searching for an electrical short. In the twelfth grade, her college fund was raided to shore up a cracked foundation. *The Monster* made every phase of a Tobin woman's life a little more difficult than everyone else's.

Yet she didn't resent the house. She loved her family home, and it would be 100% hers soon.

"Well?" Saban snapped.

Elyse did not like this woman. Something felt wrong. Saban worked too hard. Demanded too much. This was not the lonely, single millionairess she was used to dealing with. Was having the house free and clear right now worth it? Her internal alarms were going off. "We may have jumped into this a little too quickly."

Saban narrowed her eyes to little black slits. "I'll double your fee."

"It's a gift." Elyse was stunned. Two hundred thousand dollars.

"A big, honkin' gift!"

Two hundred thousand dollars. That would pay off the mortgage. That would cover Andrew's repairs. There would be enough money left over to straighten her teeth, take a year of college classes, and a vacation to Big Bear. The word *yes* wanted to fly out of her mouth, but instead, she heard Grandma Tobin in her mind. She always said, *if something looks too good to be true, you're probably screwed.*

Elyse was shaky, but she walked to the front door and opened it. "I'm sorry. I don't think this is going to work."

"Fine." Saban's skinny legs lifted her from the sofa and carried her to the door.

Elyse was surprised. She rarely said no, but every time she had, there had been a scene. When a woman gets to the point where she admits she can't attract a decent mate, tears flow, especially when a professional lets you know that you're beyond help. She was impressed by how well Saban was handling it.

Outside on the porch, Saban turned to her. "I'm sorry. I misunderstood. I was . . . I was . . ."

No, no, no. Elyse froze. Saban's eyes watered up. This wasn't happening. Not now.

"I've just been alone for so long. I don't have any real friends. I know people. People know me. But that's not friends. If I wake up at two in the morning, frightened, I don't have anyone. I've called date lines for three dollars a minute just to hear a human voice."

Elyse nodded along politely. This wasn't pretty. Maybe it would blow over quickly.

But Saban's water ducts were just warming up. Tears poured down her face. She choked back a sob. "It's probably being an orphan and having my adoptive parents gone."

"Adoptive parents . . . they passed away, too?"

"Not dead, deported."

"So you can still see them."

"If they weren't in a Dutch prison."

Elyse frowned. This wasn't making sense. Saban supposedly had a ton of money. "If money's a problem you shouldn't be . . ."

"I inherited the family business." Saban cut Elyse off. "Tulip bulbs. I have thousands of acres of them in Northern California and Oregon. I have all this money, but I'm completely alone."

Alone was something Elyse could relate to. She was the last living Tobin in her line. She felt her shoulders sink into her collarbones as she slumped to the porch rail. She didn't want to be alone, either. She feared spending her old age in solitude, without sons and daughters to buoy her through her golden years.

Even now, living by herself in four stories was sometimes hard, but she was still relatively young. She'd poured everything she had into fixing the house, preparing it. She had to. The last thing she wanted to do was bear children and then deny them the things that made childhood magical.

She would not put herself in a situation where she had to choose between a new furnace and swimming lessons for her children. Insulation in the attic or a prom dress. Rebuilding a crumbling chimney or joining the school band. As an only child in a run-down house that demanded every spare nickel, Elyse had lived that life, watching her mother and her grandmother struggle to make ends meet.

The house came first. Always.

There was nothing to forgive. It was simply the way it was for the past three generations. Elyse refused to be the fourth. No child of hers would live in a house that came second to a mother's love and devotion.

Still, the family home had extracted a toll, years of her life dedicated to its restoration. The clock was ticking. She hoped she had enough time left to have everything else.

Saban belted out three more sobs, turned, and trudged down the steps. "I wouldn't expect someone like you to know what's it's like to only have yourself to depend on. Is there a pet store around here? I need to buy a cat. Maybe three."

Elyse felt sorry for Saban, but joyous. Sometimes you don't recognize the truth until it comes out of someone else's mouth. Not about cats. About loneliness.

She didn't have that desperation. Sure, everyone thought she occupied herself with work and the house to keep her mind off being a single woman. The truth was, most date conversations were simply painful. Among the men she had reconditioned, she'd never found one interesting enough to keep.

Yet it was deeper than that. She liked herself. She was good company. In fact, she got along famously with herself. Someday she'd share herself with exactly the right man, a man who could appreciate her independent spirit and opinions. A man who liked a challenge.

The thought gave her pause. Did he even exist? Could she build those qualities into a regular guy?

She regarded the still-sobbing Saban. They were very different. This was a woman whose center was empty without a companion. She wasn't whole without a partner.

"Stop." Elyse couldn't believe she said the word. Another minute and Saban would have been off to the cat store and deranged little-old-ladyhood. Why was it her mission to save every wayward heart? It was true that she'd said no before, but in the end, she always changed her mind and gave in. No one should be alone unless they wanted to be.

Saban looked up at her. Her eyes held the glint of hope that she had seen many times after the drama crested. "I'll pay you anything."

Everything inside Elyse said *no, run away, don't do it.* "Okay. We'll get this done."

The phone rang.

"Wait here." Elyse hurried inside. She needed a break.

It was Andrew. "Hi. This is me. Andrew."

"Yeah. I'm in the middle of something. Can I call you back?"

"I just wanted to know if you might like to go out, you know, for a bite. Grab some grub? Something like that.

Food."

Andrew needed a lot of work, even at forming an invitation.

Elyse turned to see Saban peering in the front window. Her beady little eyes were framed by panes of beveled, leaded glass. Beveled, leaded glass that would soon be paid for. "Andrew, do you have a suit?"

"You betcha."

Chapter 4

In the dressing room of the J.C. Penney's men's department, Andrew stepped into his future. One leg at a time.

"I've never worn a suit," he confided to Nick, who waited outside. "Ever. I was hoping I wouldn't have to until my wedding day. Better yet, my funeral."

The dressing room door creaked as he swung it open and then paced to the three-way mirror.

"It's perfect," Nick said. "For under a hundred bucks, you couldn't do any better."

Andrew read Nick's amused expression. "You wouldn't be caught dead in this." The navy blue jacket and pants was a bad idea. What had he been thinking telling Elyse he had a suit? Or asking Nick for help? He was going to call the whole thing off, get a second mortgage from the bank, and sign up for an overseas bride. That had to be a lot easier than shopping.

"The suit doesn't matter," Nick argued.

"I thought the suit made the man," Andrew countered. He was confused. He sized up Nick's jacket. "This doesn't look anything like yours."

"I dress for a different audience. Think of this as a starter suit." Nick patted Andrew on his padded shoulder.

"I didn't know there was such a thing." Andrew fumbled with the lining and tugged on a paper tag. "Hey, this says it's one hundred percent washable polyester. Is that good?"

"No." Nick shook his head. "That's the whole point. We have to leave room for improvement. Especially with

Elyse. If you're her next project, there have to be things to fix."

"Like this suit?"

"Exactly."

Andrew mulled this over. "Why do I have to go through all this? Why can't I just tell her the truth? I want a hookup. I want a wife."

"Who doesn't?"

"But you're *Nick*. You can have any woman in San Francisco."

Andrew was surprised to see a hint of sadness on Nick's face. "Just not the one I want."

"Romance sucks. If you can't get the girl you want, I'm totally boned."

Nick exhaled, tired. "If you're an unmarried man pulling in less than a hundred thou a year, Elyse is a necessary evil. And she has to choose you. You should be honored."

"Yeah, well, I feel like a chump in a cheap suit."

Had he dressed himself? Glancing across the red and white checkered tablecloth, Elyse wasn't sure what to think of Andrew. Maybe this was the work of some well-meaning relative recycling a deceased uncle's clothes to family members in need? Maybe he'd mugged a sea captain on his way to her house and shanghaied his suit. If he wore an Admiral's hat, he could step behind the wheel of a cruise liner with no one the wiser.

This suit would haunt her nightmares for months. She'd have to remind herself to take a photo. This was even better than Andrew in his tighty-whiteys and boots. The bright gold buttons distracted her with his every twitch.

A fashion incident like this was exactly why she had chosen Mario's Pasta Emporium. For a place that billed itself as *The Bay Area's best value for family dining*, it was dark, candlelit, and windowless. The kind of restaurant that oozed hidden ghosts, seedy pyramid schemes, and extramarital affairs. But it had really good, inexpensive food. Not to mention, no one of social stature would dare set foot in the place.

Unless they were invited.

Saban, Jackie, and Madeline spied from a vinyl-upholstered booth a mere three tables away. Elyse could see the horror on their faces as the three of them watched from behind untouched red plastic tumblers and a carafe of Carlo Rossi Chianti.

Saban had insisted on a preview of *the goods*. Elyse had never shown anything but a finished product to any of her clients, but she made an exception in this case. A deal had been struck, and for two hundred thousand dollars, she was willing to break a few of her own rules.

Andrew, as is, was a classic candidate for transformation. The ill-fitting suit and self-styled table manners would have to go. She made yet another mental note. She'd transfer them all to paper once she got home.

She took a long sip of her Sangiovese. "How do you like the wine?"

He took a gulp. "Smooth."

"It's Italian."

"It's an Italian restaurant." At least it was a four-word sentence.

Andrew was like the wine. Simple.

She took another sip. "I'm glad you like it."

For the last half hour, Andrew had been muttering under his breath and tugging at the sleeves of his suit as if he were trapped in a straightjacket. Elyse sighed, wondering if she'd made a grave error.

She had to remain calm. She'd worked with worse, and the man in front of her represented her financial freedom. He was her ticket to paying off her mortgage.

Still, the less-than-scintillating conversation had been limited to two and three word exchanges: *You look nice, pass the salt*. The highlight of the evening, a lip smacking, *tasty pasta*. If it were just nervousness, that was fine. But what if this was the real Andrew?

He glanced up. "I could have driven you. My truck runs great."

"Mario's is halfway between your place and mine."

"You know where I live?"

She didn't have a clue. "In the Valley. Right?"

"More east." In an unprecedented show of spontaneity, he leaned over the table and whispered, "Can I tell you a secret?"

Elyse winced. Not at his lack of refinement, but at the possibility that she may have overlooked something in his character. To her the words *Andrew* and *secret* didn't belong in the same sentence. He had seemed so normal. Andrew was Mr. Average Joe. What sort of secret could possibly be lurking beneath his surface?

She had decided long ago that there were two types of men. Those who had agendas, like Nick, and those who laid their emotions open like a book. Andrew was definitely in the open book category. Or so she'd thought.

In most cases, even the so-called secrets were of little consequence. Most men had a James Bond or Luke Skywalker fantasy. She called them personality quirks, not secrets, and dealt with them accordingly.

"You're kidding, right?" She winked at Andrew. "Don't tell me you're an alligator wrestler."

"Seriously, I have a secret."

She hated surprises and flinched from the sudden throb of a headache. There wasn't room on this timeline for any major personality repairs.

"What kind of secret?" She remained cool, telling herself that this date was only a test run. With a first date, one had to be prepared for anything. She took a deep breath and waited for Andrew to reveal his secret.

"It's a doozy," he said.

"Then keep your voice down," she warned.

He ignored her. "Why? There's nobody in this place except the waiter and those women over there."

A stab of pain shot through Elyse's head. "Come on, spill." She speared a forkful of ravioli. Comfort food. It didn't exactly solve problems, but a mouthful of pasta bursting with garlic and fresh basil made problem solving easier.

"It's a real whopper."

"You mean you lied to me?"

"Well . . ."

"You said it was a secret. Then you called it a whopper. Is it a lie or a secret?"

He shrugged. "Both, I guess."

She frowned. Lies were worse than secrets. For the past two years Andrew had had a key to her house, he'd prattled on about pipes and water pressure, billed her accordingly and always to the penny. He wasn't the lying type. She was sure of it. After all, she knew men. It was her business to know men.

"I might as well come right out and tell you . . ."

"Go on," she said between mouthfuls. Though Elyse was grateful that he had moved beyond the single syllable chitchat, she wasn't keen on playing this game. "I'm waiting."

"This is it. Honest to God." His face flushed. "I've never worn a suit before."

"What?" she blurted.

"I just bought it at J. C. Penney," he said loudly and checked the sleeves. "I think I got all the tags off."

"What?" Saban howled from their table.

Andrew craned around to face the girls' booth. "Who

are they?" he asked, gesturing to the three pairs of eyes that peered over three laminated cardboard menus.

Elyse made a mental note to *never, never, never* allow a client a preview ever again. Saban was going to ruin everything if she kept this up.

"Andrew," Elyse said, snapping her fingers. "What do you mean you've never worn a suit before?"

Andrew scowled. "Do you know them?"

She couldn't lose control of the situation. If he found out he was being appraised, she could wave goodbye to Saban's money. A little white lie was forgivable, but revealing her ultimate plan for Andrew wasn't. Quickly, she calculated an exit strategy.

Step one: Smile.

Step two: Feign innocence. "Know who, Andrew?"

Step three: Take his hand. Softly.

Elyse had a theory about touching men's hands. The more education a man has, and the more money he earns, the less likely he is to respond positively to an intimate gesture such as interlocking fingers. They find the move too assertive on the woman's part. White-collar men want control. They assert, they pursue, and most were just plain lousy in bed.

On the other hand, men raised in middleclass families with a two-parent, blue-collar income are ideal lovers. Secure with their sexuality and open to exploring balanced bedroom dynamics. *Calloused fingers are a precursor to bold erections*. It was her mantra.

"Andrew?" She lowered her voice and stroked his thumb. It always worked.

He looked her in the eyes. "Sorry."

"It's okay." She had his full attention again.

Elyse wondered how far she'd need to go with his training. Usually, she would tease a man along through a couple dozen dates, each one designed for a specific result. Before they actually *did the deed*, she'd pull the bait and switch and the bride-to-be took the reins.

Would she need to go a lot farther, faster, to get Andrew into shape? Did she want that? Three years had gone by since she'd succumbed to Nick. After her night with him, the idea of taking another lover paled by comparison. He'd been that good.

Come to think of it, Nick most definitely had calloused fingertips. How did that happen? Maybe he had a hobby making furniture? He obviously wasn't blue-collar. She could tell simply by the way he wore clothes. The impeccably tailored Italian suits made of buttery, soft wool clung to his frame like an obsessed lover.

Elyse shook her head to clear her mind. This wasn't about Nick or love.

It was about the house.

"I'm sorry. I didn't mean to lie to you," Andrew apologized.

For a man who didn't seem to have much on his mind other than plumbing, Andrew was coming along nicely. She would let him off the hook for this little transgression, though before she could respond, a hand slapped down on her shoulder. She peered up to see a familiar white collar and bobbing Adam's apple.

Bishop Hegeland glowered at Andrew. "Lying is a sin, young man. That will be three Hail Mary's for you."

"But I'm Lutheran," he protested.

"Always trying to squeak through a loophole, eh?" The Bishop crossed his arms over his chest and turned his glare at Elyse. "And you, dating a liar now?"

Elyse feigned a welcoming tone. "It's good to see you again, Bishop."

"Weren't you dating Donnie? And Cyril? And that nice man who got married yesterday?" There was more than a little sarcasm in his words. "Elyse, you have the worst luck with men. They always seem to wind up marrying your girlfriends."

She silently prayed that one of her six happy wives had squealed about her in the confessional, and not that her Prince Charming matchmaking service was becoming too obvious. Was building six good husbands enough that people saw a pattern? She certainly didn't want everyone to know her business.

Especially the men.

Elyse smiled her most innocent smile at the Bishop. "Fingers crossed I'm next. Did you see me catch the bouquet at the wedding?"

"I'll light a candle that you don't let all your men get away. You might even love Andrew here. He may not be Episcopalian, but he's a fine basketball player and a good man."

"Thank you, Bishop," she said, even though he wasn't helping at all.

"And one more bit of advice," Bishop Hegeland said stoically, "I read in a magazine that the longer a woman waits to tie the knot, the lower her chance of getting married. You should think about it."

Taking a sidelong glance to the corner booth, Elyse noticed Saban, Madeline, and Jackie still cowering behind their menus. If the Bishop spotted them, he'd be like a money-seeking missile. He never missed a chance to pitch the wealthy on his latest charity. Elyse had to keep the Bishop's attention focused on her.

Fortunately, he was a man. But, he was also a man of the cloth and her feminine wiles didn't stand a chance. There would be no clever use of body language, no purred encouragements, and certainly no hints of possible future sex to keep his interest focused on her. There was only one thing to do—Agree.

"My God, Bishop Hegeland, I've seen the light!" Was it wrong to lie to a Bishop if you weren't Episcopalian?

Probably. Elyse did her best to well up a few tears. "Marriage eludes me."

"Me, too," Andrew chimed in.

Under the table, Elyse snaked a hand out and waved for the girls to make a discreet escape.

Bishop Hegeland shook his head in an understanding manner. "You're always the bridesmaid, never the bride. You need a man. A religious man. You need to swallow your pride. Get serious. Are you a serious man, Andrew?"

Andrew nodded. "Serious as a heart attack, sir."

The Bishop eyed him. "Good, but are you serious about Elyse?"

Andrew looked a little nervous. "It's our first date."

"Sometimes the greener grass is not the answer." The Bishop cleared his throat and focused on Elyse. "If you want to wear the veil, you have to stick to one man. Date one man. Go back to the beginning."

Elyse inhaled. She didn't like where this was going. "You think I should find Ricky Weinstein from fourth grade? That was my first kiss."

"No, I think you should call Nick Salvatore."

"Nick?" she choked. There was *that name*. Again. Unavoidable.

"You're dating Nick Salvatore?" Andrew quizzed.

"I knew it!" Saban shouted and jumped up from her booth. "Keep all the good ones for yourself!"

"I am not dating Nick." Elyse took Andrew's hand. "How do you know him?"

"Everyone knows Nick." Andrew swiveled to look at Saban. "And who's that woman?"

"No one," Elyse replied instantly.

The Bishop put his hands on the table. "Just last Sunday, Nick asked me if I'd heard anything from you. I'm a keen judge of character. I think you and Nick could make a go of it."

Elyse's heart pumped double time. This was the dating disaster of the decade, possibly her life. Her mouth hung open as excuses, still forming in her mind, failed to materialize into sound or sentences. "I've said it a million times, I am not interested in Nick Salvatore!"

"You're lying! I can tell," Jackie called out.

"Who are they?" Andrew sputtered.

"My best friends," Elyse explained.

Menus abandoned, Madeline and Jackie rose from their seats and flanked Saban. Just as the Bishop's face lit up with recognition, Jackie pushed past him.

"You've been secretly dating Nick, haven't you?" Jackie demanded, wide-eyed. "That's why you were avoiding him at the wedding. That's why you always make such a big deal about pretending to dislike him. I can't believe you've been dating him all along. I can't believe you kept this from me."

Elyse felt heat creep up her cheeks.

Jackie stared at her face. "You're blushing! It's true!"

"It's not," Elyse said defensively. It didn't sound convincing, even to her.

"If you're dating Nick," Madeline sniffed, "I have a right to know, too. It goes to image. I mean, if you and Nick are paramours, I have to decide what I do and do not reveal to you about intimate details. Loose lips sink ships. Just think of all those poor sailors drowning in World War Two. What a loss of manliness. Not that it matters since I'm married of course. How are you, Bishop Hegeland?"

"Fine, Madeline." The Bishop stood and gave her the required air kisses. "Have I told you about our school for orphans in the Congo?"

"I'll put a check in the mail tomorrow."

"Thank you."

At least they weren't talking about Nick anymore.

Elyse breathed a short sigh of relief. Nick Salvatore was the plague. In person and in conversation. No one was immune, but Elyse had to do something to save this disaster. "I have to go to the ladies' room," she said loudly.

It wasn't her finest moment, but it was the only safe haven she could think of. As Madeline often said, "When the going gets tough, the tough hit the powder room." Personally, Elyse preferred cheesecake in times of stress, but that wasn't an option right now.

On her heels, Madeline, Jackie, and Saban forced smiles, feigned excuses, and fell into step. En masse, the four women beat a hasty retreat for the far corner of Mario's, leaving Andrew and the Bishop alone at the table.

"This wasn't the plan," Elyse stammered as the door of the rest room closed behind them. Blinking hard, she allowed her eyes to readjust from the cavernous dark of the restaurant to the harsh fluorescents. "What part of *undercover* didn't you understand?"

"If Nick Salvatore is available, I want him!" Saban drooled. "Not Andrew. That plumber is an ape."

"A cute ape," Elyse countered.

"I bet he has quite the banana." Jackie elbowed Elyse. "How tall is he? Like six-two?"

Madeline nestled in beside Jackie and pulled her trademark lipstick, Rose Stone, out of an evening bag. "I read that a lot of the boxes of bananas shipped from Central America carry non-indigenous spiders, poisonous ones. Can you imagine? Who knew that a fruit market could be the end of you? Like this lipstick. Why would they discontinue Rose Stone? It's perfect. Like Nick Salvatore. So you're dating him, Elyse?"

"If I'd known Nick Salvatore was up for grabs, I wouldn't have even considered settling for the likes of Andrew," Saban huffed.

"I'm not dating Nick."

"You're protesting far too much to be believable, dear." Madeline puckered her lips and applied her lipstick.

Jackie turned to face Elyse. "If you're not dating him, what are you doing? Reconditioning him? For yourself?"

"He looked just fine to me," Saban gushed.

"Fine?" Elyse had had enough. "He may have a perfect body, perfect face, and perfect charm, but he is also a perfect ass!"

"I love his ass," Jackie said with a good amount of lechery in her voice.

Elyse looked at their faces. These women were the congregation in the Church of Nick, and she was spewing heresy. "Nick is untrainable. He will never be husband material, and I am not interested in him."

Jackie set her fists on her hips. "I smell a lie. You know I have a sense for this. Something is going on here, and I want to know what it is."

"Is it personal?" Madeline quizzed.

"Financial?" Saban asked, curious.

"Are you in trouble, Elyse?" Jackie pursed her lips.

"I know," Saban barked. "You're pregnant!"

"I wouldn't be drinking a glass of wine if I was pregnant. Stop it." Elyse slumped against the tile wall. "Everything is fine."

"If you aren't dating Nick, how come you avoid him?" Jackie wasn't giving up. "Like at the wedding."

"Ooooh, I'm writing a book on this," Madeline bubbled. "It's commitment-phobia. You're my guinea pig, Elyse. You and your odd distrust of Nick."

Elyse wanted to scream. *Nick.* His name just kept coming up again and again. The middle of her skull ached. She'd never had a migraine before, but maybe this was how they started.

"I'm not a commitment-phobic," Elyse announced. "I'm just committed to something else."

Madeline knew nothing about commitments. If it wasn't for Elyse, she'd be the patron saint of the Old Maids Society. Sure, she had a degree in psychology, but there was a big difference between passing a course and living in the real world. Madeline couldn't find the real world with a GPS.

"No, dear, this is obviously adverse psychology." Madeline finished dabbing the final touches of red to her lips. "This is my area, you know. The human mind. A mystery. The depths we don't see are like underwater mountains. You never notice them from the cruise ship deck. I love the midnight chocolate buffet. I'd weigh more if I didn't avoid it, or at least pretend like I did. That's the proof. You are adverse to Nick and therefore in love with him. The evidence is incontestable."

Elyse needed to redirect this conversation. She wasn't involved with Nick and never would be. Not for all the cheesecake in China. Her head throbbed, and she wondered if a quick recap of Mr. Salvatore's greatest society seductions, including Madeline and Jackie, would remind them of exactly why she had no intentions toward him.

Saban eyed her suspiciously. Elyse had to think fast or risk losing the deal with her. There's a time to tell the truth and a time to lie your ass off. Elyse decided that this was the time to lie. "You're right, Madeline," she began, "It *is* adverse psychology. I love Nick. Everyone loves Nick. Everyone has *loved* Nick at one point or another. I'm reworking him, but let's be honest, this is *Nick Salvatore*."

Madeline and Jackie nodded, knowingly.

"He was the best," Jackie sighed.

"He was quite the stallion muffin in his prime." Madeline giggled.

Saban squinted. "What? Everyone's slept with him except me?"

Elyse continued. "Nick will be my greatest conquest, but also my greatest challenge. Just laying the groundwork has taken three years. To land a fish like Nick, it has to seem like his idea to take the bait."

"He's been begging for the bait, Elyse," Jackie said, exasperated.

Elyse crossed her arms over her chest for emphasis. "But he's not ready to land in the boat yet. Nick is still a catch and release."

"I am so sorry," Madeline apologized. "I didn't see the whole plan."

"You are the master," Jackie admitted.

"I want him when you're done," Saban snapped.

"Fine." Elyse smiled. "I just thought you were in a hurry. See, Andrew is all primed and ready to change. Nick's a different case. Nick loves the chase. But that's all he loves. Once he's had his way, he's on his way. Nick doesn't date. He seduces."

"But he's a changed man," Jackie interrupted.

"Only because I'm breaking him down. He's a leopard, and only with a lot of time can I change his spots." Elyse didn't believe for a second a man like Nick could change, but she hoped that Jackie, Madeline, and Saban would believe it.

"I knew it!" Jackie pumped her fist, victorious.

"He might not be ready for a serious commitment for another four to five years," Elyse admitted. "Maybe longer. Until then, he'll continue to bed every woman with a heartbeat."

Saban chewed her lower lip.

"Nick isn't like that. Not anymore," Jackie countered.

"Nick Salvatore is simply not marriage material. Not yet."

"But he is."

"He's getting better every day," Elyse agreed through clenched teeth. "Nick is wonderful and headed toward spectacular."

"Good." Jackie seemed satisfied. "I just gave him fifty-thousand dollars for his Dessert Kitchen for the Homeless charity. He wrote a poem about muffins for me."

Madeline, not to be trumped, raised an eyebrow. "Only fifty-thousand? I gave him a hundred, and he gave me the most divine box of homemade petit fours."

Elyse flinched as she watched Saban take in the information. Her broad face and beady eyes revealed the mental calculator inside that whirled at full tilt like an accountant on April 14th. "How much does he charge for a biscuit with benefits?"

"Put your checkbook away, Saban." Elyse stepped up close. This girl needed some sense talked into her.

Jackie patted Saban on the shoulder. "We're not sleeping with Nick. Not anymore."

"We're happily married," Madeline crowed.

"We just like Nick," Jackie added. "A lot."

"He's good people." Madeline snapped her purse shut.

"You don't want Nick," Elyse said reassuringly. "You want a husband. And every man I rebuild is based on the Nick Salvatore ideal. Even Andrew. Trust me."

"I'm not paying a dime for that primate out there." Saban stomped her red Jimmy Choo.

"Fine with me." Elyse had had enough of this prima donna. "Wait a decade for all I care. You want a husband, so that ape is what you can have *now*."

Saban thought about it. "If Nick's ready in a couple years, can I trade up?"

Elyse was appalled. Only Saban would treat marriage like buying a new car. What's the depreciation on a husband? Is it better to lease or buy? Can I write him off on my taxes? Saban had a different set of morals.

Were her morals any better? She'd do anything to keep her house. Was that any worse? She needed the money, and Saban had it. The words came out before she could stop them. "Sure you can trade up."

That was that. Following the tradition of those before her, Elyse had sold her soul for her house.

Elyse followed Saban, Jackie, and Madeline back into the restaurant. Across the room, she noticed two tables pushed together with six chairs. Andrew and the Bishop had moved and were engaged in a lively conversation. So much for a graceful getaway, their coats had been draped over the four empty, waiting chairs.

Jackie and Madeline took seats on either side of the Bishop. Saban plopped down at the far end, and Elyse slid into the chair between Saban and Andrew.

Andrew nudged Elyse. "Your friend is looking at me funny. Like I owe her money or something."

Elyse glanced at Saban. Andrew had sized it up pretty well. Saban was staring. Her narrowed eyes were set on Andrew, and only Andrew.

"She's just a little intense," Elyse said. Believable, but disturbing.

Whap.

Elyse's eyes opened wide. Someone had kicked her under the table.

Whap.

She looked at each face in the group. Madeline, Jackie, and the Bishop were engaged in Charity Ball talk. Andrew was on the wrong side.

Whap.

Of course. Elyse's eyes darted toward Saban.

"I want him at the ball," she hissed.

The Bishop's Charity Ball. Elyse leaned close to her. "That's in less than four weeks," she whispered back.

"So?"

"It's black tie."

"Make him presentable by then, and I'll give you all

your money right there."

"That night?"

"Why wait for the wedding? You deliver me a Prince Charming, and it's cash on the barrelhead."

Everyone had stopped talking and was watching them.

Elyse winced. "Girl talk. Sorry. So, Bishop Hegeland, I bet that Charity Ball of yours is sold out. Not a single ticket available, right?"

Bishop Hegeland smirked and produced a packet of tickets thick enough to be a doorstop. "I just happen to have a few left."

Saban nodded her approval. "We're in."

That was the deal. Take it or leave it. Elyse gulped. She had very little time to turn a pig's ear into the silk purse of a husband.

Chapter 5

"This was the biggest disaster in the history of matchmaking," Elyse moaned. She paced across the carpets angled over her living room floor.

"The Hindenburg of hookups," Jackie agreed, settling on the sofa. "When Andrew saw Saban, I think the only thing he wanted to stick in her was a stake through her heart."

Elyse felt better running a hand over the mantle of her fireplace. Touching the ornately carved wood grounded her. The fireplace, along with the rest of this house, was her legacy. No matter how bad things got, this was her home, and it would always be here. Problems and personalities came and went. "I can fix it."

"How?" Jackie's expression was pained. "If things were this bad with Adam and Eve, there'd be no human race."

"It wasn't Apocalypse bad." She bent down to the grate and lit a fire starter under a pile of logs. A cozy fire might make her feel better. Give her some time to think this through.

Could she fix a mess this big? Saban and Andrew were total opposites. Saban had appraised Andrew like he was a slab of expired ground round in a butcher's discount case.

Andrew's reaction to Saban hadn't been any better. If she'd read the situation right, he looked ready to run away as far as his brown loafers and white socks would carry him.

"Where's the book, Elyse?" Jackie sat up straight, stuck by inspiration.

"I'm not taking out the book," Elyse said as she watched the flames grow.

"I love the book," Jackie whined.

"Not now." The last thing she wanted to do was haul out the book. She'd been thinking about it way too much this weekend. The book was dangerous.

"Please. *The Big Red Book of Men* makes me think anything is possible."

"Maybe." If all it took to quell Jackie was a peek at the book, then why not take it out? Elyse turned and let the fire warm her backside. "Will that make you happy?"

Jackie made an X with her fingers over her chest. "Cross my heart."

Elyse walked to the built-in bookcase separating the dining room from the parlor. Fishing an antique brass key out of a carnival glass bowl, she bent down and opened the locked cubbyhole at the base of the bookcase. This was the place generations of Tobins had kept their important papers. Marriage licenses, divorce decrees, vehicle titles, and loan statements, but never the deed to the house.

She kept none of those documents here. Instead, Elyse used the cubbyhole for the most important documentation of all, her book of men. Dozens of pages detailing the transformations of her fixer-upper husbands.

All of them. Including Andrew now.

When she sold the final husband, paid the mortgage, and got out of the Prince Charming business, she'd tuck the book into the attic. For good. The cubbyhole would then be home to the deed to the house. Just like Great-Grandma Tobin originally intended.

Sliding the key into the lock, the antique hinges squeaked a protest as the door opened. She slid the book out. The gilt-embossed red cloth cover of the old tome read: *The Daily Journal*, Vol. 16, Oct. to Dec. 1905.

As a child, Elyse had happened upon it under an attic floorboard. Its original purpose was supposed to have a bound record of the decades-defunct *Sausalito Daily Journal*. Three months of news compressed into one volume. Yet somehow this copy had escaped its intended purpose. Opening the front cover, she'd found blank page after blank page. Not a single splotch of ink or news article graced the paper. This was a book that could become anything.

Elyse hefted the book over to the couch and sat down.

"Open it!" Jackie pleaded.

"I am." Elyse lifted the cover and there, on the very first page, was a photo of a stout Pembrokeshire Corgi peeing on a Daphne bush. Under it was written: The honorable Rex Von Terrance.

Jackie laughed. "I feel better every time I look at him."

Elyse nodded. "You might be my first bride, but he will always be my first success."

Before Elyse discovered her talent for husband construction, there was Rex. Rex was the heart and soul of everything Elyse believed in. Rex was the spark that ignited the dream, that yes, men can indeed be fixed. Every woman for centuries had admitted that men can't be fixed. Rex changed that. There was a way.

"I saw that the Daphne bush is still doing great," Jackie said cheerfully. The book really did raise her spirits.

"Totally," Elyse agreed. "Rex remains redirected."

Rex Von Terrance was a Corgi with a Great Dane ego. He thought he owned Ivy Loop, which included the Daphne bush that Elyse's mother had planted a half century ago by the front gate. Unfortunately, Rex didn't value nature. In fact, he'd nearly killed the Daphne bush. Death by dog pee.

Every day for years, Rex had sauntered down the street on a self-guided walk. Everyone in the neighborhood knew him. He was an arrogant, but cute dog. Until one day he chose Elyse's Daphne bush for his *pee-mail* . . . and every other dog within twenty square blocks felt obligated to respond in kind.

At first she hoped it was a passing fancy. Maybe just

a random occurrence? Wrong. Rex had planted his flag and was diligent to refresh his claim on the bush every single morning. Without fail. Soon, the beloved Daphne bush began to wither.

She had tried everything to stop him. She tried kindness, greeting Rex in the morning, petting him and showering him with compliments as she led him past the Daphne bush. The little sneak doubled back the second she went inside. She tried treats, trails of Snausages artfully placed across the street. She tried threats, a rolled-up newspaper, but the dog instinctively knew she couldn't go through with premeditated dog battery. Nothing dissuaded him and his territory-marking buddies from dousing her dying Daphne.

Desperate, she searched online for books to solve this canine conundrum. She found her title. *Brainwashing Your Dog*. It proved to be a winner, and the eventual basis for her man remodeling techniques.

With a large dry sponge, latex gloves, and a little patience, in one short week, she had every dog in Sausalito peeing at the bottom of the hill, killing pernickety Mrs. Gruet's prize camellia. Now, years later, Elyse smiled every time Rex passed her house.

Rex had been reconditioned. She had taken his natural instincts and bent them into something useful.

Jackie flipped to the next page. "Rex is okay, but this guy is smokin'."

Elyse gazed at a snapshot of Donnie. Jackie's Donnie. But this was the original. Hair and glasses askew. A slightly twisted half-smile and a shirt that was buttoned out of alignment making his collar tip sideways. He looked like a man who had just survived a train wreck.

"He's a cutey," Elyse agreed.

Jackie ran a finger over Donnie's photo. "I don't know how you ever spotted him under, well, him."

Elyse pointed to his face. "It's the smile. It's

mischievous. And look at the eyes."

Jackie looked closer. "I can almost see a spark there."

"It's there."

"I know it's there now. I just don't know how you saw it back then."

"It's a gift." It was. Elyse could sense a man who wanted to commit to a relationship, but had been distracted by the clutter of life and career. Once found, she'd spiff him up and flip him to a worthy and generous bride. Her life would have been so much simpler if she'd discovered this talent earlier.

Jackie thumbed through the pages of notes following Donnie's photo. "You should publish this book."

Elyse shook her head. "I'm not giving up my trade secrets."

"I love the list of charms," Jackie said as she looked at hand-written notes on the page.

That was Elyse's favorite tool. Usually it only took a date or two to scrape off enough emotional paint to find out if a man had enough charms to make a good Prince Charming.

Charms were the telling elements of a man. A *good* man had six to ten charms. Maybe a dozen. An *excellent* man, many more. A love of art, one charm. The dedication to sit through a musical and look alert because he knew it was important to his intended, one charm. A love of animals, one charm. The willingness to cook, one charm. The *ability* to cook something that was not a spaghetti sauce lasagna, two charms. The lists of charms spanned pages.

Jackie's Donnie fell into the *excellent* category.

"Do you think you'll ever find the elusive PC?" Jackie asked.

Elyse sat forward. "It sure isn't Andrew."

They both laughed over that one. Andrew was light years away from PC status. PC was their shorthand for Prince Charming. PC was a man who had all the charms. Interests, arts, manners, upbringing, passion . . . the whole package.

So far only one man possessed all the charms. He was in the book, too. Buried, in the far back pages, beyond where she'd allow Jackie to look. No one else needed to know of the pages and pages devoted entirely to Nick Salvatore.

What a waste of charms.

Jackie closed the book without looking at Elyse's other five successes or Nick. "Can you get Andrew up and running by the Charity Ball?"

Elyse put her feet up on the coffee table and sank into the sofa's welcoming cushions. She glanced around the room. The firelight glow illuminated more than a century of craftsmanship around her. There'd been more than a hundred years of life in the house. She was only one generation doing her part.

She'd fix Andrew.

She'd sell him off to Saban.

She'd keep doing her part and if future generations were lucky enough, there'd be a thousand more years of life within these walls. "I don't have a choice," Elyse replied.

The next morning, Elyse sat at the dining room table with a cup of English Breakfast tea. In front of her, on a massive expanse of mahogany, she opened *The Big Red Book of Men.*

She turned the pages and sipped her tea. Jackie was right. This book gave her a feeling of possibility. She had rebuilt six flawed men from the ground up. Each one took up dozens of pages, dutifully detailed. Every date, every encounter, every subliminal lesson recorded here. Not one of the men had a clue that they had been a male restoration project.

Each successful rebuild gave her the confidence to tackle another man-project. The art restorer led to the musician, to the mechanic, to the professor, to the long haul driver, and the hot dog vendor. Now she'd have a plumber in the mix.

The beginning was hard. Finding, sensing a man with a good core who desired a lasting, stable relationship. She loved the end the most. At the finale of each man chapter, she pasted the wedding invitation and a bride and groom photo.

Elyse turned to the next blank page. She wished she'd taken a picture of Andrew in his boots and jockey shorts in the basement, or the blue suit and gold buttons in Mario's. Evidence of a transformation that no one could argue with, ever.

He'd be her last. Hopefully. Elyse knew she couldn't go on and remodel men forever. There were only so many wealthy women customers, and besides, this wasn't the sort of employment one broadcast to the world. On a tax return, what would she write under occupation? How could she explain that? Figuring out the write-offs alone would be a nightmare.

In the past, she'd always written web designer. It was more or less the truth.

Maybe less.

Which was why she hadn't gotten around to filing taxes. She didn't have an income. The brides *gifted* her their fees. Gifts aren't taxable.

In the distance, an engine rumbled. Elyse closed the book as a transmission shifted to low gear and climbed the steep grade of Ivy Loop. She knew the sound of Andrew's pickup well. Stashing *The Big Red Book of Men* in its cubbyhole, she ran to the door before the bell rang.

"What a surprise." She opened the door, pleased to see him.

Andrew, in his jeans, T-shirt and boots, shuffled on the front porch. "Yeah. I think I left a couple wrenches in the basement."

"No problem." Elyse grinned. He wasn't here for

wrenches. The fish was hooked.

"Kinda strange dinner last night." Andrew stepped past her into the entryway.

"That's the thing about San Francisco, you never know who you're going to run into."

"So what are you doing today?"

She couldn't say that she was plotting his manly renovation. "Working."

He bobbed his head up and down. "You're still doing the website thing, right?"

Had she really used that excuse with him? After two years, she wasn't sure what she said she did for a living. "That's what I do, I build websites."

"Maybe you could help me with one. Can I see some of your work?" His face was open and honest.

"Sure. Have a seat at the dining room table, and I'll get my computer."

Elyse dashed up the stairs to the second floor. Web design was her Plan B. She'd gone to college and studied programming and Internet marketing . . . and it really had been quite a useful education once upon a time. Except there was a lot of competition in the marketplace and the jobs that were out there just didn't pay enough to feed herself and renovate the house.

So she'd started freelancing.

One day, after Andrew was settled with Saban, she might dust off her skills and design websites again. She couldn't think of a more perfect job for a stay-at-home mom. She'd raise her children, and they'd be none the wiser about her man-renovating days of the past.

It wasn't like she was ashamed of her work. No. Tobin women worked unconventional jobs reflecting their grass-roots feminism. Great-Grandma Tobin built houses as a contractor. Grandma Tobin knew the trades well and studied as a welder. During the war, she worked on fighter planes.

Elyse's mother had been fascinated by the Golden Gate Bridge since childhood. For thirty years she'd worked *bridge crew* for the highway maintenance department and knew every cable, beam, and rivet on the entire span.

Entering the office, Elyse searched for her laptop. Years ago she *had* designed a few websites. Her flair for mixing color, content, and picking the right graphics made the clicks from page to page flow like an intimate dance between the customer and source. Her philosophy was that websites should be like a romance.

On her desk, the old laptop rested under a layer of dust. She brushed it off and plugged in the charger. In a few brief moments and a couple of mouse clicks, a website glowed on the screen.

InflamedHearts.com

The brainchild of Leona Banks, one of San Francisco's fringe elites, InflamedHearts was a vanity matchmaking company created to find suitors for her and her wealthy potential friends. The idea to use matchmaking as an entry to the social elite was a good idea.

The company was a miserable failure.

Leona had one great false assumption at the inflamed heart of her concept. That good men were plentiful and easy to find.

"I have hundreds of men just chomping at the bit," Leona had bragged when they first met. "You set up the database, and we're in business."

Paid by the hour, Elyse had taken her time to comb through the applicants. Plus, her mother had died the previous winter and she was still paying off the funeral home in installments. She needed the extra cash. Leona had plenty of that, or so it seemed.

Almost all the men fell into one of two categories. They were either unmarried for good reason . . . phobias, psychoses, or simply bad hygiene, or they were playboys looking to score. Elyse had preferred the insane and unwashed to the slick one-night-stand aficionados.

There was very little in between. But there was a little. Elyse found two, nine-to-five average men who seemed like decent human beings. How sad that instead of love, it was almost enough to find someone with basic morals—not to be too restrictive, if a man didn't regularly break more than five of the Ten Commandments, they were a prize.

"Did you look at these men, Bryan and Tom?" Elyse had quizzed Leona at her office. "Why didn't you snap them up?"

Leona looked over their files. "Complete rejects, darling."

Elyse couldn't understand it. "But why?"

"Look at their interests, their hobbies, their jobs. These men are dull, dull, dull."

Elyse had seen honest and hopeful. "I'd rather have dull than scheming."

"We don't say scheming in the matchmaking world," Leona corrected her. "We say they are smart and passionate."

While Elyse thought dull had potential, Leona went out of business. But not before Leona called one more time.

"The history of civilization is doomed due to the lack of decent men in the world," she whined. Sitting at her kitchen table, Elyse listened to Leona while watching Rex Von Terrence strut past her Daphne bush. "And if you haven't cashed any checks I wrote, don't. They won't clear the bank."

That's when Elyse made the decision.

Men needed to be drawn out. Encouraged. Using the techniques she'd practiced on Rex, Elyse took the whole *brainwashing your dog* concept to a new level. She decided to find men and experiment.

That's when her night with Nick happened.

An accident. An experiment. A weak moment. Whatever it was, however embarrassed she'd been by her lack of good judgment, that one night turned her life around. It led her to Donnie.

Intentionally finding a man and refurbishing him to the Nick Salvatore ideal hurtled her to success. To $100,000 paydays.

Elyse closed the laptop computer, tucked it under her arm, and raced down the stairs.

"Sorry about that," she announced, rounding the banister. Andrew paced the parlor. "Had to close out an old file. Shall we get started?"

One legal pad filled with ideas, several Internet searches, and a pot of tea later, Andrew continued to waffle on what the perfect plumber's website should look like.

"They're all too newfangled," he complained.

The website was going nowhere. At the table in the dining room, Elyse buried her head in her hands. "Aren't there any websites you like?"

"I don't even like computers." Andrew elbowed her. "Maybe you'd like to come over to my house tonight and see how a plumber lives. Then we can talk about what a plumber's website should look like!"

Elyse blinked. Dinner? This was moving along nicely. She closed the laptop. "I'll bring a salad."

Andrew smiled. "Well, okay then. I'll get my wrench and see you tonight."

Elyse strolled the stalls of the Sausalito Farmer's Market. In her opinion, it was the best market in the Bay Area. She loved the variety of vendors. There were crafters, artists, florists, ceramicists, and an organic winery.

The legions of produce growers hawked everything from organic citrus to dirt-crusted carrots and potatoes.

Hands down, her favorite part of the market was the four-man jug band. Grown men who twanged and blew their way through three sets from 2 p.m. to 4 p.m.

Standing in the front row, she watched children with rainbows painted across their cheeks dance to the *thump, thump, thump* of the washtub bass. She couldn't help but tap her foot to the infectious ragtime beat of *Diga Diga Doo*. The group's leader, a virtuoso of the kazoo, alternated to his duck call to the delight of the kids who quacked along.

Actually, the band wasn't very good. But they were an exceptional example of men having fun. Elyse tossed a dollar into their tin bucket. Not that any of these men needed money. Over the months, she had chatted with them on breaks to see if there were any potential husbands.

One was a lawyer. Another a sanitary engineer, or garbage man as he called himself. The third drove a BART train, and the last was a computer software designer. Four men who ditched weekday careers to puff bottles and pound kitchen utensils. Excellent candidates, but all married.

Married like Andrew would soon be.

That is, if Elyse packed enough lessons into the next four weeks. She'd work on food, dining etiquette, and flowers tonight. Could Andrew handle the accelerated timetable? In one night she'd have to cover areas that usually took a month to teach.

Wandering to a flower-laden market stall, she put down her bag and studied the purple snapdragons, yellow lilies, and giant red Gerber daisies. Each competed for her attention with bright colors or heady scents.

Snapdragons were her favorite, but they weren't quite right for this evening. Especially since Andrew didn't need to learn her favorites, but Saban's. Did Saban even like flowers? Every time she said *tulip,* she seemed to sneer.

Elyse spied a bucket in the far corner of the stall, shaded by an oversized umbrella. Freesias. Now there was a flower. Fragrant, but not obtrusive. Casual and still classic. She lifted a bouquet and inhaled.

"You can't sniff the smell off those and stick 'em back, ya know," the flower vendor snarled.

She looked up and assessed the man. She read the bitter frown lines on his tanned face. Surrounded by the beauty of these blooms, even a dour personality should soften and succumb to life's joys. This vendor was immune.

"Five dollars," she offered.

The vendor howled. "Twenty!"

"Meditating on the beauty of the freesia?" came a voice from behind.

A tingle raced up her spine. She knew who it was without turning around. "I would have made Nirvana, Nick, if I'd just had another second of uninterrupted peace."

"Does the world really need another Buddha?" He stepped up next to her.

Elyse met his gaze and pushed down the physical attraction that rushed her, taking her by surprise. She despised the man. She'd had her way with him. He should be out of her system. Permanently.

Her body defied logic. Heat surged between her legs as he smiled at her.

Damn. Logic wasn't working. She bit her lower lip. Nervous. Angry.

Horny.

Double damn.

Thoughts of his naked body and slightly calloused hands forced their way into her thoughts. Opening up *The Big Red Book of Men* two days in a row had been a mistake. Her tongue traced the edges of her teeth before she set her jaw, firm. She had to stop thinking about him. Somehow, looking at Nick's photos and newspaper clippings that she'd spent three years compiling in the book, corrupted her resolve to steer clear of him.

No, wait. He'd found her.

Had he stalked her outside the bathroom door at the wedding? Landed in her lap in Wedgeworth's on purpose? Unlikely, though she shuddered at the restaurant memory, and her obvious weakness for him. As he'd gotten up from the floor, casually grazing her knees and shoulders, every cell in her body had screamed, *take me, take me*.

Never.

Even if he was the last man in the world.

Well, maybe if he was the *last* man in the world. She'd only have sex with him again if it was for the good of the human race.

Elyse pushed a strand of hair behind her ear and steeled herself. Nick Salvatore was bad news.

But he looked so good.

The man even made a faded pair of Levis and casual polo shirt look sexy. She noted that neither piece of clothing had so much as a wrinkle, loose thread, or stray button. His walking shoes were scuff-less. He was, as always, perfectly turned out. No one should be this crisp, especially at a farmer's market.

Elyse scanned Nick up and down. "You look nice," she said casually. "Do you keep an ironing board in the trunk of your car?"

"I keep a dry cleaner on twenty-four hour alert." He picked up Elyse's bag of groceries. "Seems you're entertaining."

"Can't a girl buy herself salad and flowers?"

"It would seem a waste."

"A waste of what? Do you think flowers are wasted on me? Is food wasted on me?" She grabbed the bag of groceries with her free hand, grazing Nick's elbow in the process. The soft hairs on her arm stood up.

She forced herself to resist the lure of Nick. Rudeness was her only defense. Without that defense, she'd throw him in the back of the flower van, strip him naked, and take him then and there.

"You misread me, Elyse. I meant it seems a waste that no one would be there to enjoy your company."

Nick was smooth. If she smacked him with a brick, he'd just keep coming. He was relentless, and usually successful, when seducing women. Just not this time.

"You needn't worry," Elyse said, hoping to mask the lust in her voice. She shifted her weight to one leg and cocked her hip. "I'll be in good hands soon."

"I bet you will. Anything less would be a crime against humanity."

He had his routine down so well it was like having a Broadway play right here in the middle of the stall with an audience of one. In every encounter she'd had with Nick, she never knew whether to applaud, or pelt him with vegetables. At least this time, she had ammunition if she chose the latter, though Elyse hated the idea of wasting a basket of fresh organic cherry tomatoes on him.

"I think I know why you don't like me . . ." he continued.

Elyse was done with the clever patter. She had to leave. Get out of here before he wore her down. "How about I'm a smart woman in touch with myself, secure, and even when I'm not, I know that I'm strong enough to change my world without the emotional manipulations and false stimuli that you offer to project the image of a life worth living?"

Nick arched an eyebrow at her. "Has Madeline been counseling you?"

"No."

"Someday you're going to want to know why you don't like me," he chuckled.

"You can tell me at your funeral."

"I'm trying to earn a living here," the vendor cut in. "So how about coughing up the twenty bucks, and you two can go off and make kissy face?"

Kissy face with Nick? Elyse cringed.

Never again.

Nor was she about to pay twenty dollars for freesias. She wouldn't pay that much for them if they were certified organic, state fair blue ribbon winners that turned to gold after they wilted.

Elyse addressed Nick first, waving the flowers in his face. "Don't make me file a restraining order."

"Good day then." Nick nodded, swiveled on his heel and headed in the opposite direction. Exhaling a shaky breath, she watched his perfectly sculpted butt move as he strolled away through the stalls.

Had she really threatened a restraining order? God help her, the only thing that needed a restraining order was her libido. No matter how good-looking or charming the man was, he was still Nick Salvatore.

Totally off limits.

Nick paced through the winding paths between vendors. The only thing that needed restraining was the grin on his lips. Elyse Tobin's body language had betrayed her words.

Her pupils dilated, she'd licked her lips, shifted her weight—several times—and pushed her hair behind her ears. She'd fondled the stems of those freesias to the point of mangling them. The clues led him to one incontestable conclusion: he was slowly, but surely, getting to her.

But would she come around soon enough?

Nearing forty, he'd accepted that he wasn't getting any younger. He wanted to start a family. He couldn't wait forever. Elyse was the most fascinating woman he'd ever met. He was certain she was *the one*. But he couldn't pursue her forever.

So he'd made a deal with himself, *The Cheesecake Deal.*

He knew her weakness for cheesecakes and was using it against her. Over the course of three years, he'd let his imagination go wild, concocting whimsical and elaborate cakes for her. Each one a testament of his adoration. He was building the Taj Mahal in sugar, spice, cream cheese, and berries.

He'd documented and detailed each cake over the past three years. If he got to number 1,000 and she still refused to give him the time of day, he'd concede romantic defeat and give into his agent, Vicky Barnsdale.

Actually, there were two things Vicky wanted, to publish his cheesecake recipes as a book. And his sperm.

Vicky had eggs on ice.

It wasn't how Nick had envisioned his children, being raised by dedicated lesbians. At least Vicky was committed to her partner. They'd been together long before Nick ever met them. If there was a perfect couple, they were it. They cherished each other. In this world of *me, me, me*, Nick admired their complete consideration of each other. That was love.

While a plastic cup and a DVD in a fertility clinic was not his idea of a good time, or a way to start a family, it was the only offer he had that meant his offspring would get the unconditional love and attention that all children deserve.

Though he wanted badly to be a father, he'd settle for frequent visitation rights and being known as Uncle Nick. It wasn't the brass ring, but if that was as close as he could get, so be it.

Continuing down the row of stalls, he felt a surge of hope. Of progress. Nick helped himself to a sample of free-range pork sausage. It was tasty. Being grass-fed gave the meat a gamy flavor he liked, but they had added a touch too much fennel. He understood spices.

Elyse swept through his mind like a cold wind. He didn't understand her. What did she really want? The rumors and stories were clear. She loved her house. She was a matchmaker extraordinaire. But she must want more than that. When they'd made love, he sensed that there was so much more struggling beneath her surface.

He was nervous. His next cake would be 997. After that, there were only three more. He chose the number *one thousand* after teaching a course on Japanese fusion cuisine. His co-chef from Tokyo was busy making origami cranes in his spare time. When Nick asked him about it, he told him of the Japanese legend . . . if you make a thousand cranes, you will be granted a wish. The Japanese usually use it to guarantee a long marriage, healthy child, or to ward off illness. Nick tried to learn to fold the small paper birds, but it was useless. His fingers were too big.

That's when he decided to make cheesecakes. If the gods favored paper cranes, they would probably love cheesecake. One thousand unique desserts. If he didn't get his wish for Elyse after that, well, the gods must not be listening.

"Nick!" an excited voice called. "I have the berries!"

He knew the voice well. Sun was from the Sonoma Buddhist Monastery. If there was anyone who could find wild black truffles or pine nuts, it was Sun and the monks. They were Nick's source for his most unusual culinary creations.

"What have you got for me?" Nick asked as he hugged the priest who wore a flowing orange robe and deep red sash.

"Huckleberries!" Sun cheered. "They're early this year."

Huckleberries. Nick had been at loose ends trying to figure out his last four desserts. Huckleberries were exactly what the gods must have ordered. "Let's see them."

Sun led Nick out of the market to a Volkswagen van parked on the street. Two other monks waited. They opened the sliding side door with a creak. Inside were four flats of the salmon-colored berries.

Sun took a handful and held them out to Nick.

One taste, and Nick was sold. They were sweet and tart, but not like cultivated fruit. He could taste the mountain, the cold rain, and the struggle the bushes endured. "I'll take them."

"All of them?" Sun asked, surprised.

"All of them," Nick said with a friendly nod. "What are you asking?"

Sun looked to the other monks. "We were hoping to cover our gas, maybe have a meal, and take some supplies back to the monastery."

"What kind of supplies?" Nick had done this negotiation with Sun before.

"Soy beans, rice, maybe some fruit."

"Come by my place for a meal. I'll order any produce or staples you need through my distributors." Nick took out his wallet. "How about five hundred?"

"That is far too generous, Nick," Sun objected.

"Money means little to me, Sun," Nick said with a little sadness. "And your berries are pure gold."

"I'll give you ten," Elyse offered.

"Ten dollars?" The vendor howled. "You can't expect Argentinean flowers for no ten dollars."

She hated negotiating. "These came from Paso Robles. Probably on a truck this morning."

The vendor shook his head like his hair was on fire. "I swear to you, Argentina! Cold shipped! By air!"

"There's a tag." She turned the tag attached to one stem. "It says Paso Robles Floral Growers."

"You know what gas costs to drive those up here? Hundreds. Them flowers don't walk, you know."

"Ten," Elyse repeated. She wondered what made some people so bitter. Like this man. He had beauty all around him, yet he couldn't see it. Maybe there was a lesson here.

"What do you want?"

"What do I want?" he shouted. "I want a life. I want a career. Instead, I got dirt. I got flowers. You people have it so easy."

"You people?" she asked.

"Yeah," he said with a snarl. "Rich people. I work my ass off to put a roof over my wife's head, and you want to argue over a couple dollars. I bet you spend more money on shampoo than I do for food."

"I'm not rich," Elyse objected.

"Ha!" The vendor spit on the ground. "Look at that bag."

Elyse looked at her bag. "What about it?"

"I know that's one a them designer bags. A Her-mes. My wife yaks about them all the time. She wants a Her-mes. She wants a Prada. She's lucky we got our kids in community college."

"I have the bag, but I'm not rich," she argued.

"It fell off a truck, right?"

"I bought it at a rummage sale. Yeah, it was a great deal. I got a mortgage. I got problems. I'm lucky my head's above water."

The vendor studied her. "For real?"

"Yeah. You've got a wife, kids in school, and some beautiful flowers. You're a lucky man." Elyse was surprised by the earnestness in her voice. "Damn lucky."

They stared at each other before the vendor leaned close to her. "I'll take ten for the freesias, but don't tell no one."

Chapter 6

In her Prius, Elyse cruised the flat thoroughfares of Andrew's neighborhood. His house was past Oakland, out to the fringes of the vintage suburban sprawl. It was as far as a person could drive and still be considered within reach of the Bay Area. She marveled at row after row of late 1920's built homes, almost identical, but for an occasional overgrowth of foliage or a neon exterior paint job. The streets were almost identical, too, except for their names. Elm. Fir. Alder. Cherry.

Even though she'd never seen these houses, she knew them. Each and every floor plan and model. In the crawl space above her fourth floor bathroom, Elyse had discovered rolls of architectural plans detailing the modest two-bedroom designs built for less than a dollar per square foot. The plans had belonged to Great-Grandma Tobin, a construction foreman.

Between world wars, Great-Grandma oversaw massive housing developments just like this one. Her crews of skilled laborers worked twelve-hour days to build affordable homes for soldiers-turned-factory-workers. Elyse squinted as she turned into the path of the setting sun on Pine Street.

Proud of her Great-Grandmother's accomplishments, she was also grateful she'd never lived in one of these homes. The bungalows were a tribute to American ingenuity in a time of need, but there was a total absence of craftsmanship and character. To Elyse, those two qualities were everything.

She shuddered as she pulled to the curb in front of her destination. Andrew's house. A weathered single-story structure. She pictured the blueprint. No foyer, the front door opened into the living room. A kitchen at the back and two small bedrooms separated by a single bath.

Parked like a shiny trophy, Andrew's plumbing pickup sat squat on two strips of concrete next to the house with grass growing between them. Even the driveways had been rushed here.

She stepped out of the car and smoothed her white, eyelet lace sundress. Her look was chaste, even a touch virginal. The vintage dress had a high neckline and a cream colored sweater covered her arms. A faux pearl choker topped off her ensemble, adding to the overall *good-girl* effect.

Entering a man's lair often translated, in male thinking anyway, to the possibility of sex. A notion firmly discouraged.

Elyse grabbed the freesias, groceries, and her orange purse off the passenger seat. What had she been thinking bring her Hermes? She wore it everywhere, every day. But here? It didn't fit in on Pine Street any more than she did in San Francisco high society. She should have worn a basic bag, something made with rip-stop nylon or better yet, woven straw.

She hefted the bag in her hand. Even if she'd bought the luxury purse for a song in the basement of the Episcopalian church, it made her stick out like a sore thumb in the suburbs. When she was downtown, with her friends and wealthy clients, it made her one of the girls. Her handbag equaled admission to their world.

Saban had judged her by it.

Madeline had assessed her character via her handbag long before the introduction to Cyril.

Even her best friend, Jackie, might not have given her the time of day at the charity event three years ago if it hadn't been for the Hermes.

Deep down, she wished women would stop judging each other through designer accessories. A purse or shoes didn't reveal a person's true character or intentions. Women needed to see beyond decorations, to the core of the person, like Elyse could see into men.

Balancing the groceries, flowers, and handbag, Elyse stepped across the lawn, grass crunching under her kitten heels. At least the lawn didn't need mowing. It was dead. The grass was the light brown color it turns when it's never met a sprinkler. How could a lawn be dead in June?

Andrew opened the front door and greeted her. "Don't mind the lawn. I poisoned it. I'm going to lay in gravel."

"No mowing," she said, cheerfully horrified.

"And guests can park on it." Andrew held the door open wide.

Andrew clearly took pride in his home. A simple house and a simple man, both on the cusp of being all they could be. Let the fast track to transformation begin.

"This house was built around 1930?" Elyse asked. She made it sound like a guess, even though she knew better.

"1928," he answered and puffed out his chest. "If I have some time off this summer, I'll paint it. I was thinking brown."

This was exactly what she wanted to hear. Taking care of the things you love is definitely a charm. Clutching the groceries, Elyse stepped through the doorway. Inside, without air-conditioning, felt like a sauna. The smell of bread and tomato sauce wafted across the living room.

"Take your sweater?" Andrew offered.

As he hung it up in a tiny coat closet, Elyse set down her purse and surveyed the living room. A futon sofa and a pair of Ikea chairs. Ikea shelves. A nook was set up as a dining area with Ikea table, chairs, plates, silverware, and glasses. She felt like she'd been transported into an Ikea showroom.

"You're a fan of Ikea," she observed.

"One-stop shopping." Andrew hurried through a doorway into the kitchen and returned with a plate of meatballs on toothpicks. "I have snacks."

"Ikea?"

"Heat and serve. Don't worry, I'm cooking something special for dinner."

Elyse inhaled. The odor of garlic was strong. She followed him through a pair of swinging shutter doors into a narrow galley kitchen with a back door at the far end. In the door was another smaller door at the bottom. A dog door. Had he mentioned a dog?

The back door and walls were painted sea-foam green to match the original sea-foam green tile countertops. Countertops that looked like an Italian kitchen battlefield. She shivered, knowing what was to come. If you walked into a bomb maker's kitchen, you'd probably find dynamite, plastic explosives, and timers. This was more disturbing. There were empty jars of spaghetti sauce, a box from dried noodles, a plastic powdered Parmesan container, an empty tub of cottage cheese, and the wrapper from a generic block of Mozzarella.

"I'm making lasagna," Andrew said proudly. "Even better than Mario's Pasta Emporium."

Spaghetti sauce lasagna. The college staple of seductions, lost virginity, and whispered promises of forever. She'd been down that path before. What was it about a jar of Ragu and some cheap cheese that could make a stable, young, right-thinking girl lose all direction?

She was not fond of lasagna.

"There's garlic bread, too." Andrew hopped to the oven. He pulled out a charred and smoking foil bag.

Setting the groceries and bouquet on a small patch of uncluttered counter, she decided to start off with flowers. "Do you have a vase?"

Andrew pulled an Ikea glass tube off the top of a cupboard as she handed him the freesias. "What are these?" he asked, inhaling the flowers' scent. "They smell great."

Elyse liked his eagerness. "They're *freesias*."

"*Freesias,*" he repeated, "I'll have to remember that. I thought the only flower was, like, roses. They come in a million colors."

This was a wonderful opportunity. "Roses are an all around good flower, and each of the colors means something."

"Red are love, right?" he said, sure of himself.

"That's right," she agreed. "White are innocence, and yellow, friendship."

Andrew tipped his head, taking it in. "That would have to be a pretty good friend to spend the bucks for a dozen yellow roses."

"There are other flowers, too, that aren't expensive," she continued. "Daisies are a nice surprise. Chrysanthemums are the royal flower of Japan and last a long time. And alstroemeria look like little orchids."

"I should write this down."

"Feel free." Elyse breathed out, relaxing. That he wanted to remember had potential. Memory for flowers, and the desire to give them was definitely charm-worthy.

Andrew filled the vase with water. "Are you ready for dinner?"

"Let me get out the greens."

"Greens?" he said, puzzled. "We're talking salad, right?"

"Yes."

"I usually get the pre-washed stuff in a plastic bag. Wham, bam, here's a salad, ma'am."

Wham bam? She'd have to get rid of that phrase. "When you care about someone, you want to give them the best of everything. Don't you agree?"

"Sure."

"So a fresh salad takes a little longer to make, but it says a lot to the person you serve it to."

Andrew peered into the grocery bag. "You could feed a hundred rabbits for a month with all this lettuce."

"*Greens*," Elyse repeated for effect.

Andrew nodded along. "Which is just a fancy way to say lettuce."

Elyse needed to guide him a bit more. Make some physical contact to open his mind. She slid a hand onto his firm bicep.

A flicker of doubt crossed her mind. When she touched Andrew's arm, it was just an arm. A very nice arm, but an arm all the same. When she'd touched Nick this afternoon, it was like a small electric shock. If anything, it was probably Nick's Italian leather shoes building up a static charge. Simply science.

Definitely not attraction.

"Not just lettuce," she said, shaking off the thought of Nick. "We'll begin with an arugula and baby spinach mix with a champagne and pear vinaigrette. I'll spice it up with some Oregon raspberries and slivered almonds."

"This is a long way from meat and potatoes," Andrew admitted. "But I'm in."

"Okay." Elyse rinsed the vegetables and berries in the sink.

Andrew watched. "Do you think they served iceberg lettuce on the *Titanic*?"

"Is that a joke?" she asked as she shook the water off the arugula.

He bobbed his head. "Get it? Iceberg, *Titanic*?"

"I do."

"Then it's a joke."

Elyse would only give him half a point for humor, but a full charm for trying.

"Oh," Andrew said, excited. "I almost forgot. I got us a bottle of wine. With a cork." He hurried to the refrigerator and took a bottle from the freezer.

She glanced at the long, slim neck of the icy bottle as Andrew battled the cork with the screw on a multi-tool can opener. No charms for wine selection. Red sauce and Riesling?

Men who drank beer, trying to impress their intended women by not serving beer, probably made up ninety percent of cheap Riesling sales. Not that she disliked Riesling. There were some that made a nice dessert wine. But this wasn't dessert.

He filled two glasses.

"That might be a little too cold," Elyse warned.

Andrew clinked his glass against hers and took a massive drink in one big gulp. His eyes opened wide, then he slapped a palm against his forehead. "Brain freeze!"

One step forward, ten steps back. Her stomach twisted in a knot. She'd been too confident. Too optimistic. She could feel her blood pressure ratcheting up past healthy. She suppressed a howl of frustration. Elyse couldn't believe that he chugged it.

Closing her eyes, she wondered if it was too late to cut and run. Could she find an Andrew replacement? Impossible. Andrew was the clay she'd been given to mold. Saban had seen him and had accepted the package.

Elyse pictured her house, perched at the edge of Ivy Loop. If she wanted her dream, she needed to deliver the goods. She opened her eyes and took him in. Tall, muscular, average looks, a full head of hair, employed. He'd gotten off to a good start she just need to get him back on track.

"I always remember the three 'S's when I try wine," she said in her best teaching voice.

"Three 'S's?" Andrew asked. "I saw a tasting thing on TV. Everyone spit out the wine. Is one of the 'S's *spit*?"

"No. Well, maybe later. It's not one of the main 'S's." At least he was trying.

Andrew's face brightened. "Suck it down? That's another 'S'."

"It's swirl, sniff, and sip," Elyse said strongly. She

turned her glass so the wine swished around inside. "This helps you look at the color and the viscosity. If it clings to the side of the glass, it has legs."

Andrew swirled his wine. "Legs are good?"

"Yes. Legs are good." She put her nose to the rim of the glass and inhaled. "Next is smelling the bouquet."

"Like flowers?"

"It's the fragrance of the wine."

Andrew sniffed his drink. "It smells like wine."

"But are there other aromas?" she challenged. "Do you smell fruit?"

"Yeah. Grapes."

"Other than grapes. Maybe a hint of raspberry?"

"That's probably coming from the salad you made."

"It isn't." This was getting tiring. "Finally, take a small taste in your mouth and then inhale a little air over the top of it."

Andrew took a gulp, held it in his mouth and made a gargling sound. "It makes my teeth ache."

"Just take a little. Like this." Elyse took a sip and inhaled a small stream of air over it making a soft gurgle.

After swallowing, Andrew followed her lead. "Wow, that makes the wine taste a lot different."

"Exactly." This was good. He was falling in line. He might never be a wine connoisseur, but he could at least look like he knew what he was doing. With Andrew, not shouting *brain freeze* at a tasting would be enough.

Andrew was improving by leaps and bounds, but was it possible to sand off enough rough corners to make him palatable to Saban by the Charity Ball? There were a lot of rough corners.

"Cheers," Andrew toasted. He raised his glass and gulped the rest of his drink. "We should go to the wine country."

"I'd love to." Elyse warmed to the idea of teaching

him the basics over a leisurely afternoon driving through the hills of Napa and Sonoma. Country highways through the Russian River Valley and some pinot noir. Beautiful scenery and a Pinot Gris. There was a tasty little white.

Andrew set down his glass and pulled the lasagna from the oven. With a spatula, he scooped it onto plates. Elyse applied the dressing to the greens, and they settled at the dining nook table.

The lasagna was the usual disappointment. Soggy noodles. Spongy cheese.

"What do you think?" He dug in.

"It's a classic." Carving her fork through the layers, she made the best of the situation. Even though she loathed his choice, it was great that he was working hard to impress her with a home-cooked meal.

Andrew shoveled another load of noodles into his mouth. "I learned how to make this when I was in college."

Now there was an opening Elyse could exploit. He must have had lots of interests then. Political science. Literature. To match up with Saban, it wouldn't hurt if he had a minor in agriculture. "What did you study?"

"Plumbing."

"And?" she asked. There had to be something else.

"Math. I loved math. Do you know how long it would take a one point eight gallon toilet tank to flush through a two inch pipe?"

"No."

"I can go get a paper and pencil and figure it out."

"Maybe after dinner."

Elyse tallied her work so far. Flowers, greens, wine. Not complete disasters. The restaurant didn't count since there'd been no training. Still, there was a lot of ground to cover.

A distinct bang from the kitchen made her jump. "What was that?"

Andrew jumped up and turned to the doorway. "Brace yourself."

She didn't have time.

A clatter of claws on linoleum, then a flash of fur came bursting in. Andrew tried to catch it, but it shot between his legs, skidded into Elyse's chair, and buried its nose between her legs. Its huge, feather duster tail wagged excitedly.

Elyse recoiled.

"That's Riley." Andrew wrapped an arm around the dog's torso and pulled him away. "He's kind of a crotch rocket."

Elyse stared down, horrified. The dog shook and wiggled, breaking free of Andrew's grip and lunged at her privates again.

"Sorry," Andrew apologized, grabbing Riley again. "He failed obedience training. Three times."

Other than Rex Von Terrance, she'd had little interaction with canines. It wasn't that she didn't like them, she did. Adopting a rescue dog from the local shelter was on her list of things to do, right after paying off the house, making herself a Prince Charming, and having children. Children and dogs went together like peanut butter and jelly. They were meant for each another.

Elyse just didn't relate to big dogs. And she wasn't relating to Riley, though Riley seemed to love her, or at least her crotch.

"Leave it," Andrew commanded and hauled him away through the kitchen. Elyse listened as the back door opened, Riley was booted out with a dog treat, and a lock flipped closed on the dog door.

Andrew returned to the table and sat down. "He hates missing a chance to beg."

Elyse looked down at her lap. Black fur clung to her dress. A wave of panic swept over her. If she recalled correctly, Saban was a cat person. "Does Riley like cats?"

"He likes chasing them up trees." Andrew laughed and speared another forkful of lasagna.

Maybe his dog and Saban's cats could learn to get along? What a nightmare. Pets weren't part of the matchmaking package. Andrew and Saban would have to figure that out on their own.

"So, what do we do now?" Elyse put her fork down. She'd had enough. Enough spongy lasagna, burned garlic bread, enough dog fur. Time to make some real progress, and the sooner, the better. Time to talk.

"Are you thinking about my website?" Andrew asked.

"You really want one?"

"I thought it might be a way for you to work off some of the money you owe me."

Elyse's mind braked to a stop. If this was all about money, she'd read everything wrong. Could she have misjudged the situation that badly? Had he only invited her over to dinner to discuss finances? Sure, she owed him a lot of money. And he'd be paid in full. After she deposited Saban's check into her account.

"I think I'll use the ladies' room," she announced. She needed to get her thoughts together. Regroup.

"Through the living room to the right." Andrew pointed.

Andrew rubbed his face, relieved to have a few moments to himself. Nick warned him this might happen. Elyse had high standards. He could tell she hated his lasagna. What was that about? His lasagna was really good.

All the fancy words were giving him a headache. *Freesias? Arugula? Alstroemeria? Vinaigrette?* He'd never had to study this hard for anything.

Sheesh. He was a plumber, not some monocle-wearing, Mr. Money aristocrat. He couldn't pretend to be like Nick. No matter how hard he tried. Nick was smooth. He wasn't.

Andrew scooped up the last of the noodles from his plate, leaned back in his chair, and chewed thoughtfully. What was Elyse looking for?

Why didn't she just tell him? Say, read the newspaper, watch television talk shows, stop saying words like *cheap* and *friggin,'* and say *inexpensive* and *abominable* instead. *Really* had to be dropped, too. Then he had to think about the big stuff like wine and politics.

He bristled. Nick mentioned these things. A sort of primer for having Elyse choose him. Yeah, he was supposed to remove *sort of* from his vocabulary and *yeah*.

The man he was didn't measure up well in the real world of women. At least the ones Elyse knew who wanted to get married. He enjoyed hot dogs, garage sales, and court TV. He preferred minor league sports to stadiums filled with tens of thousands of fans. He thought George W. was a fine president, and he didn't like high-falootin' people.

He wouldn't have liked Elyse much, either, except working on her house for two years gave him a pretty good look at the woman. Just because she walked around with a fancy purse and rich, glamorous friends didn't mean she was high society.

The funny thing was, even though she didn't fit in, her friends seemed to genuinely like her. She was a good person who did good things.

He'd discussed this with Nick after their weekly basketball games. Sometimes they went out for a beer. Nick, being the worldly guy he was, even told him how much that silly orange purse cost if she'd bought it in a downtown shop. Why would anyone carry a purse worth more than their car?

Still, he knew she didn't buy it downtown.

The rummage sale price tag had fallen out of the side pocket when she was digging around for her checkbook. He picked up the tag and handed it to her. She'd confessed, right there on the spot, where she'd bought the bag. She was honest about it and her roots.

So why couldn't she be honest about what she did for a living?

He wanted her help. He just didn't want to get bulldozed or have to jump through flaming hoops.

Nick had coached him on what to wear, how to act, and when to speak. Less was better. Except for clothes. And scent. Another thing to remember. He had to use just the right soap, too. Women liked that sort of thing.

So far, Nick had been right every time. Andrew just prayed that Elyse was not going to come out of the bathroom and do what Nick said she was going to do. Everything would be fine as long as she didn't say the four deadly words. Four words that usually led to complete and utter defeat. Four words that meant she might throw in the towel.

As Elyse checked herself in the mirror of the small bathroom, she noted the top-of-the-line fixtures. Andrew had gone all out in here. The toilet was a low-flow model she'd admired in a showroom. The pedestal sink, though narrow, balanced the space. The big draw of the room was the jetted tub, complete with a multi-function showerhead.

A hodgepodge of bottles perched on the edge of the tub. Conditioner. Dandruff control shampoo. Flea soap. Yuck. But there was something else, too. Tucked in the corner, hidden by the shower curtain. Body wash.

Body wash?

Curious, Elyse leaned over the tub and tilted the plastic bottle with the gold lettering. Expensive soap from France. Flipping the lid back, she inhaled its heady scent. There was something familiar about the spicy aroma with a hint of citrus. She'd smelled this scent recently. Racking her memory, she recalled the wearer.

Nick.

Elyse stared at the bottle in her hand. Ridiculous. This had to be a coincidence. Maybe this soap was a fad among guys. Like single men who flocked to the latest pheromone-infused fragrance that promised to drive women wild. Men were susceptible to marketing, too. She grinned and put the bottle back.

Andrew got a huge charm for trying.

She smiled her confident, in-control smile. There were problems, yes. She'd find solutions. One at a time.

Everything was dependant on this last husband transaction.

So what if Saban wasn't a dog person. Worst-case scenario, Elyse would adopt Riley herself. Rearrange her ideal of children before dogs and just go for it. Why not?

Saban would get her man. Elyse would get her house, and maybe a dog.

A big black crotch rocket. Oh well.

He'd certainly discourage visitors. But would Andrew understand?

She knew what she had to do. She'd open the door to the bathroom, march out there, and take control of this evening. Damage control. Salvage. There'd be no talk of websites, money, or plumbing.

This dinner had been a runaway horse, and it was time to seize the reins.

"Andrew?" Elyse called as she paced through the living room.

"In the kitchen," he answered.

She moved to the doorway. At the counter, Andrew scooped a generic brand of Neapolitan ice cream into two bowls. "I'm making dessert."

Elyse steeled herself. *Time to take control.* "We need to talk."

Andrew stood up straight, eyes wide, like an invisible person had just kicked him in the butt. "We need to talk?"

"We need to talk."

"I think we're moving too fast," Andrew said the words like he was reading them off a script.

"Too fast?" With the schedule Elyse had in mind, it wasn't possible to move too fast.

"We need time together. Quiet time. Time for me to know you better." With an honest tenderness, he reached forward and touched her hand. "First, we have to work on the friendship."

What? Men didn't want to be friends. "I think we're great friends," she said, trying to steamroll this speed bump off her highway to financial freedom. "We're the best. Everything is great. Let's go to the living room so we can sit down and talk. Really talk. You and me."

"Tell you what, I want to show you what I can do." He raced to the front hall closet and got her sweater. "Let's call tonight a wash and have a real day together next Saturday. The whole day. Give me a second chance."

Andrew thrust her sweater at her, then picked up her purse and pushed it into her arms.

"That's a week away," Elyse protested. She spread her feet and took a stance, like Andrew had when his dog bolted inside. She wasn't going anywhere. She held out the sweater, refusing to put it on. "We haven't had a chance to talk."

"Absence makes the heart grow fonder." He opened the front door wide.

If she hadn't heard it herself, she would have sworn that Nick was speaking through Andrew like a ventriloquist. Was her influence changing Andrew, or was Nick somehow behind this? She wasn't sure.

As the gentleman that Andrew was, he took the sweater from her, draped it over her shoulders, then led the way to her car. She had no choice but to follow. Reluctantly.

With an awkward peck on the cheek, they said goodbye.

As she drove away, Elyse glanced at the rearview mirror and watched Andrew wave. Had he just put her out?

Wearing yoga pants and T-shirt, Elyse sat alone on her overstuffed sofa. With her mail stacked up on the coffee table, she'd begun the tedious task of sifting through each piece. More madness than method at this point, she separated the magazines and advertising flyers from the utility statements and other random bills. The pile threatened to overwhelm the coffee table. While she probably didn't need to do it this second, dealing with the dreaded mail was better than thinking about what had happened with Andrew.

What had happened, exactly? If she occupied herself with a mundane task, the answer might just come to her. It might float into her mind, relieving her anxiety. *Next Saturday?*

She needed Andrew now.

Grabbing a fistful of correspondence, Elyse sorted one piece after the next, flinging it into several piles. *Water, March. Electric, May. Postcard from the Swiss Alps*. She flipped it over. It ended with, *Love, Madeline. Wait . . . January?* How long had she been avoiding her mail?

The house was quiet, as it had been since her mother passed away. She pulled another handful of mail out, tipping the pile. Mail spilled over the edges of the table. Frustrated, she leaned back in the cushions.

Funny how the house was the same, but felt so different. So empty. Growing up, the house had been full of life. When she was very young, her grandmother was still alive. Three generations of Tobin women under one roof.

There was always something going on. Arguments over what to cook for dinner, what bills were due, who should mow the lawn, clean the gutters, or pick up after her grandmother's dog. The Bassett Hound's baying had disrupted any moment of peace or solitude, annoying the neighbors who called animal control on a daily basis. The dog couldn't bear silence. Elyse missed the never-ending chaos down to her bones.

The house had been still too long.

Throwing the mail back on the table, she conceded that she didn't have the energy to deal with it. Not now.

What she wanted was *The Big Red Book of Men.* Unlocking the cubbyhole, she slid the book from its hiding place and went to the kitchen. She set a pot of water to boil for tea and laid the book on the table. This was just what she needed.

A smile traced her lips as she turned pages. Past Rex Von Terrance, past Donnie and Cyril and everyone else. Charting a course for the back pages, she craved one comfort, Nick.

He wasn't hard to find. Then again, the art of being Nick Salvatore was equal parts mystery and total availability. His past was cloaked in rumor and intrigue. His present was plastered across newspapers and Internet.

Elyse kept tabs on him and did web searches. She dutifully clipped press photos and, God help her, she'd even bought his books. In secret. Even the children's cookbooks, her excuse being that she'd have children of her own someday and knowing how to get them to eat broccoli and peas was part of parenting.

Not that she cooked. Her only skills in the kitchen were tea making and egg boiling. A lack of culinary expertise kept her slender. Unfortunately, her addiction to La Sals' cheesecake meant she hadn't been able to zip up her favorite jeans since December. Even her yoga pants felt a tad snug these days.

Mental note*: Avoid La Sals.*

The kettle whistled. After pouring her favorite jasmine tea into an oversized cup, she took a sip. Yes, this was exactly what she needed right now. Comfort.

Settling back down at the table, she turned more pages. She'd rebuilt six men, perfect Prince Charming husbands, in Nick's image. Without the gigolo part, of course. Six men dedicated to commitment and spending their lives in wedded bliss.

Down the side of each page, she'd kept running lists of Nick's charms. He was perfect at everything. Except commitment. She wondered if he'd ever had a serious relationship.

The gossip mills always churned with news of his latest conquests, but for the past couple of years, maybe longer, the usual wagging tongues had been stilled. Now, Nick news consisted of glowing reports. His charity work. Volunteering at soup kitchens. Reworking the menus for homeless shelters. Funding basketball courts and skateboard parks around the Bay Area for disadvantaged youth.

Every time she opened the Sunday paper, his face beamed out at her from the society column. Under his name, he always listed an email address and telephone number. If anyone wanted to donate or help, *Call Nick.* The need was greater than ever, and he happily coordinated armies of volunteer workers for his latest projects.

She'd cut out every picture and pasted it here, in the book. Tracing his name, email, and phone number with her fingertip, she savored his tenacity. She allowed herself to enjoy Nick Salvatore from the safety of her kitchen table. Elyse sighed, blissfully.

She only had one problem right now. Confirming that Nick's soap was the same one she'd discovered in Andrew's bathroom. It certainly smelled the same. Over the past few days, she'd been in close proximity to Nick several times.

As soon as she found out, she'd be sure to swing by a department store and pick up a sample of it. Another sensory layer to add to her men in her quest for perfection. Wrapping her hands around the mug, Elyse took a long, thirsty sip of tea.

Was she Nick obsessed? Or was this legitimate research?

If she had to ask herself that question, she didn't want to know the answer. Was she a million miles away from her goal of paying off the house, building a made-to-order *Nick* of her own, and having children? Or was her happiness and security waiting just around the next corner?

The next morning, Elyse was sleeping blissfully when the doorbell rang.

Then it rang again.

And again.

She wanted to pull the covers over her head and stay in bed forever, but there were plans to make and a man to train. Andrew. She hoped it was Andrew at the door. Then again, he had his own key. She grabbed a robe, slid her feet into slippers, and plodded downstairs.

As she rounded the corner to the foyer, playing back last night in her mind, a doubt gnawed at her. Men were smarter than she gave them credit for. How much had she missed? Was the spaghetti sauce lasagna a trap set to spring on a woman's maternal nature? What if men were naturally evolving to a Nick Salvatore level of awareness?

The doorbell rang yet again.

For the first time in her life, the doorbell was beginning to annoy Elyse as she unlocked the door.

A small, bald, rotund man in a cheap tweed suit paced her front porch. He smoked a cigar that smelled like an old boot. "Jeez, lady, you think you could come down from your ivory tower any slower?"

"I was sleeping." She yawned.

"It's eleven o'clock. I coulda got down off the

Matterhorn faster than you got to the door."

"Can I help you?"

"You Elyse Tobin?"

"Yes." She watched him fidget. He was like a toy with its spring wound too tight, on the verge of exploding into a million pieces at any second.

The little man fumbled in his pockets. He tried the inside pocket of his battered jacket. He stuffed a meaty finger into his shirt pocket. Finally, he pulled a crumpled envelope from a back pocket and handed it to her. "You been served."

"What?"

"You know, a summons."

Elyse ripped open the envelope and unfolded a single page. "It's a summons!"

"Yeah. Go figure."

"This is a tax audit," she objected.

"You answer the stuff they mail you, they wouldn't a sent me. It's a good job, though. Thank you."

"I can't be audited." Tension flip-flopped in her belly. "I don't have time."

The man threw his hands in the air. "Not my problem."

Elyse turned to scan the overflowing pile of bills on her coffee table. Surely she would have seen an envelope marked Internal Revenue Service. She hadn't gotten that far behind in her mail. Only a few months. Obviously the IRS hadn't contacted her. This was an error. On many levels. She faced the man again. "This is clearly a mistake. Besides, I haven't had to file a return in three years."

"I don't write the summons. I just deliver them."

Elyse stared at the paper. "This says I'm supposed to be there today! I didn't do anything!"

The small man studied the end of his cigar. "All I know is they don't call you downtown for nothing. It's been a pleasure serving you."

With that, he bounded down the steps and opened the

front gate just in time for Elyse to spot Rex Von Terrance, the once incorrigible neighborhood Corgi, trotting past. But he didn't go past. He stopped, eyed her defiantly, raised his little terrier leg and fired away at her Daphne bush.

Elyse watched, horrified. All her work was coming undone. As the dog's thin stream of pee trickled across the cement walk, she sensed that everything in the universe was turning against her.

Chapter 7

Wherever Elyse's luck was today, she was certain it wasn't hanging in her closet. In her second floor, south-facing bedroom overlooking the Golden Gate Bridge, she held up a decade-old orange pantsuit. "What about this?"

"It looks like a prison uniform. Slap a number across the back, and you're ready to find your cell." Jackie sat on the antique four-poster Princess bed piled with rejected outfits. "Find something that says, *I'm innocent*."

"I haven't been *innocent* for a very long time," Elyse noted, wistfully.

"Oh God, no," Jackie howled. "You are not going into the *Darrel Kincaid, law student* story? It was a time of unrequited love, of hope, of youth . . ."

"Don't be so jaded. It was romantic," Elyse argued.

"Until he left."

"Well, it was romantic until then."

Jackie leaned back on a dozen decorative pillows. "You lost your virginity ten years ago. Now it's time to find an outfit that brings it back."

"An old prom dress is not going to get me through this." Elyse stepped through the narrow closet doorway to the packed rods and shelves of clothes. She pulled out a navy blazer with epaulet shoulder trim. It reminded her of Andrew in the Italian restaurant, and she carried it out to the bed. "This might work."

Jackie shook her head. "If you're a captain going down with her ship."

Elyse threw it on top of the other rejects. "I can't wear

white. Too obvious. I can't wear black. Too guilty. I'm going crazy."

"Calm down. There's a whole rainbow in between."

The only bright spot in this horrid day was her best friend rushing over. Elyse stepped to the closet for another round. "I could use some leprechaun luck and a pot of gold."

"Gold is out. You need to look poor." Jackie rolled on her side for a better view. She propped her chin in her hands.

"I am poor," Elyse complained. "I haven't even finished paying off my bathroom yet."

Jackie rolled her eyes. "You live alone in a four-story Queen Anne with a view that any real estate agent would give up a kidney to list. When you come into more money, you should really change the wallpaper in here."

Elyse marched out of the closet, empty-handed. "I love this wallpaper," she objected. "My mom let me pick out this wallpaper when I was seven. Strip by strip, we glued it up. It took two days!"

"It looks like a bordello." Jackie snickered. "Is that what you were going for?"

"I was thinking fairy-tale castle. And no one is putting my house on the market. Not for a kidney. Not for anything. It's family property."

Jackie's face twisted into a sly grin. "Then you better start a family."

"Don't you dare bring up Nick," Elyse warned.

"You said it, not me."

"I have bigger problems than Nick." Elyse slumped next to Jackie on the bed. "I am so screwed."

Jackie draped an arm over Elyse's shoulder. "I'm sure that everything will be fine. It's probably an audit lottery. Your name just came up. Maybe they'll say, *hello, thanks for coming in, sorry for the inconvenience, see you in ten years*."

"Aren't you Mary-Freakin'-Sunshine?"

"It's my nature. What's that red dress in the very back?" Jackie pointed a manicured finger toward the closet.

Elyse felt her cheeks color. "Not that one."

"Is that the dress I think it is?" Jackie quizzed. "You haven't worn that in years."

She hadn't. The vintage Halston, another rummage sale score, had a history of trouble. The Nick Salvatore kind of trouble. She hadn't worn it for three years, since the night she'd wound up in bed with Nick. As dresses go, it was dangerous. It was a loaded gun of seduction. There was nothing innocent about it, which was why she banished the disco-era cocktail dress to the far reaches of her closet. She should have retired it to the attic. Elyse closed the closet door. "It's a little low cut."

"That's an understatement. I love that dress." Jackie hopped off the bed, flung open the closet door and pulled out the dress. "It's fabulous!"

"For an uninhibited night on the town, maybe," Elyse argued. "It's completely wrong for an audit."

"You are so wrong," Jackie chided her. "Ninety percent of IRS employees are scruffy little accountant men locked in cubicles with calculators. Wear something that says *Hello, Mr. Auditor, here are my boobs, everything is fine.*" She twirled in a circle holding the dress against her.

Elyse shook her head. "Maybe something wool? Something with total cleavage coverage. Wool armor. And maybe a nice Pendleton plaid chastity belt?"

"You can't wear wool," Jackie gasped. "You'll sweat like a pig. A tax-evading pig."

"I'm sure the Federal Building has air conditioning." Elyse went back to her closet and dug out a ski sweater with snowflakes patterned across the chest. "This is good. Snowflakes. Pure as the driven snow."

"You'll itch and fidget. Nothing says *lock me away* like fidgeting. Wear the red."

Undeterred, Elyse held up her favorite pair of Levi 501 jeans. The ones that didn't fit. *Damn cheesecake.* She burrowed into the shelves searching for a butt-shrinking foundation garment. "I'm always comfortable in jeans."

"Too casual. Go for sexy. Wear the red dress." Jackie waved the Halston in her face. "Trust me. This is your winning ticket."

Elyse cringed. "It's at two in the afternoon. Who wears a red dress at two in the afternoon?"

"You."

Turning back to the closet, she sifted through a half dozen skirts. "How about this brown one and a button-down shirt."

"You're not applying for a job."

"I have an idea. Just give me a minute." Elyse closed the door to her walk-in closet. Inspiration struck. She pulled her hair back and pinned it up, tight. She rooted out a Victorian-inspired blouse from the 50's with a high, starched collar. The sleeves had lace trim that peeked out from the cuffs of a boxy gray jacket. Paired with an ankle-skimming skirt, black hose and pumps, the outfit suggested a woman with a high moral code.

Elyse stepped out of the closet, beaming. "It's perfect!"

Horror flickered across Jackie's face.

"What? You don't like it?"

Jackie pointed past Elyse's shoulder. On the wall behind her were framed family photographs. The most prominent being Great-Grandma Tobin, a scowling woman in dark clothes, tight hair, and a Victorian blouse. "You've channeled your great-grandmother!"

Elyse swiveled to the oval portrait and stared, speechless.

Jackie piloted her black Prius, that looked almost identical to Elyse's black Prius, through the streets of downtown San Francisco. "It's going to be okay."

"Nothing is okay." Elyse, wearing the red dress, sank deeper into the passenger seat. Her orange purse sat in her lap. They'd spent over an hour going back and forth on whether or not the Hermes was appropriate. For starters, it clashed with the dress.

On the other hand, she did buy it at a rummage sale and still had the $25 price tag tucked inside the liner pocket. Proof of her thrifty ways. In the end, the clock made the decision for them. There wasn't time for Elyse to find another bag and transfer the contents over.

They stopped in front of the Federal Building.

"Aren't you going to tell me about how beautiful this building is?" Jackie forced a smile. "It's got iron and cornices and all kinds of stuff."

"It's just another building." Elyse felt weary, but opened the car door and got out.

"I'll catch up to you inside," Jackie called over the beep of impatient horns behind them.

As Jackie pulled away from the curb, Elyse unfolded the summons and double-checked the address. This was it. She stared up at the Federal Building. It was an imposing structure. Cold. Weathered. Gray. Her red pumps felt heavy as she trudged up the steps.

If she had been in a better mood, she might have appreciated the foyer. The walls were a mix of stone and warm dark wood. The door handles were brass, polished in places by the thousands of hands that had pushed them open. The interior had the comforting feeling of a great castle.

Pacing to the elevator, she rode the lift to the third floor. Glancing at her reflection in the gleaming steel of the elevator door, she was terrified. What was she doing showing so much cleavage?

The doors opened, and she slunk down the sterile hallway of the third floor. She hunched her shoulders inward, trying to make the meager fabric cover more of her chest. The eerie silence of the place made Elyse's stomach flip flop. No place should be this quiet. It was like a morgue. A place where taxpayers go to die, or at least beg for mercy.

Painted letters across the window on the door of *Room 341, Auditor* told her she'd arrived. A small sign read, *out to lunch.*

Next to the unlit office, benches lined the hallway. Elyse settled on the closest one. Hopefully the auditor was having a wonderful meal that would put him in an understanding mood.

How could she describe what she did? Did she even need to mention it? Maybe they just wanted to know why she hadn't filed a tax return for a few years. Elyse tried to think positive. She'd iron out any financial hiccups, hire an accountant, and fix the problem. What more could she do?

As Elyse worried, a woman about her age in an off-the-rack business suit plodded down the hall and landed an armload of files on the bench. She smiled a desperate smile that was beautiful and kind at the same time. "Don't you just hate this?"

She did. Looking at the woman, her caring brown eyes, Elyse knew she was a sister-in-arms, a comrade facing the same enemy. "I don't belong here," she sighed.

"No one does," the woman replied.

"Are you early or late?"

"I'm always late. It's a genetic disability."

"You're lucky they take long lunches here." Elyse wiped a drop of sweat from her forehead.

"Are you all right?" the woman asked.

Was she all right? She wanted to laugh out loud, a deranged cackle puncturing the eerie quiet of this building. Elyse, beyond scared, was half out her mind with fear. She quaked in her bright red heels. She'd never met a historical building she didn't like. Buildings were like men, most held potential.

This one held only dread.

She'd probably break out in hives at any second. Running out and never looking back seemed like her best option, and she would have done just that if Jackie wasn't on her way up. Where the hell was she? Jackie had promised to hold her hand and get her through this nightmare.

"You look a little pale," the woman observed.

"I am in so much trouble," Elyse wailed. She couldn't hold it in any longer. "I didn't know what to wear. I look like I'm auditioning for a porn movie. You did so much better. Nothing says I don't have a million dollars like a polyester suit."

"J.C. Penney," the woman crowed. "Their suits last forever."

"They do. Why did I wear this?" Elyse looked down at her cleavage. "Stupid. I don't even know why I'm here. I haven't made any money."

"You don't have any income at all?" the woman quizzed.

"Well, some of my friends gave me gifts."

"Gifts? Like your purse?"

"This?" Elyse held up her bag, feeling more at ease. Clearly the inexpensive suit hid a woman with a keen eye for quality. She was certain that this was a woman who'd appreciate a bargain. Fishing out the battered price tag, Elyse held it up for inspection. "Third Saturday in May, every year, St. Mark's Episcopal hosts a new-to-you sale."

The woman nodded, appreciative. "That's a great deal, but what about these gifts?"

"They're *thank you* gifts. I have a talent for rebuilding men. After I do, my friends marry them and then thank me with a little money."

"How little?" the woman inquired, raising an eyebrow.

"My best friend gave me ten thousand dollars. Now they give me even more." Elyse shifted on the bench.

"Those are nice friends."

"It's complicated," Elyse confessed. "Most are nice, some not so much. Other than Jackie, I don't feel like I belong. I'm not San Francisco high society. I only do it because I'm trying to save my house. I love my house. It's been in my family for four generations."

The woman looked sad, reflective. "I wish I had just one friend."

The delicate click of heels ended the conversation as Jackie hurried toward them. "Did I miss anything?"

Elyse shook her head. "We're both waiting for the auditor to show up."

"I said I was late," the woman remarked. "I didn't say I wasn't the auditor."

Elyse felt like the floor had fallen out from under her. She had bared her soul to the IRS. That was it. Game over. "Why did you let me go on?" she whined as they followed the woman inside a small, dark office.

The auditor shook her head. "It doesn't matter, dear. I find out everything anyway. That's my job."

The auditor turned on the lights and pointed to two wooden straight-back chairs facing a plain, government-issue desk. Elyse and Jackie sat. The auditor settled behind the desk.

"Whatever Elyse said is not admissible as evidence," Jackie stated. "No one read her her rights."

"No one is under arrest." The auditor opened a file. "Yet."

"I didn't do anything wrong." Elyse took a deep breath. Her mother had always been big on seeing the sunny side and counting one's blessings, even to the end of her life. Elyse had not inherited her optimism.

Everything was going wrong. Her work, Andrew, Saban, Rex Von Terrance, even the house. She loved the house, but sometimes it weighed on her like an anchor.

"Elyse?" Jackie said, her voice rising. "You aren't breathing."

She wasn't. She put a hand against her chest and gulped. This was it. Death was imminent. While this might be a better end than, say, dying trapped in a bridesmaid dress in the foyer bathroom at a wedding, it still wasn't how she pictured going out. In her mind, she always thought she would be surrounded by family. Daughters and granddaughters. Then she'd quietly and gracefully drift off.

"Don't you hate it when this happens?" the auditor asked. She pulled open a desk drawer and took out a crisp, new brown paper bag. "Breath into this. It's just a panic attack."

Elyse snapped up the bag and puffed the last bit of air from her lungs into it, then waited. She wasn't inhaling. Her head spun. Finally, her throat opened and the oxygen rushed in. The bag collapsed and expanded, again and again as she relaxed. "Does this happen often?" she mumbled with the bag still over her mouth.

"I buy these bags by the thousand." The auditor closed the bag drawer. "You can call me Iris."

This was definitely not the IRS Elyse had expected. This woman in front of them had humor and gave out paper bags for panic attacks. She was compassionate. She was human.

"What are you doing in a place like this?" The words popped out of Elyse like a champagne cork.

Jackie looked like she was going to faint.

The question took Iris by surprise. "It's a good job. Security. Benefits. But this is about you."

"Does anyone ever say thank you? Do you see any happy people?" Elyse inquired. "I'd think you'd feel about as welcome as the Grim Reaper. How can you stand it?"

Jackie elbowed Elyse, hard. She mouthed the words, *shut up.*

Iris studied them for a moment, not sure if they were sincere or not. "Miss Tobin, let's keep this on a professional level. Shall we?"

Jackie jumped out of her chair, angry. "She bared her soul to you under false pretences. Now you want to be professional?"

"It's okay," Elyse said and pulled Jackie down to sit again.

"It's not okay!" Tears welled up in Iris's eyes. "I don't want to be professional. I never did. I hate it here."

Elyse didn't know what to say. "The lobby downstairs is nice."

"It's all horrible." Iris unburdened herself. "Everyone hates everyone. It's not only the people we audit. All the workers hate their jobs, and they hate each other. No one is happy."

"So why do you stay?" Elyse asked.

"Pension. Nine-to-five hours. No layoffs. Ever." Iris sighed.

"That's true," Jackie agreed. "There are only two sure things, death and taxes."

Iris wiped her eyes. "I thought this would be better than a job in a mortuary. Now I think dead people would be more fun."

"There's more to life than your job, Iris." Not that Elyse's life was any better. She was as unhappy and trapped as Iris.

"Not anymore," Iris argued. "The first couple years weren't so bad. My sister and her family lived in town. We had holidays and celebrations. Then they moved back East.

I still had friends from college, but year-by-year they moved or married or just drifted away. Now, the only people I see socially are on Friday after work. We go to a bar, drink, and complain. I don't have a life outside the job."

"Have you tried dating?"

Iris stared at Elyse. "Who'd date me? I'm a walking lie detector. It's what I do. I ferret out the truth for a living."

Elyse shook her head, sympathetic. "Not an attractive quality."

"Don't you have an off switch?" Jackie asked.

"I wish I did." Iris sobbed quietly. "What I have is fifteen more years before I can retire."

Elyse knew what had to be done. She stood and tapped Jackie on the shoulder. "When there are no solutions, no hope, there is only one thing in the entire world that will help."

Jackie smiled. "La Sals?"

"Don't look at the prices." Elyse tugged the gold embossed menu from Iris's fingers.

"You'll have a heart attack," Jackie cautioned.

"I think I just did," she gasped. "I can't afford a cup of coffee here!"

"Just trust me on this. I know what I'm doing." Elyse scooted forward in her chair and placed her menu on top of Iris's. There was no need to peruse the gourmet offerings. They were here for one thing and one thing only.

Iris didn't argue. Instead, she gawked at the opulent French country surroundings. Antique crystal chandeliers hung above clay jars of sunflowers. Simple print tablecloths covered the tables. "I've never even heard of this place."

"Most people haven't," Elyse admitted.

"No one from Wedgeworth's will come here," Jackie agreed. "There's no valet parking."

"It's more than that," Elyse added. "Did you notice that there's no sign. No awning on the street that says *La Sals*. You either know to come here . . ."

" . . . or you don't," Jackie finished the sentence.

"Is the food good?" Iris asked innocently.

"Heavenly." Elyse licked her lips. "Not that we can afford it. Dinner here would take your whole paycheck."

"So why did we come?"

"Because La Sals is more than just a mere restaurant."

Jackie leaned forward. "They don't even take reservations. Everyone has to show up and be judged as to whether or not they're worthy to eat here."

"That's elitist," Iris huffed.

"Not that way," Elyse calmed her. Rumors circulated it was the mysterious and highly eccentric owner of La Sals that commanded Martine, the maître d', to choose diners who reflected the world's broad cultural and socio-economic spectrum. "No one knows who'll get seated and who'll get turned away."

"Half the time I can't get in." Jackie pouted. "They turn away some of the richest and most influential people in the city every night."

"If the OPEN sign is on the door, the place is packed."

Jackie leaned over and said with more than a little suspicion, "But they never turn Elyse away."

"Why?" Iris asked.

"For the life of me, I don't know." Elyse didn't. It was true, though. She had never been denied her cheesecake.

Iris was confused. "You come here all the time, but you said we can't afford to eat here?"

"We can't afford to eat *dinner* here," Elyse corrected. "Anytime is right for dessert." Her overly tight jeans in her closet at home were proof of that.

She was infamous for her late cheesecake lunches like today, midnight cheesecake runs, cheesecake breakfast takeout. Not that they were open for breakfast, but if she knocked hard enough and long enough on the back door, eventually she'd be hooked up with her cake. Like today. It was between lunch and dinner, which meant La Sals wasn't officially open. But Martine had seated them in the empty restaurant. They knew they had her.

She was a cheesecake junkie. Totally addicted. Only a La Sals cheesecake would do because all others paled in comparison.

She was a woman who would not be denied her cake. Her monthly tab had been in the hundreds, which didn't make much sense because if she paid menu price, her tab would have run in the thousands. Maybe they gave her a bulk discount? Not that she'd ever seen a bill. All she knew was she signed for the cakes. Having been strapped for cash three years ago, Martine opened a tab for her. One that never came due.

She didn't know why. Or care. Elyse greedily took her cakes every time.

And ate them, too.

"Martine," she called out, twisting around in her chair. The waiters hadn't yet begun their shift. The maître d' approached the table and smiled.

Despite the fact that, in her current financial state, Elyse most certainly could not afford to be here, she instinctively knew that there was only one cure, one solution, one reparation for the hostilities of life that had been heaped upon Iris and her.

Cheesecake.

What made a La Sals cheesecake special were the inventive recipes. The base was always a classic New York cheesecake, but beyond that, the sky was the limit. Just last week, she'd taken a bite of a delicately flavored cake covered with a Mango compote.

Each divine mouthful was almost orgasmic.

"The usual," she ordered. "Times three."

"Feeding me isn't going to change my audit," Iris said seriously.

"I don't expect it to," Elyse conceded.

Iris frowned. "Then let's get to the details."

Elyse folded her hands on the table in front of her. "The first money I ever got was from Jackie."

"I gave her ten grand for my Donnie."

"After they got married."

Iris studied Jackie. "You're friends?"

Jackie nodded. "Best friends."

"That's all right then." Iris shrugged. "Ten thousand is a lot, but from a friend, definitely a gift. Is that all?"

Elyse winced. "The next two women weren't such good friends."

"At ten thousand each?" Iris asked and took out a calculator.

"More," Elyse confessed.

Iris's fingers poised over the calculator. "How much more?"

"Fifty, then seventy-five. After that, it went a little higher."

Iris's eyes were wide as she punched the keys. "I need a number."

Elyse looked down to the table, embarrassed. "A hundred thousand."

"Dollars?" Iris choked out the word. "For each one?"

Elyse nodded. She wished Martine would hurry. She desperately needed something good to happen.

Iris took a deep and labored breath. "Do you have anything going on right now?"

Jackie held her hands to her face. "She has a friend that wants to pay her two hundred thousand by the end of the month."

"I can help you then." Iris perked up, relieved. "I'll need copies of the checks, bank statements, and a sworn affidavit and apology, but a payment of two-hundred thousand against what you owe should solve everything."

Elyse stared. She'd be broke, but free. "What about my house? My mortgage?"

Iris made a *tsk-tsk* sound. "Would you rather go to jail and put the house on the auction block?"

Martine landed a silver tray with three Limoge cups filled with coffee, then glided away silently.

Nausea gripped Elyse. Three weeks away from doing what no Tobin in history had ever been able to do, she'd failed.

"Take the deal," Jackie advised. "This is a setback, not a defeat."

Elyse nodded, sadly. Saban's money would keep her out of prison. She could negotiate a new mortgage with the bank. There'd be more grooms, more wealthy and desperate brides-to-be.

She'd put her own goals and dreams on hold.

She would live in a quiet house.

Put off having children.

It felt like an endless treadmill. Uphill. Steep. All for the house.

It wasn't fair. She was as alone in the world as Iris. And just like Saban, her ovaries were ticking away, two little time bombs waiting to blow her last chance at motherhood.

She wanted the house full of life and love and noise. She wanted it to be a living thing again. How many years would it take to pay off the house this time?

Martine returned. He settled a slice of cheesecake in front of each of them. The wedge-shaped servings were tiny. Maybe four inches long and an inch and a half wide. The cake, if you could call the creamy confection mere cake, was a pale white, like a first snowfall. On top, a layer of jelled, salmon-pink compote nestled with tiny berries. The finishing touch was a baby leaf of basil.

Elyse leaned in and smelled the delicate compote and blinked back tears. *Huckleberries!* Great-Grandma Tobin always insisted huckleberries were lucky. Huckleberries had brought her a man and love. Huckleberries had led her to the building site for the house. In her journals, she'd sworn huckleberries had preceded the conception of Grandma Tobin. Though the huckleberry bushes of Ivy Loop were long gone, Elyse had a soft spot in her heart for the elusive, wild berry.

Perhaps, in some mysterious, universal way, Great-Grandma Tobin was speaking to her through the cheesecake. *Everything will be okay.*

"This is just cheesecake," Iris said, deflated.

Jackie clutched Iris's hand. "It's not."

"It's La Sals' cheesecake." Elyse raised her fork, victorious.

"This is the cheesecake of the gods," Jackie added.

"Cheesecake is cheesecake." Iris shifted her eyes, suspicious.

"Try it," Elyse ordered.

Iris shoveled a bite of the concoction into her mouth and froze. Elyse loved seeing someone discover this food bliss for the first time. It was the next best thing to an orgasm. Iris's face did not disappoint. This was a cake to contemplate.

Elyse knew the sensation well. Many times she'd rolled it in her mouth, allowing it to coat every taste bud. The sweet. The tart. The mélange of organic sugars and lighter-than-air cream cheeses. And finally, the swallow.

Iris set her fork on her plate and grabbed the edge of the table to steady herself. A moan escaped her lips. She needed a moment before she could speak. "This is really good."

"Try the coffee," Elyse suggested.

Iris obeyed. Elyse knew what she was feeling. The

warmth of the coffee mingling with the cream of the dessert. It was cleansing. Bitter, but rich. Then ready to reload with the sweet. Another bite.

"I get it." Iris swooned, picking up her fork again. "This is so right. It makes me realize how much of my life is so wrong."

Uh-oh. Elyse had another convert to the church of La Sals, but Iris's eyes misted up. Tears were coming and nothing could stop them. "It'll be fine."

"It's not fine," Iris cried. "People hate me."

"No, they don't." Elyse said the words, but knew the truth. No one likes an IRS auditor.

"It's what I do. Every day I pick apart people's lives. *Where did your aunt's inheritance go? No, your dog is not a dependent. Yes, your child's hospital bills are deductible, but not for liposuction and a nose job.* Everyone hates me," Iris sobbed. "I hate me."

"It'll be fine now," Elyse comforted her. "Once you realize something, then you can change it."

Iris sniffled. "You're right. I can change my life. I met you. I can make new friends. I can call my family and put that back together. I could even ask that nice janitor that comes by my office every night out to dinner."

Elyse handed Iris a tissue from her purse. "I'm an expert. Janitors are great."

"Salt of the earth." Jackie winked. "And they'll sweep up."

Elyse glided a fork into the cheesecake and took a bite. The explosion of flavor took her tongue by surprise. Rich and firm, yet fragile and delicate. The berries melded with the creamy depth, and she swooned, just like Iris had.

Things were looking better. La Sals' cheesecake really could fix anything.

Beside her, Jackie's eyes rolled back in her head as she chewed. Her fork hovered in the air, ready for a follow up.

"La Sal, whoever he might be, has outdone himself."

Elyse took a sip of coffee. "Iris, the only thing that puzzles me is, how did you know to look into my case in the first place?"

Iris paused, mouth open and ready for more dessert. She took a breath and said quite matter-of-factly, "Someone turned you in, dear."

Nick set his coffee cup down and grabbed the phone on his steel and glass desk. On the security monitor in his private office, he watched Elyse at a table with Jackie and another woman he didn't know.

"What's up?" Vicky Barnsdale arched a brow from the opposite side of his desk.

"She's back."

"What number is this?"

He waved her off and spoke into the phone. "Martine, break out 997 and keep 998 in reserve."

Vicky stood and put both palms on his desk. She gave him a steeled look that was all business. "Just give her the four damn cakes, publish the book, and make up your mind."

Nick loved Vicky, but she was about as cuddly as a Great White. "The cakes will not go out until they are called for, I'll publish the recipes when I'm damn good and ready, and *maybe* you can have my sperm."

"Well, hurry up and decide," Vicky ordered. "Tawna's ready to go. If you're not up for it, we have a former president, an ex-Olympian, and a nuclear astrophysicist waiting in the wings."

There were things Nick wanted. When he was ten, he wanted a life outside the Bronx and his immigrant family. He loved his family. He still talked to them every week. He just didn't want to grow up to be a janitor in his local elementary school. If it hadn't been for the cook taking an interest in him when he waited for his father to finish work, he would probably be pushing a broom at this very moment.

In the school kitchen, Nick discovered a love of cooking. On an industrial level. When he was sixteen, he wanted more. With his parents' blessing and a student loan, he got an early admission to the Cordon Bleu.

For more than two thirds of his life, everything he wanted had something to do with food. Now, if food did not save the day, he would be done with it.

Vicky sat down and sipped a coffee. "You know, I could sell your memoir if you'd write the damn thing."

"I don't think anyone wants to know about me," he replied. Why would people want to read about him? He wasn't any different than Andrew or Vicky. All of them wanted the same thing. A family.

If Vicky had asked him five years ago what he wanted, it would have been a different answer. After the breakup of his marriage and the loss of his cherished Broadway Bistro in the divorce, he was at loose ends. But it only took one night with Elyse to make him realize that love was not in the arms of a hundred different women, that there was something inside him that wanted to be loyal again.

To trust again.

Vicky thumped her coffee cup on the desk. "If you're going to do this, then do it."

"I will."

"Good. Go."

"I am." He didn't know why he was so flustered.

Vicky leaned forward and ran a hand over his mid-day stubble. "Before you go get all puppy-dog-faced with her again, you should shave."

They both knew that Vicky was his fallback position. If Elyse didn't realize that his cheesecake creations were a labor of love, if she didn't see the real Nick Salvatore with his blue-collar roots and solid family values, if he had to give up the dream of them being together, he would agree to be Vicky's sperm donor.

He had four cheesecakes to go.

Four cheesecakes and the dream would live or die.

Four cheesecakes of fate.

Nick ran an electric shaver over his face, then rubbed a handful of his signature aftershave over his smooth chin. "Better?"

"Go get her, stud."

Elyse continued to stare at Iris long after any of them were comfortable with it. "What do you mean someone turned me in?"

Jackie's mouth hung open. "Someone squealed on you! They ratted you out! There's a stool pigeon!"

"I understand the concept, Jackie." Elyse rubbed her eyes. "Who would do that?"

Iris sipped her coffee. "It was an anonymous call. Usually an ex-husband or an enemy tattles on you, but you'd be surprised how often it's a jealous friend."

"Don't look at me," Jackie said quickly. "I love you, but I'm not jealous."

It made no sense to Elyse. She didn't have any enemies. Everyone liked her. All the wives and husbands were happy. There was no one that wanted to destroy her life like this, was there?

"Ladies." Martine stood in front of them with three more helpings of cheesecake on his tray and a sterling silver pot of coffee.

"Excellent timing, Martine," Elyse said as she forked up the last bite of huckleberry cheesecake. "You are a mind reader."

"It's not my timing. These are compliments of the gentleman."

"Free?" Iris perked up.

"Indeed." Martine set the plates down and refilled their coffee cups. "Huckleberry, but this time with a Belgian chocolate swirl."

"Huckleberries and chocolate, too?" Jackie clapped her hands.

"Which man?" Elyse asked, forcing herself to tear her eyes away from the plates of cheesecake. Chocolate and huckleberries were a dream come true. Scanning the tables of La Sals, she searched for signs of life. All the tables were empty except for theirs. The restaurant wasn't even open for another hour.

"You looked like you could use a refill."

Iris, Jackie, and Elyse turned toward the voice. There he was. Nick Salvatore. "I'm sorry if I'm interrupting . . ."

"Join us!" Iris couldn't get the words out fast enough. She smiled a mega-watt smile.

Elyse's face crumpled. Some dreams were too good to be true. He was the last man she wanted to see right now. Her current problems were like a tidal wave. On Nick's worst day, he was beguiling. On his best, a distraction threatening to derail her cheesecake bliss. "Who let you in?"

"I have my ways, Elyse."

"I'm sure you do," she muttered. He'd probably bedded every female staff member. She watched him glide around their table and pull out a chair for himself, but he didn't sit.

Elyse couldn't help but note that he was the essence of perfection. The tailored suit, manners, thoughtful nature. The heat she'd felt in the farmer's market returned. A surge of lust, of longing, rattled her to her core.

She couldn't take it.

He even smelled fantastic. Almost as good as the cheesecake.

Think of something else. She had to. Focus. Her life was in limbo. The house was going back into mortgage hell, her livelihood was up for grabs, and she had to crank out a husband-to-be in record time or go to jail. On top of all that, someone was out to get her. She cleared her mind of Nick.

Until she looked at him again.

She remembered the newspaper clippings in the back of *The Big Red Book of Men.* She could see his picture and the lettering. *Call Nick.* She wanted to. Desperately. The one thing that was better than cheesecake for obliterating a horrible day was a dozen mind-blowing orgasms.

Had she sunk that low? Again?

Nick offered his hand to Iris. "I'm Nick."

"Nick." Iris squealed his name.

"I don't want to intrude," he soothed.

"Intrude! Intrude!" Iris encouraged.

With that invitation, he sat between Elyse and Iris.

"That is a stunning dress, Elyse." She could feel his eyes as they lingered over her exposed flesh. "It's very familiar."

"This isn't the best time," Elyse said. She wanted to change the subject. What was she thinking wearing this dress? At least he was after her and not Iris. She certainly didn't need Iris getting ideas about Nick. At this moment, she was her most important friend, one that held her financial interests and freedom in her hands.

"Life is a funny thing," Nick said and leaned an elbow on the table toward Elyse. "One minute you're on top of the world, the next you lose everything. But then sometimes you get extra cheesecake."

Iris bobbed her head, mesmerized.

Elyse stared, her eyes popped wide to the revelation of what he said. It hit her like a lightening bolt. *One minute you're on top of the world, the next you lose everything.*

She was the only one who ever stood up to Nick.

The only one who confronted him.

He must see her as his arch nemesis. Nick was smart, and now he was playing hardball. How would he deal with an enemy? Distract them with charm. Destroy them with information gained through his seductions. Elyse was sure of it.

Nick Salvatore had turned her in to the IRS and ruined her life.

He looked straight at Elyse, then his eyes dipped to her chest and back. "I've had dreams of you in that dress. I know why you don't like me . . ."

Fury screamed through her like a monsoon. All the rage and frustration of her day released itself through her lungs in one long howl. "You bastard!"

Nick sat back, stunned and a little nervous. "What?"

"I know everything. And I know you, Nick. The real you. I see under the manners, under the clothes. You put out an image and everyone buys it because that's what they want to see. That's what they need." Elyse wagged a finger in his face. "I know what you've done!"

Nick eyed the closest exit. She had him squirming now, which was a first. Nick never lost his cool, but she could sense it, he wanted to get away. Run.

"You started this, but I'm going to finish it," Elyse said, voice rising. "If you're out to destroy me, you're going to have one hell of a fight on your hands."

Nick's nervousness vanished. "Wait a minute. You think I'm out to destroy you?"

"You turned me in to the IRS!"

"It wasn't me, Elyse. I swear. Why would I do something as stupid as that?"

She didn't buy his excuse for a second. "Because I'm the only woman who hasn't succumbed to your charms."

"Well, technically, you did once," Nick corrected her.

Jackie jumped up. "You slept with Nick? How come you didn't tell me?"

"It didn't count," Elyse argued. "I was drinking . . . and lonely . . . and vulnerable. He took advantage of me."

Nick smiled. "As I recall, you paid for the room."

Elyse felt the anger rising inside her again. She did pay for the room. She wanted him, badly, then. She still wanted him now. Even if he was a rotten bastard who ruined her life. "I'm not mad at you for that night. I'm mad at you for turning me in to the IRS!"

"I'm lonely and vulnerable." Iris leaned against Nick.

Elyse reached out with a hand to Iris's shoulder and eased her back. "You don't need him, Iris. No one needs him."

Nick stood. "Maybe I'd better leave you girls alone to sort this out. Nice meeting you, Iris."

As Iris pushed her IRS business card into Nick's palm, Elyse felt her temples pound. Anger coursed through her. Nick Salvatore was about to make an elegant getaway yet again. Well, not this time. She eyed her options on the table, a sumptuous plate of cheesecake, wonderful shade-grown Blue Mountain coffee, and a glass of water. She seized the water.

The world stalled into slow motion.

Usually, the best moments flash past in an instant and disappear, but this one held. Elyse felt the weight of the glass in her hand as she jabbed it forward. She could see Nick's eyes shift down to the impending liquid, then back to hers in disbelief.

Iris's mouth opened wide.

Nothing could alter her action, resolve, or the outcome. No one did this to Nick. Everyone loved Nick. It was time someone put things right.

Splash!

Nick stared down at his water-soaked crotch.

Elyse felt a smug glow of satisfaction from her assault. "This is the first time I've seen you without a clever retort." She hadn't felt this good in days.

Nick looked down at his pants again. "I guess this was

meant to dampen my ardor?"

Elyse set the empty glass on the table. "That's the Nick I know. Gracious to the very end."

"Yes. You made your point quite clearly." Nick winked at Iris. "Good day then, ladies." He turned and strolled away toward the entrance, dripping across the floor.

Iris shivered and sighed.

Patting Iris's shoulder, Elyse took her seat again. "Don't worry, there's a world full of decent men out there."

Iris glanced after the retreating Nick. "Who wants decent when that's around?"

Elyse took a victorious bite of cheesecake. If the last piece had been orgasmic, this one was even better. Like two orgasms. Simultaneously. She savored the chocolate and berries. Even if it was from Nick, to let a piece of La Sals' cheesecake go uneaten would be a true injustice. Not to mention, she'd need the calories to fuel her efforts to reform Andrew, pay off the IRS, and save her house. She couldn't afford any more mistakes, any more distractions.

She couldn't afford Nick.

Iris and Jackie ate their desserts and moaned appreciatively. After a few minutes, Iris giggled. "I've never seen anyone make a scene before. At least not in a nice place like this. I'm surprised the owner didn't show up and ask us to leave."

Jackie looked up, interested. "No one knows who the owner is. That's one of the big mysteries of La Sals."

"There are a dozen new rumors every year," Elyse joined in.

"I heard there were two billionaires who would have bought the place lock, stock, and barrel if the owner came forward," Jackie whispered.

"I read about a secret restaurant in a gossip paper," Iris spoke in a low tone. "Someone said a European heiress, pregnant and unmarried, settled in San Francisco to have her love child away from tabloid eyes. She couldn't find any food good enough in town and started a hush-hush supper club."

Jackie nodded. "That's one of the rumors, too."

Elyse loved these stories. "My favorite is the East Coast chef who fell in love with his sous chef, married, divorced, and lost the restaurant in the settlement. Bitter and alone, he started La Sals, then faded into seclusion, letting his recipes fund his life on a sailboat in the bay, where he ponders the meaning of life to this day."

Iris sighed. "That's so beautiful."

"That's my favorite, too," Jackie agreed.

"No one will ever know," Elyse sighed. "But we still have the cheesecake."

"And Nick." Jackie smiled.

"The rat," Elyse added.

Iris shook her head. "I'm not saying he's not a rat, but I do know he didn't turn you in."

"It couldn't be anyone else. I'm sure it was him."

"Maybe," Iris said with a mouthful of dessert, "But the person that called me was a woman."

Chapter 8

You know who I am, or you wouldn't have called. In Modesto on a job. Back soon. Beeeeeep. The tone sounded after Andrew's message.

Elyse hung up, disappointed.

Fearful.

Frustrated.

Having left eight messages over four days, she ran the risk of scaring Andrew off. *Damn him.* She needed him more than ever. Her freedom, her home, her future were all riding on her being able to deliver him to Saban as the perfect husband. And what had he done? He'd up and left. He wasn't even returning her calls.

He'd gone to work.

She had half a mind to drive to Modesto, hunt him down, and bring him back. Anyone could reef on wrenches and install fixtures, or whatever he did down there. Though denying him the job he loved and his livelihood wasn't the answer. The man lived for pipes. He probably dreamt of pipes, *the New York sewer, the Alaskan pipeline, the Roman aqueducts*. As a plumber, he did spectacular work. Her house was proof of that.

On the fourth floor of her home, immersed in her hammered copper tub full of piping hot water, Elyse inhaled the lilac-scented steam drifting off the surface.

She inhaled again, deeper, desperately seeking calm.

It wasn't coming.

Calm wasn't even in the same zip code as her racing brain. The sight of the early morning mist rolling over her beloved Golden Gate made her pulse quicken and her heart beat faster. Not in a good way. Everything in her life was wrong.

An unknown enemy was trying to take her down, and she'd made an ass of herself in La Sals accusing Nick of turning her into the IRS. Throwing water on him hadn't been her finest moment. Worse, she'd sat there and gobbled down a second helping of cheesecake, too proud to apologize.

Had her grandmother seen that appalling display of manners, she'd have disowned Elyse on the spot. Tobin's, while not rich, were always polite. *Genteel*, her grandmother had counseled her as a child. She heard her grandmother's words in her head. *It doesn't matter where you were born, or what your station in life, if you have manners, if you hold your head proud, you will succeed.*

At La Sals, Elyse had failed. Even if Nick was the most annoying man on earth, he still deserved better. He deserved an apology. Sliding deep into the bath water, she felt worse than ever.

Under normal circumstances, a bath had the power to put everything right. She hadn't been the first in history to seize upon the therapeutic benefits of hot water. The Japanese reclined in onsens, the Finnish had steam rooms, and Native Americans gathered in hot springs. The effect was the same. Relaxation, healing, and regeneration.

Other than a great orgasm at the hands of a master lover, there was nothing like a good soak to clear the mental channels and restore inner peace . . . under normal circumstances.

In the meantime, she had no choice but to wait for Andrew to return.

For four days, each morning, afternoon, and evening she made a new plan. In *The Big Red Book of Men* she wrote her detailed lists. Manners. Speech. Conversation. She didn't even know if he could dance. She'd written and rewritten

Andrew's ideal *charm* list at least thirty times.

There was a lot of work left to do.

What if he got to the Charity Ball, stomped all over Saban's feet, then slurped down a beer and belched? She could picture him eating a handful of crab puffs and wiping his hand on the lapel of his tuxedo.

Startled by the doorbell, Elyse sat up in the tub.

She wasn't expecting anyone. Especially at 6 a.m. With the exception of her favorite church rummage sales, she preferred not to schedule any guests or business before noon.

The doorbell rang again.

"Coming," she called.

Pulling the plug on the tub, she slipped into a robe and plodded down the three flights of stairs. At the front door, Andrew stood tall in a work shirt and overalls.

"Hey," he said in his jovial manner.

Thrilled to see him, Elyse flung her arms around him in a bear hug. "I'm so glad you're back."

He was here. The training would commence. He wouldn't leave her sight until the Charity Ball. From this second on, nothing would be left to chance.

Andrew looked puzzled. "You had some plumbing trouble while I was gone?"

"Ummm." She let go. Recovering her composure, she took a step back.

Maybe she'd left a message or two on his voice mail about pipes breaking, hoses splitting, and flooding on a Biblical scale. Anything to get him to return her call.

"Everything's fine now." Elyse forced a smile. "Want some tea?"

"How about we start our day?" Andrew gestured to his still-running truck at the curb. "You know what they say about early birds."

"They get the worm?" She chewed her lip. Where was he taking her at 6 a.m. on a Saturday morning? It didn't matter. It only mattered that he was on her porch. In the flesh. "I'll get dressed and grab my bag."

Elyse dashed up the stairs. Prince Charming Number Seven had returned to her fold, ready and waiting to be transformed. In the coming days, he'd be prepped and ready to meet his future wife. Andrew, unbeknownst to him, was going to save her bacon.

On the 101 headed south, Elyse looked ahead through the windshield. The big, white expanse of hood stretched out in front of the truck. Inside, a tree-shaped air freshener swung from the rearview mirror in a poor attempt to mask the scent of grease, sweat, and a thousand Styrofoam cups of 7/11 coffee. Elyse felt tiny. Like a child. Riding high on the passenger seat of the quad-cab pickup, she looked down on passenger car roofs in the other lanes. To the sides, a sea of suburbs flashed by as Andrew drove to their destination.

They rumbled along for over an hour. The city fell far behind. The houses, three and four bedrooms on double levels, all seemed the same. None had the character of the homes on Ivy Loop.

"Where are we going?" she asked. The silence was killing her. She shifted. This was all wasted time. She hadn't planned any lessons that could be taught rocking along in a noisy pickup.

"It's a surprise," he said. He sounded pleased with himself.

Still tired from a long night of fretting over possible solutions to her problems, Elyse folded her arms over her chest and slid down in the passenger seat. She was happy to see Andrew. She would apologize to Nick. The IRS problem would work out. And sooner or later, she'd figure out who turned her in. Knowing she had an enemy lurking somewhere in her insulated social circle nagged at her. It made her stomach knot up. She really needed more positive thinking.

She needed more Andrew.

Shifting her gaze over to him, she noted his thick biceps peaking out from the edges of his freshly laundered white T-shirt. Sun-bleached strands of his sandy-brown hair, cut short, caught the morning light and glinted.

In another time or place, Andrew might have been the sort of man she wanted for herself. His good nature shone in everything he did. Kind and attentive, he'd planned this day. Just for her. She could sense that he was a guy to confide in, to reveal all concerns to without fear of judgment. Someone to share a life with.

Saban had better appreciate him. Andrew was a good one.

A keeper.

Elyse had spent a good part of the last four years without male companionship, steeling herself with the knowledge that, as a forward-thinking woman hailing from generations of feminists, she didn't need a man. She wanted one, of course. But the more men she reconditioned and married off to eager brides, the more she came to realize that relationships weren't simply a dictation of terms and conditions. They were a team effort.

Her job was to act as a scout and coach, but beyond that, the actual day-to-day marriages were equal parts love, understanding, and looking out for one another.

The love part was easy in college. She'd been deeply committed to Darrel, and for a long time she thought he loved her back. Gambling her happiness and future, she'd put him on the back burner when her mom got sick. The diagnoses got worse with each medical appointment. Leaving her mom's side wasn't an option. Neither was joining Darrel on the East Coast.

The distance became more than miles. Months, then

years, slipped by. An emptiness grew slowly within her, until the night spent in the arms of a man who couldn't possibly love her back. One night of feral lust with Nick Salvatore had been her turning point.

She needed more, and so did every woman who came to her seeking a committed relationship. She gave to others what she continued to deny herself.

It was time to break the cycle.

It was time to stop.

"We're here." Andrew braked at the top of a freeway onramp and made a right hand turn toward a rundown drive-in movie theater.

Elyse sat up as the truck bumped through a pot-holed parking lot to a spot near a rusted, corrugated metal fence that kept the world from peeking inside. At an entrance gate, a big, yellow shade umbrella perched near a sign that read: Admission $1. "We're where?" she asked.

"The most magical place on earth." Andrew grinned and pointed up, toward the backside of the towering screen.

This hardly seemed magical, but she gave Andrew the benefit of the doubt and craned forward. Staring up, a thirty-foot banner announced, WEEKEND SWAP MEET.

Elyse was horrified. "This is your idea of romancing a lady?"

"I'm not romancing a lady." He sounded a little hurt. "I'm romancing you."

Elyse scowled. Maybe she wasn't a grand dame like Madeline, born to wealth, but that didn't make her any less a lady. She was just more of a blue-collar, flea market lady. Okay, maybe Andrew had a point.

He had driven her a million cultural miles away from San Francisco, back to what she had always been. He had delivered her to the world headquarters of quick-buck-artists and squalor.

She panicked.

Saban wouldn't stand for jumble sales or any other second-hand notions of entertainment. "How did you know I'd like this?" she asked.

"You love flea markets. I've seen you sneak out on weekends, then stash your treasures in the basement." He turned off the engine.

"I do not," she protested weakly.

"That's not your box of 1960s Dream Pets stuffed behind the furnace? What about your Starbuck's city mugs? Or your grapevine wicker backyard furniture?" he said as he jumped out of the pickup and jogged around to her door.

Elyse felt her cheeks color. The sad truth was, she did love flea markets. And rummage sales, tag sales, yard sales, and white elephant church bazaars. She'd tried to break herself of the habit many times, but the lure was greater than her resolve. Flea market finds and eBay had fed her through college. She wasn't proud of those years and loathed the term they used for her kind, a *Picker*.

"I think you've spent too much time going through my basement." She pouted as he held the door open.

Andrew took her hand and helped her out of the pickup. "You know what they say, a woman's basement is the window to her soul."

She followed Andrew toward the yellow umbrella and turnstile entrance.

"Early-birds pay double," barked a middle-aged woman sitting in a lawn chair.

"This place is great," he admitted as he paid the admission and they walked inside. "You can always find something you didn't even know you needed."

"Or a million things that other people must have." Pacing beside Andrew, Elyse surveyed the market. Row after row of vendors set up their wares.

Some sellers had a couple card tables pushed together and a few shiny baubles spread across a crumpled expanse of velvet. Others looked like they were here for the long haul. Theatrical productions folded out of the back of vans. Display racks and signs advertised products and services. From scented candles to knife sharpening. Sports cards to palm reading. Bobble heads to key cutting. Stall after stall boasted everything from household goods to vintage swag. It was like a caravan of itinerate junk gypsies cursed to wander the earth in search of the next buck. The mélange of squalor and desperation, mixed with the smell of chemical toilets and cotton candy, presented a fetid world to Elyse.

She felt sick.

With excitement.

Under all the dust, noise, and stench were possibilities. She loved the place. Andrew was right. Discovering that hidden attic or garage treasure was pure addiction. If she'd never found anything, it would have been easier to kick the habit, but with her Hermes purse always by her side, Elyse was a modern day pirate searching the rummage seas for booty.

Funny how her old life colored her everyday observations. While her friends were among the elite, Elyse often felt tainted by knowing the value of nearly everything they owned. A crystal bud vase would fetch $350 at auction. That old beaded purse would sell online at $175. But the knockoff figurines? Couldn't they see they were fakes? She was often surprised at the forgeries nesting in the nooks and crannies of the grand houses she visited.

Luckily, she didn't limit her appraisals to possessions. She could sense a good man at a hundred yards when no one else could see him. Instead of buying a chair or a desk cheap and flipping it for a higher price, she flipped men.

"My guy is way in the back." Andrew took her hand to lead her through a particularly dense patch of buyers at the open rear door of a U-haul truck. The center of attention, on the tailgate of the truck's massive storage area, was a bedraggled man.

"I got a Mixmaster here," he shouted, holding it up.

"Five dollars!" someone called.

"Sold!" the man yelled and handed it down as he grabbed the money. "I got a sewing machine."

Voices shouted *five*, *ten*, *twenty dollars*.

"You got it." The man passed the sewing machine down and took the twenty.

"I hate these sales," Andrew muttered as they edged through.

"They're just things," Elyse replied.

"This happens here a lot. It's a divorce sale. The wife gets the house, but the husband empties it and brings the stuff here. It's awful."

Elyse felt badly for any marriage that didn't make it. "People get petty, I guess."

"If I ever get married, and then have to get divorced," Andrew confided, "I'm taking the high road. The whole liquidate-the-assets-so-the-woman-gets-nothing is just low. I say, give it to her. Give her everything."

Elyse knew it was easy to take the high road when you were on the outside looking in. How would Andrew feel if Saban wanted to trade up in a couple years? Her guess was that Andrew would find himself here, broken-hearted, with a truck full of hot tulip bulbs.

"It's really sad," Elyse agreed as the bedraggled man hoisted up a battered bust of Woodrow Wilson. Not that anyone at the flea market other than her recognized the features memorialized in plaster.

"I got an old bust of somebody famous," the man shouted.

Andrew frowned at the crowd. "They're like hyenas feeding on the carcass of a marriage."

"Twenty dollars!" Elyse hollered. It wasn't the wisest move, but she had to have the bust.

"Sold," the man bellowed.

On Andrew's heels, Elyse lugged Woodrow through the thinning crowds. Andrew was not amused. Then again, it wasn't her job to amuse him unless it directly impacted his training.

"I can't believe you bought that thing," Andrew snapped. He was headed to the back fence of the flea market.

"I needed him." She cradled the bust. "It's President Wilson."

"The poor guy was selling off a relationship," he huffed.

"I know what I'm doing," Elyse argued. "Besides, it's just stuff."

"Stuff you bought." Andrew stopped and turned to her. "Sometimes, I don't think I know you at all."

Elyse stewed. He didn't know her. Not really. But that wasn't what bothered her. This went to the issue of trust. She had to make him trust her again, and to do that she'd have to do something she hadn't tried before . . . confide in him.

She took a deep breath. "My great-grandmother had one of these."

"What does your great-grandmother have to do with this?" He poked a finger at the statue's ear, and a flake of bronze paint fluttered to the ground.

"She was a suffragette." She held up the bust. "Woodrow Wilson backed the Nineteenth Amendment, and even though my grandmother said he was a waffling little weasel, all Tobins loved him for pushing it through."

"That's the women's vote thing, right?" Andrew asked, unsure.

"Woodrow's the man. When I was a child, Woodrow was always in the corner above the piano. It wasn't until I was ten that I realized he wasn't a composer. He always watched me practice. My mother traded him to a contractor to fortify the foundation of the house when I was twelve."

Andrew eyed her. "You don't have a piano."

"It went to have the front porch rebuilt when the boards rotted out. I was fourteen."

"Tobin women will sell off anything to keep that house, won't they?"

There it was. The truth of her life set out for display in the harsh and unforgiving light of day. There was no denying it. No pretending it wasn't true. Nothing was sacred. Everything had a price and had probably been for sale at one point or another during the last 100 years to keep the Tobin family home on Ivy Loop.

Elyse shrugged. "It seems so."

Andrew was satisfied. He draped an arm over her shoulder and aimed Elyse at a ratty pickup truck. The back bed was covered with a tarp. A lout wearing a soiled undershirt glowered. Andrew stepped up to the lout and shook his grimy hand. "You got it?"

"You got the money, I got the pipes."

Andrew flashed a ten-dollar bill. The lout nodded and flipped back the tarp. The back of the truck was filled with faucets. Old faucets. Elyse peered over the truck's side panel. Bone handles. Brass. Bathtub fixtures with connected showerheads on a four-foot long pipe.

The metal bits and pieces caught the sunlight. Dizzy with hope, Elyse gasped. "Those are the exact same era as my tub."

"Jasper's on the demolition crew for the old Fountain Hotel." Andrew dug into the plumbing pile to find the best. "They help themselves at night and sell it here on weekends."

Elyse remembered the Fountain Hotel, a throwback to the Barbary Coast. Built as a brothel, the basement bar of the four-story structure became legendary for jazz in the 1920s. In the Depression, it was a place for men with no hope to find courage in a bottle and a flea-ridden bed. In the sixties, it was called the Acid Hotel. That was its last popular incarnation. In the last few decades, abandoned, an empty hulk. But it had history. A tawdry one, but history all the same.

The Historical Preservation Society tried to step in, but earthquake-proofing the structure proved impossible. Some of the great buildings couldn't be saved. Not at any price.

Andrew emerged from the pile holding a faucet up like he'd discovered the Holy Grail. Elyse was pleased and troubled at the same time. Andrew had found the last piece of the puzzle that was her house. Soon it would be one hundred percent authentic and restored. Gratefulness washed through her. She blinked hard as tears pressed the backs of her lids.

This was the single-most romantic gesture any man had ever made for her. He'd taken her on their big date to shop for used plumbing.

Back in Andrew's pickup, headed for civilization again, Elyse stroked the chipped and pocked features of her President.

Andrew noticed. "I guess the flea market wasn't a total *bust*."

"That's a terrible joke," she groaned. She had to get used to the idea that Andrew was going to need some special work. Fast work. He had a solid foundation to build from, but the reality was she had weeks to turn a frog into a prince. "So, is this it?"

Andrew beamed. "Not by a long shot."

That sounded hopeful. Maybe he had a picnic lunch hidden behind the seat. She'd take the first opportunity she got to start in on lessons. Elyse didn't have time to give him a long leash, but she could wait a little while longer to see what he could do.

If nothing else came of this day, she had Woodrow. She turned the bust over in her hands. It was far from mint condition. Much of his paint was faded or worn down to the plaster. His nose, obviously broken and poorly repaired, gave him the air of a hockey player who enjoyed a good brawl. Yes, she had the Rocky version of Woodrow Wilson, and she loved him.

After everything settled down with Andrew and Saban, she'd spray-paint Woody gold again and set him on the table next to where her piano had once been. Someday, when the house and finances allowed, she'd put money toward another Steinway. Music always made the house feel more alive.

"I hope you're hungry," Andrew said and pulled off the 101.

Elyse balanced the bust in one arm and carried the bag of burgers in the other as she stepped up the front walk of her house. Behind her, Andrew juggled a tray of soft drinks, his toolbox, and the faucets.

"Let me get this stuff laid out, and then we'll eat," he said. Setting down the drinks, he jogged inside and up the stairs.

Hurrying to the kitchen, Elyse eyed the bag of burgers. They threatened to leak grease through the paper sack and onto her carpets. Wary of Andrew's claim that these were the best burgers on the West Coast, she wondered if she should pop an antacid while he was still upstairs. Distant thumps and clanks from far above echoed through the walls as she spread paper towels on the table and settled the food. If you called double cheeseburgers from a greasy spoon *food*.

Andrew appeared in the doorway. "I can hook it up in no time." He plopped down onto a chair and tore the wrapper off a burger. "Let's eat."

Elyse sat across from him and delicately unfolded her sandwich. It was a mess. The bun was mashed into a gooey mass of cheese, fried onions, and bacon. "Is that an egg?"

"I got 'em with the works." Andrew gripped his with both hands, took a huge bite, and chewed. A look of pure rapture crossed his face, followed by appreciative grunts.

Forcing herself to nibble an edge, she took a pensive bite. Actually, it wasn't bad. The burger merited a heart disease warning label from the Surgeon General, but the onion rings and pepper jack really gave it a kick. "This is good."

"Told ya, they're the best," he mumbled, mouth full.

Oh, no. Was she that far behind? This was kindergarten manners 101. No talking with a mouth full of food. No exceptions. She had to break him of this habit immediately.

From every man she'd ever trained, talking was the least effective way to communicate a lesson. Action always spoke louder than words. Elyse took a second, huge bite of burger.

Moaning and chewing, she mashed the egg, meat, cheese, and bacon into a paste in her mouth. "Mmmmmm."

Andrew swallowed. "I told you these were amazing."

It was time to teach. "Yes!" she agreed loudly with her mouth so full, it was hard to get the word out.

The word wasn't the only thing out. Burger and bun and egg bits sprayed the table. They sprayed Andrew's food. They sprayed Andrew's shirt.

"Ewww," he gasped, sitting back.

"Sorry," Elyse apologized with a sly smile. "I shouldn't talk with my mouth full."

"I guess we know why," Andrew agreed and shook the masticated food off his paper burger wrapper and shirt.

Not her finest moment, but as they ate the rest of their food, Andrew didn't talk with his mouth full, not once. A small victory, but one she'd chalk up in her win column. Hopefully it would only take this one reminder. There'd be lots of chances to test drive his table manners coming up. Starting tonight? "I was thinking we'd go to a wine tasting later, then dinner."

"I didn't tell you, did I?"

"Tell me what?" She tilted her head.

"The Modesto job. I got another week on it. I'm heading back tonight." Andrew smiled innocently and chomped away at his burger.

"You're leaving?" Elyse felt lightheaded. "Again? But you just got here."

No, no, no. This was not happening. Dread plowed through her like a bulldozer, burying her plans for him. She needed Andrew here, under her control. To make the transformation from plumber to suave, polished handyman required daily lessons.

Everything was riding on her delivering Andrew to Saban. It wasn't just the house anymore. Her freedom was at stake. Without a gentleman plumber, she had nothing. She'd even lose her beloved cheesecakes, the impossibly delicious dessert that had comforted her through all her crises of the past three years. She was fairly certain La Sals did not deliver to the Federal Prison.

Desperate times call for desperate measures. She'd break every rule in her book to make sure Saban got her man. Unbuttoning the top button of her blouse, she leaned over toward Andrew and ran her hand over his muscular forearm. A fine layer of arm hair prickled her fingertips. Her eyes danced across his broad chest. *Is that ketchup on his shirt?*

"Andrew, let's move this to the next level," she purred, trying to ignore the stain.

His eyes bugged out of his head. He choked on his burger, but recovered and chewed furiously.

"Let's go upstairs," she added with a wink.

There was work to do. If the promise of sex wrangled him into her control, then so be it. She'd never gone *all the way* with her previous Prince Charmings. It was bad form to sully the merchandise. Though she had to do something.

She steadied her gaze on Andrew, serious. Inside, she was terrified. What if he said *yes*? If she started this, could she stop it before it went too far? Could she trust herself? What if she didn't want to stop?

She looked at the stains on Andrew's shirt from her hamburger-chewing lesson and shuddered. It would be worth getting him out of that shirt just so she could wash it. Elyse had an aversion to stained clothes. Because of the house. Since childhood, her wardrobe came from rummage sales and thrift shops. Why buy new clothes with money that could go against the mortgage? At an early age, she learned about stain removers, bleach, and pre-soaking.

Which was another reason she found Nick so appealing. He was always impeccably groomed.

The truth was she wanted to strip Andrew naked and take him to another level. The basement. She wanted him in her laundry room. There wasn't anything sexual about her fantasy of washing Andrew's clothes. Thoroughly.

Were clean clothes too much to ask for?

But what if she lost Andrew to the pipes of Modesto? Then what?

She had to clear her mind and make a decision. "Andrew, I want you."

Andrew, stunned, swallowed his food with purpose, then spoke slowly and clearly, mouth empty. "I gotta take a whiz."

Seagulls dipped and dove around the docks. Their cries announced each boat that came and went. Sometimes, just for fun, Nick brought biscotti and tossed it out to them. Though most people saw the birds as a nuisance, he liked their calls and surly attitudes. It was life and drama. Something sorely missing inside his sailboat home.

That didn't mean he didn't love living on the water. Solitude was part of him, too. He centered on finding his balance. Given his strange week, he needed to meditate and sort things out. Big changes were coming with Elyse, Andrew, and Vicky.

He needed his calm. A simpler time. A time before his businesses demanded constant attention. Before book deadlines, charity work, and produce deliveries. He had very little time to himself, for himself. There were always interruptions, cell phone calls, emails, and text messages.

Nick needed a day off.

To unplug.

Which was exactly what he should have done with his cell phone. The phone lit up, ringing out its tune. Nick sighed.

He'd left instructions with Martine that he was not to be disturbed unless it was an emergency. Looking down at the screen, he realized this wasn't business. He clicked to accept the call. "Andrew, what's up?"

"I think she wants to have sex with me," came the nervous reply. "You said she didn't have sex with the guys she matched up."

"Are you sure?" Nick searched the far shore with his eyes as he tried to think of the right advice to give Andrew. None came.

"It was pretty clear," Andrew whispered. "She's cute and all, and you should have seen her eyes light up when I found the handles for her bathtub, but what if she grades me on my, y'know, performance?"

Nick had kept tabs on Elyse and her operation for the last three years. From all reports, her work was always about the happiness of the couples. Sure, she'd tease the poor slobs to get them to improve their manners or learn to dance, but she never slept with her grooms-in-training. "I don't see where you have much choice," Nick said, hating his own words. "Give her your A game."

There was a long pause. "What if I don't have an A game?"

Nick suppressed a chuckle. Andrew was having performance anxiety before there was even a performance. He felt bad for both of them. Andrew didn't want to sleep with Elyse, and Nick did, desperately.

But Elyse Tobin was a free woman, and he had no claim on her. She'd falsely accused him of turning her into the IRS and thrown water on him. She'd stomped on his every effort to get to know her better, and he loved her even more with each slight.

Underneath all of her denials, he knew the truth. The night they'd shared was more than just sex. Granted, his years spent pleasing women might have left him with a reputation, but it also made him the man who could fulfill all of Elyse's desires. He was the perfect partner for her. The one and only. Why couldn't she see it?

Pride or anger wasn't going to end this union before it began. No, it was something she had inspired in him. Three years ago, he was a man at moral loose ends. She had changed all that. She had opened up to him and made him think. He could see himself through her eyes, and he didn't like what he saw.

While he was the son of a janitor, his father was more than that. His father was a good man. A gentleman with a personal code of ethics.

That night with Elyse triggered Nick's own code of ethics into being.

In those few hours together, he wanted to be more. The desire turned to resolve, and the resolve became virtue. Nick Salvatore had evolved from an attentive male consort to a real man.

It was so obvious to him, he couldn't believe Elyse didn't see it. She prided herself on sensing a good man, of recognizing potential and progress. How could she be blind to what was really happening? Her lessons didn't make men great, the introduction of love did. Once a man has committed to love, all else changed. How could a man in love act selfishly? How could he not do his best? How could he not be courageous?

But as a man has a life span, so can love. Unrequited love dies as surely as a flower denied sun and water. She would take his cheesecakes, but not his heart.

"What do I do, Nick?" Andrew pleaded.

"Tell her the truth," Nick suggested. "Admit everything."

"Even you helping me?"

Nick settled onto a deck chair and hit *save* on his laptop publishing file. His 999th cheesecake recipe. The book was one recipe away from completion. He was tired of all the games and deceptions. "I would."

"But I'm not you," Andrew admitted. "I think I still got a shot at a wife. I don't want to do something I'd regret forever just to get married."

This was torture. Andrew was right where Nick longed to be. Nick listened carefully to a knocking on the door over the phone. Then came Elyse's door-muffled voice. "Are you in there, Andrew? Is everything okay?"

"I'm gonna have to do this, aren't I?" Andrew asked.

"Give me two minutes," Nick replied. "I'll see what I can do."

Disconnecting, Nick hit his speed-dial keys. A moment later, the call went through. "Vicky, I need a favor, and I need it fast."

Elyse knocked on the bathroom door again. What was going on? Andrew had locked himself in and refused to open up. "If you can put Modesto off for a week, I'll make it worth your while."

"I'll be out in a couple minutes. I promise," Andrew yelled.

She would have sworn he was talking to someone in there. Maybe he couldn't handle a hamburger with the works. Or something else was wrong.

For her, everything was wrong. One minute they were having a meal together, and the next, he blindsided her with the news that he'd be gone for another week. She couldn't afford to lose another week.

It was now or never. She had to get the situation under control. Plan B.

If Andrew opened the door, she'd come clean and tell him everything. The six previous grooms, the brides, even the money. She'd offer Andrew a cut, paying him out of the re-mortgaged-for-the-zillionth-time bank loan. Not a great solution, but a solution all the same. Hopefully, he wouldn't be so appalled by her real profession that he'd walk out the door, disgusted, leaving her in the lurch.

To find another groom on such short notice would be impossible. She knocked on the door again, harder. "Andrew, open this door right now. We need to talk. This is serious."

"Forty five seconds," he shouted back.

What kind of schedule was he on? The last thing she needed was another problem or distraction.

The phone rang.

She didn't want to answer it, but what if it were Iris? Grabbing the phone in her office, she was floored by an onslaught of rapid-fire words. *Something-must-be-done-Loose-lips-sink-ships-Relationships-are-as-fragile-as-flowers-Elyse?*

"Yes, Madeline," Elyse replied. She steeled herself for another barrage of language, but it didn't come.

Madeline only said two words. "Wedgeworth's now!"

The line went dead. In the years that Elyse had known her, this was the first time Madeline had put two words together that made perfect sense. Something was up. Something big. She was in no position to refuse Madeline, no matter what was going on here. But she couldn't afford to lose Andrew, either.

Elyse returned to the bathroom door. "Andrew, I have to go out for a while. We'll talk when I come back. Promise me you'll stay . . . please?"

From the second floor bathroom window, Andrew watched Elyse drive down Ivy Loop. Nick was some kind of magician. He said two minutes, and two minutes later the phone rang and Elyse left. Amazing.

Unlocking the door, he hiked up to the fourth floor. His pipes and tools were laid out in the bathroom. Picking up a wrench, he knew what he had to do. Quickly.

Handing off her keys to the valet, Elyse jogged up the marble steps into Wedgeworth's. The girls were at their usual table. Madeline, Saban, and Jackie.

"Isn't it exciting?" Jackie cheered.

Elyse took her seat. "What?"

The waiter landed a bottle of champagne at the table as Madeline pushed a book toward Elyse. "My agent is feting my new book tonight. It's a surprise book launch party just for me. You can't believe how long it takes to make a book. Weeks. I swear publishers are like tortoises. The turtles on land. Sea turtles are much faster, well, in the sea anyway. Has anyone tried the fish today? I read you should never order fish on a Monday, but it's not Monday. I love my new book."

Her mind swarming with regrets, Andrew, and the IRS, Elyse picked up the book. This was about a book? That's it? Not some earth-shattering announcement or problem? She stared down at the title, *Instant Intervention: A Guide to Saving Your Friends, Family, and Coworkers from Themselves.* "You wrote this in a few weeks?"

"Of course." Madeline waved for the waiter to pour the sparkling wine. "It's not hard at all. I had a secretary follow me around while I talked about all the people I knew. Did you know that secretaries make less than maids? At least my maids. You can't have just anyone washing your sheets. After we had scads of words, tens of thousands, we sent them to an editor. I love editors. They're like gold miners. They find the gold, re-jigger everything and presto, a book."

Elyse flipped the book over. On the back cover was a photo of Madeline in a crisp business suit. "You look very professional." She didn't have time for this. She had work to do. Andrew work.

Jackie held up her glass of water. "To another success!" They toasted.

Madeline frowned. "I really should wait for my agent, but we'll pop another bottle then. Someone has to keep the economy moving. Do you think these were fair trade grapes? I'd hate to think of poor Frenchmen toiling in the sun and then not getting health insurance. Speaking of France, are you leaving the country, Elyse?"

"What?" The question took her by surprise. She shot a look at Jackie. "I'm not going anywhere. Who told you that?"

"I had to tell," Jackie confessed, setting her glass down. "We're all involved."

Saban glared at Elyse, suspicious. "They're not going to hunt you down and put you away before I get my man, are they? I have a lot invested in this."

"You don't have anything invested yet," Elyse objected.

"It's an emotional investment," Saban snorted.

"No one is putting me away," Elyse said, downplaying the situation. She'd come too far to lose this deal now. The big payday was two weeks away. Two-hundred thousand dollars for a husband. For Andrew. "I just have to pay a little fine. That's all. Everything is peachy."

"Very well." Madeline settled back in her chair. "It wouldn't do for everyone to know our man business. Jackie, tell the story again. I love it. It's like a TV show. The IRS, cheesecake, love, drama, and La Sals. That could be a show."

"You told them everything?" Elyse questioned Jackie.

"What?" Jackie sighed. "It's a great story."

"Great for TV," Saban agreed and belted down her wine in one gulp. Maybe she *was* a good choice for Andrew.

"This is even better than Shakespeare," Madeline trilled.

"Thank you," Elyse said, standing. "Congratulations, Madeline. It's been a pleasure, but as you can guess, I have a lot of work to do. See you all soon." She air kissed everyone and hurried for the door before anyone could object.

Elyse hummed her Prius across the Golden Gate Bridge. Sunlight showered the Bay below. Every ripple glinted a silvery crest. She couldn't look for too long. Just a few glances at the hypnotic water below.

If there'd been a bright spot in the Wedgeworth debacle, it was that Saban was still onboard. One hundred percent committed to taking delivery of Andrew at the Charity Ball.

The stress gnawed at her. Would Andrew be ready for the big night? She was hoping against hope that he'd still be at her house. Finding out was the only thing keeping her on course for home and not veering toward La Sals. At times like this, she'd give just about anything for a La Sals' cheesecake.

No. She had to be strong. Show resolve.

No cheesecake.

She was going straight to Andrew.

Besides, she had a new plan. Instead of a fully

functioning, attentive, conversing, engaged male, she'd change the pitch. Andrew was the strong, silent type. The perfect man who would look good and wait in a corner at a cocktail party sipping a scotch. Everyone loved that kind of manly man.

If it worked, she wouldn't have to come clean with him. Or cut him in.

Braking hard, she turned the corner to Ivy Loop and stopped in the middle of the road.

Andrew's pickup was gone.

Her pulse quickened as she parked her car and paced up the stone steps to her front door. Taped to the beveled glass of the window was a note. She ripped it down.

Finished your bath. Plumbing emergency in Modesto. See you next Saturday.

A plumbing emergency? What kind of emergency could plumbing have? A pipe breaks, you turn off the water.

She hurried inside and dialed his number. Having punched in his number so many times over the past week, she'd memorized it. What was she going to say? Tell him the truth over the phone? *Bad idea.* That wouldn't work. She'd sound like she was pimping a male harem out to horny socialites. *Welcome to the club, Andrew. You've been sold to a Flower Heiress. You leave for Argentina tomorrow.* Maybe just Oregon.

Pacing back and forth across her living room, phone in hand, she tried to think of the right words to say, a reason he needed to return to the city. Who was she kidding?

Her plans sucked, and Andrew was gone.

Maybe she'd think of something upstairs. That was it. She'd take a bath. It was the next best thing to cheesecake, or a simultaneous orgasm. Neither of those were an option right now.

Tossing the phone back in its cradle, she jogged up the three flights of stairs to the fourth floor bathroom and stopped dead in her tracks. Elyse gawked. Her knees wobbled as she straddled the doorway.

Her bath had changed.

She stood transfixed by the most beautiful example of turn-of-the-century plumbing she'd ever laid eyes on.

Andrew had been busy before he left. Where once there was a simple chrome tap and spout that filled the tub, now stood a monument of nickel and copper. Gleaming pipes fed a spigot, but two more pipes rose high above and ended in a saucer-sized nickel showerhead. Perfectly authentic. Her new plumbing was a tribute to shower evolution.

Elyse sighed as all her fears and doubts drained away. Grabbing the phone beside the tub, she dialed Andrew's number and listened for the beep. "Hi, Andrew. This is Elyse," she began. Gratitude swept through her. He had a special skill. Andrew deserved more than some lame excuse to return to the city. He was doing what he loved most, even if he was doing it in Modesto. "I just wanted to say thank you. The shower is a miracle. You're the best plumber a girl could ever hope to find."

She hung up the phone, lost in the gleaming beauty of the antique fixtures. A truer plumber had not crossed the threshold of the Tobin residence in a hundred or more years. If ever. Andrew was a master.

Plumbing was more than just a job or skill to him.

Inspired, Elyse ran back down the stairs to the bookcase. With a twist of a key in the lock, she pulled out *The Big Red Book of Men*. Cuddling into the sofa with the book, she began to make notes. She didn't have a photo of Andrew yet. But she knew exactly what she had to do.

After writing Andrew's name at the top of a blank page, she paused. For the first time in three years, *plumbing* had become a charm.

Plumbing. Who would have guessed?

Tears came to her eyes, but she wasn't going to cry.

She wasn't usually this emotional, but seeing the shower and knowing that the plumbing was, at long last, complete, brought an enormous sense of awe. She'd turned a corner. The house was complete. The leaky plumbing, rotting floorboards, damaged downspouts, and the cracked foundation that had plagued the house decade after decade were gone. The structure was pristine.

She'd won.

The house was solid, and she had everything she wanted in life. Almost.

As her mother would advise, she needed to count her blessings. She owned a home. So she had a mortgage. Everyone did. She also had heritage. An entire family tree of strong, decisive woman who refused to give up when the going got tough. Tobins were survivors. She had cheesecake. Maybe not in her refrigerator at this second, but she had the cheesecake's address.

The things that were missing weren't out of reach. She'd have her family, just as soon as she straightened out this IRS mess. Elyse flipped through the pages of grooms. Absolutely no one did what she did. She should write a book or something, or start a charm school. Sure, she couldn't train guys forever, but maybe there was a way to mass market her unique skill set. The answers would come to her.

Admiring her massive fireplace and mantle, she knew there were possibilities. Opportunities. They'd come to her if she let them. She let her fingers stray to the pages in the back of the book. Her favorite pages.

Turning to her collection of dust-jacket author photos carefully glued in order of year, she stared at Nick Salvatore's smiling face, authentic and original. Elyse flipped another page. More Nick. Nick at a fundraiser. Nick judging pies at the county fair. Nick playing in a charity golf tournament.

She still remembered her night with him. Even if it wasn't a real relationship, even if he had been pretending, he still did all the right things. He was a walking, talking textbook of what to do to make a woman feel special.

Elyse wanted that feeling again.

She turned another page, and there was a picture of Nick in a basketball uniform. A flyer recruiting players for Bishop Hegeland's team. At the bottom, very clearly, in bold, were the words, CALL NICK. Under that was his phone number.

"Call Nick," she giggled. *As if.*

Then again, she did owe him an apology.

Call Nick. The words spoke to her. But she couldn't call Nick.

Never.

Eventually she'd run into him like she always did. He seemed to be lurking around every corner. When he appeared again, then she'd apologize to him properly.

She would *never* call Nick.

Chapter 9

Elyse picked up the phone and dialed. It rang. Snuggled in and safe on her sofa, she traced Nick's dust-jacket photo with her fingertip.

There was a click, then "Hello." Nick's voice sounded tentative.

She took a deep breath. *Hang up. It's not too late.* "This is Elyse." The words rushed out, defying common sense.

"I know. Caller ID," he replied.

Was she insane? Had she finally lost her mind? No. Elyse steadied herself. She was calling to apologize to Nick. That was it. Nothing else. This was not, *absolutely not*, a booty call. "I'm surprised you answered."

His voice was even and controlled. "I believe that screening calls is the lowest form of cowardice."

"Yes, a coward screens a thousand calls, but a brave man answers but once." She loved their banter.

"So?" he asked.

A single word. Spoken low. She thought she heard an inviting tone in it. Or was it sexual innuendo? *So?* The man made every syllable of the English language sexy. *So?* Elyse crossed and uncrossed her legs, squirming in her seat, her thoughts ripping the clothes off his body.

Oh God, she was making a booty call!

"What do you want, Elyse?" Nick questioned.

What did she want? There were a million answers to that question. She wanted the deed to her house, once and for all. She wanted her mother back, alive and well, not buried in the Sausalito Cemetery. She wanted Saban to take joyful delivery of Andrew and pay her accordingly. She wanted her tax audit to vanish, along with the boxes of paperwork stacked up in her kitchen. She wanted a life. Her life.

She wanted to start over.

From the beginning.

With a La Sals' cheesecake in her refrigerator.

Elyse squeezed her eyes shut and clutched the receiver with both hands. The cheesecake always made her feel a little guilty, but not as guilty as what she was about to ask for. There were a lot of things she wanted.

She wanted to apologize. That was the reason she called Nick. He was due a sincere apology. Which really should be delivered in person, not over the phone.

Okay, she wanted Nick. She admitted it. Now she just had to convince him. "Would you like to come over?"

Nervously, she entwined her foot around the throw pillows beside her. She swore she heard a chuckle on the other end of the line. Maybe it was a choking sound. After that, there was a long pause. Was he laughing at her? Did he need a Heimlich Maneuver?

"This isn't April Fool's Day, is it?"

"It's June." She didn't blame him for being wary. She'd rebuffed his every advance for three years. Her cheeks burned with shame. She had to say something to make him trust her. Why not the truth? Or part of the truth. "I want to apologize. The thing in La Sals. It was a mistake. You weren't the one who turned me in to the IRS. I'm sorry."

This time she distinctly heard a soft chuckle. "I thought Tobins weren't capable of apologizing."

"I've evolved." Lust rocketed through her. She'd denied herself for too long. She deserved this indulgence. She deserved *him*. "You never answered my question."

"Which was?"

He wouldn't deny her, would he? Did he want her to grovel for his forgiveness? Well, he could forget that. She might as well lay it out there. "Do you want to come over?"

"I'm already in the car."

With cheesecake #999 riding shotgun, Nick double-checked the address on his GPS. 358 Ivy Loop. He pulled to the curb and set the parking brake on his Ford Explorer. It wasn't a fancy car, but he didn't need leather seats to haul crates of raspberries and cases of wine. It was a working car. It was like him.

He sat in front of Elyse's house and breathed deeply. He had to calm down. He had to be in control. While he had always thought Elyse would call him, he'd almost given up. Three years was a long time. A long time to prepare.

Doubt shot through him. He'd redeemed and remade himself into a gentleman. More than that, the perfect lover. For Elyse. Images from their last encounter played through his imagination. Her surrender to their mutual sexual frenzy was burned into his brain, but tonight had to be more.

Much more.

If it was only physical, he suspected she'd have her orgasms and put him out. Again. That wasn't the plan. After three years, he wanted to show her he could be a partner. He was rolling the dice for a lifetime commitment.

Everything was riding on this night.

He had one chance to change their worlds.

Cheesecake #999 was his last hope. #1,000, if there was a #1,000, would be the end. He slid the cake box into a cloth grocery bag and opened the trunk.

Gathering two more shopping bags of groceries, sundries, and surprises, he headed up her steps. He'd thought about bringing champagne as well, but decided against it. He wanted her clearheaded. He wanted her to see the real him.

The bags weighed heavy in his hands. They'd waited a long time for this day. Little by little, gleaning information from Andrew, Jackie, or Madeline, he'd collected oils here or a recipe there, all aimed at this eventuality. At this date.

This was Nick's chance to prove his virtue, his skill and dedication. It was time to show his merit and the mettle of which he was cast.

Booty call! Elyse danced across the hardwood floors victorious. Jubilant. Empowered. Giddy at the prospect of the evening ahead, she wondered why she'd denied herself the carnal pleasure of a night with Nick for so long.

Too long.

Tugging the lace curtain back with her finger, she pressed her nose to the beveled glass window beside the front door. He had arrived in all his dark-haired-swarthy-good-looking magnificence. Was he carrying bags?

She felt a tingle race through her as she recognized the distinct shape of her favorite cheesecake box in one of the sacks. If Nick had expanded his sexual repertoire to reading minds, she was in deep trouble. Then again, her cheesecake addiction was common knowledge. Before she had a chance to chicken out or come to her senses, Elyse flung the door open.

"Bio-degradable cloth bags," she observed. "How ecological of you."

"No one says you can't have a good time *and* save the planet."

Leaning in close to peek in the bags, her skin prickled with heat. She inhaled his masculine scent. More than just his woodsy, citrus smell, there were more layers this time. Soy sauce, ginger, the ocean. "I should warn you, Nick, tonight is a one time thing."

"That's what you said last time." He smiled broadly, showing off two perfect rows of teeth. Entering the house, he looked around. "Kitchen?"

"That way." She nodded to the hallway. "There's chilled champagne in the fridge."

She was saving the bottle for the day she paid off the house, but now that was impossible. Tonight qualified as a worthy occasion, and she knew that Nick would appreciate a fine wine.

"No need for that," he said, landing his bags on the counter with a *thump*. "I want you to have your wits about you."

Not wanting to appear too eager, Elyse sidled up to him and watched as he put several containers in the fridge, including the suspect box with #999 written on top of it. "Is that La Sals'?"

"One course at a time." He turned, brushing against her.

Her nipples rose to attention. Sex and cheesecake. He *was* a mind reader. She wanted to crush her mouth on his and wrap her arms around him. Instead, their eyes met. He stood still, unmoving. She hated this. He should be all over her, taking her into his arms and carrying her off to the bedroom. What was wrong with him?

He turned away and worked with expert confidence at the counter, taking items out of the final bag. Jars of dried leaves. Bottles of oil.

These must be the tools of his new and improved seductions, she assumed. "Let's get this show on the road."

"Patience, Elyse." Popping the top off a bottle of carbonated mint-flavored juice, Nick poured the liquid into two wine glasses and handed one to her.

"I'm not the patient type," she replied as she raised her glass and took a sip. The liquid fizzed on the tip of her tongue, delicious, unlike anything she'd ever had.

Nick clinked his glass against hers. "I'd say waiting three years between dates is patience."

"More like abstinence." She polished off the drink. "We had a toast. We talked. Let's go upstairs."

He stepped up to her. Their chests grazed and arms touched. Elyse felt a shiver of longing warm her deep inside. His hot breath played across her earlobe as he raised his hand and gently pushed her hair back. "I was thinking we'd go for more romance this time," he whispered.

"You want to take it slow?" She tilted her head up. His lips were inches away from hers. His dark brown, Mediterranean eyes bore into her, like they were searching her soul, seeking the very depth of her being. If this was all part of the renovated Nick seduction technique, it was working.

But what if it wasn't. What if he really wanted more? Was it possible that San Francisco's most notorious playboy had more in mind than just a quick roll in the hay, another notch on the bedpost?

No. Not Nick. She dismissed the thought. This was the Nick Salvatore Show.

He lifted her hand and rubbed the tips of her fingers against his strong jaw before gently kissing her palm. "Don't you think we should take the car out of the garage before we stomp on the gas pedal?"

Damn it was a good show. Her nipples tightened, tension building. So that's the way he wanted to play this, slow and torturous. She reached a hand down to his belt, her fingers grasping his buckle. Two could play this game. "Do you need help getting your car out of the garage?"

The kitchen floor was about to become the Tobin 500 Speedway to orgasm. He'd have no option but satisfy her after she took the driver's seat. Better yet, after she had her way with him, cake. God help her, celibacy and diets did not work. Not apart. Not together. She was a starving woman ready to devour her prizes, Nick and the cheesecake he rode in on.

"Elyse," he said, firmly. He took her hand and wove his fingers between hers. "I thought we'd start with a bath."

"What?" She straightened. Was this just a guess, or part of his new routine, or did he somehow know about her bath? Was it Jackie? She blabbed about everything. Elyse didn't want to think about that now. She didn't want to think about anything. "I'm very particular about my baths."

"I'm not going to give you *a* bath." He paced to the counter, leaving her. Their bodies no longer touching. "I'm going to give you *the* bath."

Sinking a fist on her hip, she was annoyed. Who did he think he was? This was her house, her seduction. Wasn't it? Still, she was curious. "Knock yourself out. The tub's on the fourth floor."

Nick jogged up flight after flight of stairs with one of his cloth bags. He had to get out of the kitchen before his pants set the place on fire.

He wanted to strip Elyse naked, make mad sweet love to her, then spoon-feed her cheesecake until she fell asleep in his arms. He had to deny himself immediate gratification. This was the big test he'd been preparing for. Three years. If he rushed it, he knew he'd be out on the curb.

Entering the fourth floor bathroom, he marveled at the workmanship.

Andrew hadn't been exaggerating. The converted attic was a bathing utopia. Centered in the room was a hammered copper tub. Next to it was a 1920's fainting couch and shelves with oils, foams, and powders. Against one wall, a pair of dressing screens. Behind them, towels.

Opening the curtains over a window, Nick stopped. The postcard view was incredible. The Bay and Golden Gate Bridge stretched out to the twinkling lights of San Francisco in the distance.

Working quickly, he turned the antique tap handles, and hot water rushed from the spigot. Unpacking the bag, he lined up candles, a lighter, plastic bags of herbs, and jars of liquids.

The room still didn't feel exactly right. It needed a little more focus. Pulling the fainting couch to one side, he lined up the dressing screens to frame the view of the Bay from the tub. Lighting the candles and turning off the overhead light made all the difference in the world. The room looked magical.

Next, he turned his attention to the tub again. Humming an old song his dad sang to his mother, Nick measured handfuls of bath salts and herbs into the water. The steam and scents made him a lightheaded. Or maybe it was just being here. As he understood it, no one was allowed in here with the exception of professional services like carpenters or plumbers. He was the first man to be invited into Elyse's inner sanctum as something other than a contractor.

And he hoped to be the last.

With that thought, he began to relax. This was his element. Spoiling Elyse was what he was made for. The words of the song came to him, and though he seldom sang, the lyrics erupted from his soul like a primal love call.

Growing impatient, Elyse tiptoed up the stairs to the fourth floor landing. She paused, straining to hear. Was Nick ... singing? She peeked over the top step. He was hovering over her bath.

And he was definitely singing.

She recognized the song from old romantic comedy movies and grinned.

The man was full of surprises. He showed up, brought food, suggested a bath, and now sang in a totally disarming, slightly off-key baritone. Who would have guessed that Nick had a flaw?

The night was getting better and better. Elyse slipped

back down the stairs to the second floor and her bedroom, leaving the door open wide. She stripped off her clothes and pulled on a Chinese silk robe embroidered with peacocks. She could still hear Nick singing two floors above.

His voice sounded louder as the water stopped.

Stretching across her bed, she waited for him. How many nights had she lain here and thought of Nick as she touched herself and pretended it was him? She'd always sworn their one night of passion would never be repeated. Yet here she was.

Again.

This wasn't the same. She was a different woman now.

Three years ago, overwhelming grief, anger, and loneliness had churned into a perfect storm of lust. She was the aggressor then. Her mission . . . to seduce Nick and make love to him relentlessly until her emotional firestorm subsided. Her mother's death, her broken long-distance engagement followed by her fiancé marrying another woman, her inheritance of a broken house with leaky pipes. Her world had been out of control and there was only one way to stop it. Problems, pain, and uncertainty had poured out. Every orgasm had brought her closer to the truth of herself and the answers she sought. Sex had been the bridge to a greater realization of her purpose in life. It was also when she knew that Nick wasn't part of her overall vision. He was simply a very pleasant means to an end.

Elyse lay back in the pillows and ran a hand over her breasts, then lower. Her fingers caressed her thigh and the edge of her robe, then closer to the moistness growing within her.

"I've heard you can go blind touching yourself like that." Nick stood in the doorway. His skin had a sheen from the steam of the bathroom and droplets of water, sparking like diamonds, clung to his eyebrows.

"I wouldn't have to touch myself if I had a lover worth

a damn." She cocked a mocking smile at him.

"I'm always up to a challenge." He paced toward her.

Elyse arched her back and propped herself up with an elbow. Her robe gaped at her chest, revealing the curve of her breast. "Did you give up on the bath?"

"I don't give up. Not on the bath, not on you." Kneeling beside her, Nick took matters into his own hands. Or rather, his arms.

She felt light as a feather in his embrace. Eyes closed, she nuzzled her head into his shoulder as he lifted her, then turned and carried her out of her room and up the stairs. Each step was a smooth rhythm as he took her higher into the house. Her house. Her bath.

"We're here." Nick's words were barely a whisper and his hot breath on her neck made her shiver. The room was humid from the bath, but there was a scent to the steam that she didn't recognize. He gently landed her on the fainting couch. The tie on her robe hung loose. She opened her eyes.

There were candles everywhere, giving the room a flickering glow. Her tub was filled with bubbles. Many towels were at the ready. In the distance, through the window, framed by the dressing screens, the towers of the city shone against the water.

"You rearranged my furniture," she stated lazily.

"It's a great room," he replied without shame.

Elyse stood in front of him and let her robe drape open. "Don't tell me you plan to take up interior decorating?"

He glanced down at her chest and lower, much lower, to her curly brown hair. "Not as long as I see something more beautiful right in front of me."

She rolled her shoulders and let the robe slip away, completely. "See anything you like?"

"Indeed." He lifted her off her feet again and eased her into the foam of the bath, soaking the front of his shirt.

"Hey," she objected. "How come I'm the only one

who's naked here?"

"Making love is a process that should consume all the senses," he said as he removed his shirt. "Relax."

She inhaled deeply as the water swirled around her. Losing her focus to the fragrant bath, she lay back. The hot water covered her body. Her thoughts turned in slow circles. The perfumed scent of . . . what was it? Spice? Every muscle in her body eased. "You pour a good bath."

"I haven't even started yet." Nick strode out the door.

While Nick was an expert in the bedroom, he was more comfortable in the kitchen. Setting a pot of homemade dim sum dumplings to steam on the stove, he opened the refrigerator.

Cheesecake #999.

The inspiration for the bath and tonight's food came from one of his many fantasies of Elyse. In this one, they were honeymooning in the Chinese islands dotting the ocean south of Macau. Late night, after a long day at the restaurant, he loved to watch the travel channel. Someday, with the right person, he'd traverse the world.

Lifting the lid of the box, he gazed at the cake. It was a departure for him. Usually he relied on local farmers or gourmet artisans. With this effort, he went farther afield than he ever had. The Mandarin Orange. It had taken him hundreds of oranges and weeks to find a way to reduce their essence to an extract. It was an uncharted culinary horizon. By making his own extracts, he had a control over food that he didn't have in other areas of his life. Like love. Like Elyse.

He ran a knife under cold water and cut a perfectly proportioned slice as the lid on the steamer rattled from the heat within. He was ready.

Elyse didn't know if he was gone a minute or an hour as waves of steamed aromatics washed over her. Her lilac bath was an exact science, but this was something else. An adventure in her own tub. That was a lot of Nick's allure. Even in a home that she grew up in, Nick found a way to make it something new, something unexpected. Just like his cookbooks. Traditional dishes were spiced up with unimagined combinations of flavor like curry hotdogs or mac 'n cheese soufflé. While she rebuilt men in his image, the carbon copies paled to the real man himself.

Her body and thoughts were suspended by the bath as Nick stepped into the doorway. He stood there, stripped to the waist, his muscular build supporting a plate of hors d'oeuvres in one hand and a piece of cheesecake in the other.

"You look like the cover model of a romance novel," she observed.

"The Wanton Waiter?"

She shifted in the tub for a better look. Waves of scented water splashed against the rim. "I like this story."

Moving close, Nick landed the plates on a small table next to the tub. "Dim sum, Milady?"

"Indeed, Farnsworth."

"Farnsworth?" he questioned. "That sounds more like a stuffy butler."

"You would deny me butlering?"

"I would deny you nothing." Nick expertly lifted a dumpling in chopsticks. "The dim sum are meant to complement the Chinese bath."

"I was wondering what it was," she said dreamily.

"It's made by a Chinatown apothecary. A cleansing bath. Tripled-distilled rice liquor, salts, spices, and Asian pear soap." He held out the dumpling.

Elyse opened her mouth. Nick slid the morsel between her open lips. As she chewed, her eyes rolled back in her head. "Ginger, ground pork, soy sauce, five spice."

"In an ephemeral veil of dough."

"No one does take-out like you, Nick." She swallowed. "Do you have more?"

"More than you can handle." He speared another and lifted it to her.

"If you can keep this up, you might just be here in the morning." She raised a soapy hand and stroked his broad chest, then ran her hand lower. "I see keeping it up isn't a problem. Are dim sum an aphrodisiac?"

"Second only to spaghetti sauce lasagna." Nick fed her another dumpling.

"What?" she mumbled.

"The ultimate seduction meal," he repeated. "Every man in the world knows that."

She sat up, foam clinging to her breasts. "A jar of Ragu, tough cheese, and soggy noodles makes a man irresistible to women?"

"I don't know who figured it out, but it works," he admitted. "It says, *I'm pathetic and need your guidance, but I'm trying really hard.* Most women fall for it."

Elyse was bowled over by this revelation. Men made traps based on the whims, emotions, and apparent overconfidence of women, then communicated their success to other men. That spoke to organization. Maybe she had been underestimating them. Though this was not the time to contemplate the puzzle that was modern man. This was time for more spoiling. "What's coming next?" she asked. "I hope it's going to be me."

"Soon." Nick picked up the plate with the slice of cheesecake on it.

Elyse was shocked. It was orange. Bright orange. "La Sals doesn't make an orange cheesecake."

"Maybe it isn't La Sals'." He cut the end off with the edge of a fork and held it out.

"I'm very particular about . . ."

"Shut up and eat," Nick ordered. "This is the plane, and your mouth is the hangar."

This was the strangest seduction of her life. As he hummed an airplane sound and swooped the cheesecake close to her, she bit it off the fork.

The flavor was overwhelming. Intense. "Oh mama, that's good." She thumped the side of the copper tub with her hand.

"It's just a cheesecake."

"And Picasso was a house painter." She rolled the confection in her mouth. It was creamy like La Sals', but it didn't have a topping like she was used to. Everything was blended perfectly together. "It's tangy and sweet and sour with a punch of citrus that makes my mouth pucker." Her lips puckered.

Nick leaned over and pressed his lips to hers. "It's the kissing cake. You have to kiss after each bite. It's the law."

Elyse gulped down the bite in her mouth. "Cheesecakes come with codes and covenants now?"

"The rules are written on the bottom of the box." He held another bite on the fork, taunting her.

"You can't fight City Hall." She accepted another forkful, and the kiss that followed.

Altogether, there were twelve bites of cheesecake and twelve kisses, each a little longer and more intimate than the last. The final kiss was soft, with a nice amount of tongue . . . tongues that both tasted like orange cheesecake. She smiled as he sat back and studied her.

"What are you thinking, Elyse?" he asked honestly.

"I was thinking, if you're out of cheesecake, what else are you going to woo me with?"

"Me," he said as he bent over the edge of the bath and drove a hand down into the foamy water between her legs. She gasped at the sudden, bold move, then relaxed as he pulled the stopper out.

As the water drained away, Nick wrapped her in a big white towel, then swept her into his arms again. The short trip down two flights of steps led to her room, her bed.

He lowered her to the open sheets. She looked up into his dark eyes as he stood over her. He seemed to hesitate.

"There's a point of no return," he warned her.

She opened her towel. "I passed that when I picked up the phone and called you."

"I'm just glad you finally did." Nick unfastened his pants and slid them off, then joined her on the bed.

The next hour was a scramble of images in Elyse's mind.

Their lips met gently, then harder as the passion built inside them. He still tasted like cheesecake. He explored her entire body with soft caresses and delicate kisses. He teased her most intimate places again and again until the anticipation drove her over the edge.

Finally, she returned the service to him, making him writhe and moan as she had. When neither of them could stand much more, she straddled him.

He stood ready between her legs as she positioned herself, then lowered herself down bit by bit. Had it really been three years since she'd been with a man? This man? She could see the expectancy in his eyes, the yearning. He wanted her, badly.

Three years was a long time. She wasn't certain she was up to accepting his full girth. She wanted it, though. She wanted all of him.

Pleasure flashed through her body as she took his length. It was like the first time again. With Nick.

They were united. One.

She slowly rose. He exhaled as she did, then inhaled sharply as she dropped again. All the way. Again. Again. Up and down. Soon they were in their own rhythm. A dance of life, of love, all in her house.

Her thighs began to ache. Her muscles weren't used to this. He seemed to sense it and they rolled. It was his turn to set their pace. She relaxed, surrendered, and he was in no hurry.

The moon shone in the window as they climaxed. Sweat poured off their bodies as they rocked against each other, consumed by their needs and fulfilling them in each other.

Gasping, they lay side by side.

"Oh my god," Elyse exclaimed. "I'm out of shape for this."

"You were perfect in every way." He grinned at her. It was an exhausted, goofy smile of complete satisfaction. She'd seen it before.

"You haven't noticed a few extra pounds on me since last time?" She eyed him. Would he lie?

"You were too thin." He lifted the sheet to check. "Your hips were a little bony before. Now, you have just the right amount of padding and a bit more curve. My mother always says, *Anyone who's too thin hasn't learned to enjoy life.*"

The comment struck her as odd. She couldn't picture Nick having family. She was sure he didn't just spring from a magical gigolo well when some poor woman made a wish and flipped in a coin, but family? "Do you see your parents?"

Nick rolled over to study the ceiling. "I was raised in New York. My dad was a school janitor. It was a good life."

"Where are they now?"

"Retired in Italy. They never got over leaving the old country. I don't see them as much as I should."

"I'm sorry." She was. She knew what it was to be alone. "I lost my mom just over three years ago."

"I know. A lot of things happened then. You were troubled."

Elyse nuzzled in under his arm to cuddle. "I was a flaming ball of raw emotion."

"Well, I'm glad you crashed into me."

She was, too.

Three years ago her world had fallen apart. Her first love from college, Darrel, had whispered promises of marriage. Eventually. They'd met at Berkeley where he studied law, and she used the library. After graduation, he worked for a Boston firm while she built websites on weekdays and went to rummage sales on the weekends, cobbling together an income.

Elyse would have followed him immediately if her mother hadn't taken ill. Continuing the long distance relationship, months turned to years as her mother slowly declined. Darrel insisted he'd return to San Francisco, they'd marry and start a family . . . just as soon he passed the California bar exam.

Days after her mother died, a wedding announcement fell through the mail slot and into the foyer. Darrell had married another lawyer in his office.

In one week, everything except the house was taken from her.

Then she met Nick.

There was a deep longing in both of them, and they fed each other's fires.

But that was three years ago, and this was now.

"Thinking about the past?" Nick asked and held her close.

"I wasn't very happy with myself when I first met you."

"And I was a cad," he admitted.

"A useful cad." Elyse elbowed him playfully. "Sometimes it's good to find one."

"That was a long time ago."

"So you've upgraded from cad to gigolo."

"I'm a reformed gigolo."

Elyse laughed. "There's a twelve-step program for that?"

"Yes." Nick laughed, too. "We have weekly meetings,

drink coffee, and burn our little black books."

"Is there anything else I should know?"

"I have an ex-wife."

"Were you faithful to her?"

"Long after the marriage ended. In my mind, I wasn't with anyone else until I met you."

They kissed again. They kissed because they were alone. Separate. They kissed because they wanted to be part of something more, something bigger. They kissed and made love to be part of each other.

Elyse awoke alone in rumpled sheets with the sun streaming through the window. She waited and let her head clear. Was last night a dream? Had she really called Nick? Had they made love, repeatedly? It seemed like a dream.

One that had left his pants next to the bed.

The exotic smells of Chinese five spice and ginger were gone, replaced by other scents. She inhaled deeply. Coffee, bacon, and pancakes. The aroma reminded her of waking up on Sunday mornings as a child when Grandma Tobin cooked everyone a huge breakfast. From below, on the first floor, dishes clinked and pans clanked.

He was still here.

Elyse pondered this new event. She thought that Nick was much more likely to skulk away in the night after he'd gotten what he wanted. He hadn't. He was downstairs cooking.

So if sex wasn't his main objective, what was? Maybe she'd read him wrong. Maybe he really was a reformed gigolo. It was time to let someone into her house, into her heart. There were a lot worse men in the world than the original Prince Charming. He was an incredible lover. Elyse drew the sheets around her, secure. She deserved something wonderful.

Listening to the distant sounds in the kitchen, everything was right with the world. There was life in her home. And he was cooking her breakfast.

Elyse sat up in bed. Torn between going downstairs, and waiting to see if she'd be served breakfast in bed, she took a second. Maybe after a snack, Nick would be up for a morning romp. That had a definite plus side. She loved everything about this new and improved Nick.

With the exception of his pants.

They were ringing.

Invasion of privacy. Those were the words that flashed through her mind. Never ever, under any circumstances would she answer another person's phone. On the other hand, the phone *was* in her bedroom. The call might be critical. Life or death. By not at least seeing who the caller was, she might be liable.

She fumbled with his pants and took the cell phone out of his pocket. It wasn't ringing now, but it beeped. There was a text message. Elyse opened the phone. The message sender was identified by one name. Vicky.

Vicky? She didn't know a Vicky. There wasn't a single Vicky she knew in San Francisco. If she were to hit a single button, she would know what Vicky wanted. Then again, Nick was reformed. Checking what Vicky wanted would prove that he was on the up and up. She'd do it for his sake.

Finger trembling, Elyse pushed the *view message* button.

There's a million $ on the table for 1,000 Cheesecakes of Seduction. See you tonight, Lover-boy – Vicky

Elyse knew better, but she'd read it anyway. Nick was a dog. Completely. Totally. What was she thinking believing him for even a second? Stupid. With the single click of a key, she had popped her dream of settling down with Nick.

She should have never let him into her house. Or her.

There was a lot to process for one little text message.

1,000 Cheesecakes of Seduction. Oh god, she'd seen the number on the top of the cake box. #999. She'd be his 999th conquest in the book!

She hated Nick.

He'd used her again.

And he was still in her house.

Nick was shocked at the lack of food supplies in Elyse's house. That would change soon enough. He'd thought far enough ahead to raid his own refrigerators. Bacon and eggs were staples. With a little flour and sugar, he had crepes as well.

Maybe next week he'd surprise Elyse with an updated set of cookware. Nothing too fancy. Everyday pots and pans. There was also a severe absence of utensils. No whisks. He'd had to scramble the eggs and beat the crepe batter with a fork.

While it was inconvenient, he loved it. Elyse needed him. He'd have her cozy kitchen shipshape in no time. He could picture cooking big family meals here. Thanksgiving turkeys and Christmas hams.

He admired the bright sun that shone through the windows on the table. Should he put the food on a tray and deliver it to her in bed? What if he set a precedent and had to do it every morning for the rest of his life? He smiled. That was the plan.

"Nick," Elyse called from the doorway.

He turned to face her, proud. "I made breakfast. After last night, I bet you're hungry."

Elyse flung Nick's pants at him. "Get out, you bastard!" she shouted. "Nine hundred and ninety-nine seduction cakes?"

His eyes went wide. "I was going for a thousand. I thought you'd be impressed."

"Impressed?" she howled. "That you could bed a thousand women? That you'd make me second to last? What an honor? And you have number one thousand lined up for tonight!"

"I don't have anyone lined up. It was all for you," he objected.

"Give it up, Nick. You're scum. I should have known better." She threw open the back door. "Don't make me call the police."

"But I'm innocent," he protested, stumbling onto the back porch and into his pants.

"Tell it to Vicky." Elyse slammed the door in his face.

Nick slumped behind the wheel of his SUV parked against the curb on Ivy Loop. What happened? Everything was going better than he could have expected. How did she know about the cheesecakes? She obviously hadn't made the connection between La Sals and him.

He flipped open his cell phone. Maybe Jackie knew something. Or Madeline. Then he saw that he had a text message. One that had already been opened. He flinched as he read it.

Though it was a complete misunderstanding, he had no idea how to explain it to Elyse. If he told her the truth, she'd never believe it. *He* barely believed it.

The only solution was to make the 1,000th cheesecake and publish the book.

If she read it, maybe she'd believe him.

If not, the 1,000th cheesecake would be the end of it. Of them.

Elyse poured a cup of coffee and sat at the kitchen table.

The breakfast looked wonderful. She tried a piece of bacon. Thick and chewy with crisp edges.

Stupid, stupid, stupid!

How could she have let Nick fool her so easily? She knew better.

Nick Salvatore would never be loving-partner material. Was he even that good of a model for her rebuilds? There must be a least a million other men out there. Good men. Why did she have such an attraction to him?

She blinked back tears as she opened the refrigerator. The blurry outline of the cheesecake box, clearly marked #999, taunted her. She was just a number to him. A number way up in the three digits. She wasn't special. She was like a tiny peanut in a huge sack of peanuts that Nick had gobbled his way through.

Elyse slumped to the floor, eye level with the box in the open fridge. It certainly looked like La Sals'. Nick wasn't even a real cook. He'd clearly bought this cake. Probably all of his supposed recipes were lifted from real chefs. Nick was a sham.

Even knowing it, she wished it weren't true. She longed for a Nick that did not exist. Sobs of heartache racked her chest. There was no stopping them.

She'd gambled on love.

And lost.

Again.

Chapter 10

After two hours of crying and three pieces of mandarin cheesecake, Elyse knew what she had to do. Nick was a drug, and she had to go cold turkey.

It was her only hope.

Like sudden sobriety, throwing away cigarettes, or quitting carbs, she would expel all romantic thoughts of men. She would also limit her cheesecake exposure.

She had to steel herself, be dedicated, and work through the pain. Tough. Hard. Unfeeling. This was survival.

At least she had a mission, a focus. With five long days before Andrew returned, she'd organize her finances and sift through receipts. And hopefully find enough deductions that Iris might help her keep a little of Saban's two hundred thousand dollars.

It was worth a try.

Elyse secured the doors and pulled the shades. She was in lockdown.

By Thursday night, Elyse was pleased with herself. The task had taken days, but sitting in her kitchen nook, with stacks of paperwork in front of her, she punched the final numbers into her calculator.

The keys of the 1970s relic clicked, and an electric paper feeder churned out a long ribbon filled with inky black numbers. Beside her, a calming cup of jasmine tea. Steam rose from the surface, fogging the window that overlooked the carriage house.

She'd screened her calls and ignored Saban, Jackie, and Madeline. Elyse did not have the time or energy to deal with anyone. Except Iris. Iris was an angel. Squeaking out a few thousand in deductions, she'd have enough to live on. Strangely, she looked forward to meeting Iris the next day to go over the paperwork.

Working from her kitchen table, the only drawback was the siren call of cheesecake. She should have thrown it at Nick. Or thrown it away. Or out the window. Instead, she'd eaten it. Tiny piece by tiny piece, she'd nibbled every bite. Guiltily enjoying each morsel. It was just a cheesecake; it had nothing to do with Nick.

With barely more than a week to the Charity Ball, she'd need to starve herself if she wanted to zip up her favorite gown.

Elyse sorted through the last of the checks, receipts, and mileage reports.

Her last $100,000 check had covered several mortgage payments and Andrew's materials. Minimums were paid on her credit card balances, and she settled the utilities. After a check for the property taxes, the money was gone.

Being a responsible adult was overrated.

Now, every penny counted.

Elyse leaned over and thumbed through the last box of papers at her feet. The receipts were the worst. Gas, meals, a tie here, a pair of not-white socks there. She'd only conquered the most important mail so far, finding several notices from the IRS. Shoving the rest into a wicker laundry hamper, it, too, waited for her attention.

First she'd deal with the IRS.

Next, she'd tackle Andrew. Figuratively. He'd be back any day now, and she'd have a week to work with him, one on one, right up until the night of the Charity Ball. Her life and the house were on the line.

Ding-dong.

What now? Elyse looked up from her calculator. She had half a mind to ignore whoever was there. The bell rang again. Why did everybody always ring again and again? Once was enough. She needed to place a sign above the bell, *If I'm not answering, I'm not here. Stop ringing the doorbell!*

Of course, she *was* here, but had no intention of answering. Still, few people wandered down the dead end street. As always, curiosity got the better of her. Peeking around the corner, through the living room and haze of curtains on the front windows, she could make out two women standing on her porch. Saban and Madeline. Elyse groaned. As long as she stayed quiet, they'd never know she was inside. Sooner or later, they'd give up and go away.

Elyse spun around to a rustle at the side of the house.

Jackie shoved a bush aside and peered in through a dining room window at Elyse. "She's in there!" she called toward the girls on the front porch.

"No, I'm not!" Elyse shouted back.

"You unlock that door," Jackie yelled and backed away through the brush.

There was no getting away. Trapped. The last thing she needed was company, but she couldn't very well turn them away if she wanted to look them in the eye again. Less than a second after she clicked the lock open, Madeline and Saban barged past.

"Darling," Madeline brayed, "you would not believe the day we're having. Worry, worry, worry. First, my Bentley dealership only has the new model with leather seats. I told them, I'm not sitting on a dead cow while I drive. Cows have feelings, too. Which reminds me, Sabby is a wreck. Worse than a cow waiting to be made into seat covers. Jitters like she'd drank every cup of coffee in Columbia. I think it's just wonderful we have that fair trade thing where all the farmers down there get a living wage. I mean, can you imagine feeling guilty every time you drank a cup of coffee?" She stopped in the living room and spread her arms wide.

Elyse glanced around the room, nervous. Had she picked up all the bills and late notices? *Late notices* weren't something to share with friends. Not even the very best of friends.

"Well," Madeline huffed, locking her gaze on Elyse, arms held out.

Elyse inched forward, unsure. Was this an invitation to a hug? Body-to-body contact? "You want to hug me, right?" Madeline was not, by any means, a hugger. She was an air-kisser extraordinaire, who had not so much as grazed a cheek in decades.

Madeline frowned and dropped her arms. "I thought I did. But just for a second. The moment passed."

Elyse breathed a sigh of relief as Jackie stamped her feet on the welcome mat and stepped through the door. She looked Elyse up and down. "This is far worse than I thought. You're seconds from wearing your fuzzy slippers, aren't you?"

"There's a story." Madeline clapped her hands together. "Fuzzy Wuzzy was a bear. But he wasn't fuzzy. Don't you dare wear those slippers. They'll ruin your arches. Thank god we arrived in the nick of time."

"In time for what?" Elyse was confused. She closed the front door, wondering if opening it had been a mistake. As for the aforementioned slippers, so what if she wore them when her feet were cold? Luckily, she'd forgotten them upstairs.

"Why are you hiding from us?" Jackie quizzed. "We're your friends."

"We have work to do," Saban chimed in. "What's happening with my man?"

"Not now," Madeline chided her. "First we have to fix our little man renovator, then we'll put her back to work."

"Fix me?" Her stomach lurched.

Jackie slid a copy of Madeline's latest book out of her

purse and flipped the pages. "Where do we start, Madeline?"

Elyse's pulse sped up. Growing more ticked off by the second, she didn't understand why the whole world couldn't leave her alone. She'd fix herself, thank-you-very-much. She'd been doing just that before her doorbell rang. "This better not be an intervention."

"It is!" Jackie cheered.

"Let's see," Madeline continued. "Skip the chapter on making contact and comforting the . . ."

"Victim?" Elyse finished the sentence and crossed her arms, annoyed.

"Loved one," Madeline corrected. "We're here because we love you, and you are off the rails. Like a train without tracks. It's time for the engineer to sail this ship into port."

Jackie scanned the table of contents from the book. "We've got eating disorders, kleptomania, shopoholism . . ."

"Shopping?" Madeline asked. "Why would we want to stop anyone from shopping?"

"It's your book," Jackie replied.

"Keep going," Madeline ordered. "I'm sure there's something pertinent in there."

Jackie read the options. "Hoarding, felonious behavior, gambling . . ."

Madeline leaned to look over Jackie's shoulder. "Nothing on sloth or frumpy dressing?"

"No."

"Fuzzy bunny slippers?" Elyse offered. "They're really cute, shaped like rabbits with long ears and little whiskers, too."

Jackie scowled.

"Well, back to the beginning then," Madeline commanded. "Make contact and comfort. Someone has to slap her."

"Let me!" Saban pranced forward, lifted her hand, and smugly slapped Elyse across the cheek.

"That hurt." Elyse massaged the side of her face.

"The pain helps bring you back to reality," Madeline said.

"It's all in the book," Jackie squealed. "You did read the book?" She handed Elyse her copy of *Instant Intervention: A Guide to Saving Your Friends, Family, and Coworkers from Themselves*. "You can keep it. I have another copy."

"Anyway, a friend in need is a friend indeed. Let's get started." Madeline landed an oversized, monogrammed bucket bag on the coffee table. "Now that you have been physically brought to your senses, very good work on that Saban, we'll need ice."

Elyse didn't feel like she had come to her senses at all. "Ice?"

Madeline sat on the sofa, rolled her eyes, and began to unpack her bag. "For the martinis. If you'd read my book, you'd understand." She took a bottle of British gin, a half bottle of Italian vermouth, a shaker, and four martini glasses out of her bag. "It could be done with domestic gin and tonic, but that seemed pedestrian. Not that I'm against walking. Last year tens of thousands walked over the Golden Gate Bridge. Which doesn't surprise me with the tolls going up all the time. Nice that walking is free. Like your walk to the kitchen to get the ice."

Saban and Jackie plopped onto the sofa flanking Madeline.

"Fine," Elyse conceded. She went to the kitchen and filled an ice bucket. Back in the living room, the girls were whispering as Madeline flipped pages of her book.

"Let's get to work." Saban held out a glass.

"Tonic on the rocks for me." Jackie fished a small bottle of soda from her bag. "It's a new diet."

"Wait!" Madeline howled. "This one looks like a doozy. Chapter Eight."

"The Commitment-phobic Intervention," Saban read

over her shoulder.

"Commitment-phobic Intervention," Madeline parroted. "Did I write that?"

Jackie continued reading from the book. "What to do when your friends are making foolish decisions."

Elyse cringed. "I'm not doing anything foolish. Yet."

Determined, Jackie went on. "First, we make our loved one confess everything that is going on so that calmer minds may guide the situation. This can only be achieved by isolating the intended interveenee, relaxing them, then pumping them for information."

"I knew we brought the gin for a reason!" Madeline cried. She dumped half the bottle of gin into the shaker, added the ice and Vermouth, then handed it over to Saban. "Sabby, would you do the honors? I don't shake. Bad wrists. It's all the gardening. I have *dahhhlias*, you know. Love them as if they were adopted children. So many orphans in the world today, but not you, Elyse. You have us."

She couldn't fight it. She'd just have to let them run their course. Elyse slumped in an armchair across from the three women and watched as Saban shook the martinis with vigor. More than vigor, she shook them with a vengeance. Elyse liked Saban less and less. She was pushy. So was Madeline, but Madeline had an underlying kindness to her. Saban had an underlying hostility.

Madeline took the honors and poured three martinis. Elyse didn't object when she made hers twice as big as the other two. She'd need the fortification to make it through this so-called intervention.

They all raised their glasses.

"To friends who will never give up on each other." Jackie raised her glass of tonic over ice.

"Very appropriate," Madeline agreed.

"When do we pump her for information?" Saban snipped.

Clearly there had been a typo on the cover of Madeline's book. The title should have read *Instant Inquisition*, not *Intervention*. Elyse took a long drink. The gin seared her throat and warmed her belly.

"So what's your problem?" Saban sneered.

"We're your friends," Jackie said. "You're supposed to tell us everything."

"Get it all out," Madeline admonished. "And mix another batch, Sabby."

Saban emptied the gin and vermouth bottles and shook the martinis. The ice made a comforting thunking noise in the shaker.

"Why aren't you taking our calls?" Jackie whined.

"We've had three lunches at Wedgeworth's without you this week," Madeline admonished. "Three!"

"This is fantastic gin." Elyse evaded the topic, picking up the empty bottle. "They use nineteen botanicals. Let me read them to you."

"Herbs, schmerbs," Jackie snapped. "We want answers."

Madeline, Jackie, and Saban glared across the coffee table in unison.

Elyse looked at the three of them. Were they really her friends? She was closest to Jackie, but if there hadn't been the mistaken assumption that she was a *woman of substance* because of a rummage-sale Hermes bag, even Jackie might not have given her the time of day.

They stared. Waiting.

She didn't have an answer, at least not one she wanted to give.

Did these women really care for her, or was she only tolerated in their circle because she was their ticket to male companionship and marriage? Did she tolerate them? Not really. Deep down, she actually loved them. Both Jackie and Madeline, who in their own quirky ways were true blue.

As for Saban, okay, maybe two hundred thousand dollars equaled a lot of reasons to put up with her.

Elyse remembered her college days. She had five or six friends. Now the only contact was mass-mailed Christmas newsletters. For better or worse, these three women were her nearest and dearest.

And they expected something big.

Madeline refilled the glasses. "So what could be more important than us, darling?"

"Tick tock." Saban squinted, looking meaner than usual. "And while you're spilling your guts, I want to know what's going on with my little primate plumber."

Elyse met Saban's beady eyes.

They wanted answers? They'd get answers. There was only a single subject more interesting to society matrons than the possibility of a good scandal, one thing that trumped all else in their ultra-privileged world.

"I made a terrible mistake," Elyse wailed. She flopped back into her chair and threw her hands over her face. She'd try to work up a tear or two while she was at it. Even if she'd already cried out all her tears over cheesecake, she'd force a few more out of her ducts.

The one topic that could divert any interrogation was the Prince of Passion himself, Nick Salvatore. The very mention of his name, along with a tantalizing tidbit of information, might even be enough to stop an intervention dead in its tracks.

"You've made a lot of mistakes," Saban snickered.

"Well I made the Nick Salvatore mistake," she confessed.

They all gasped and took big gulps of their drinks.

"You slept with Nick?" Jackie feigned surprise. She raised her hand and covered her lips. *Again*, she mouthed the word to Elyse.

"I should have seen this coming." Madeline giggled. "Opposites react. It was fate. Like magnets."

"You slut!" Saban stood up and stomped her foot. "I was supposed to get Nick next."

"Sit down, Sabby," Madeline barked.

She obeyed.

"Worse than that," Elyse said as dramatically as she could. "I love him."

Jackie leapt from the couch and wrapped a sympathetic arm around Elyse. "It's okay. Everyone loves Nick."

Madeline nodded. "For goodness sake, dear, you had your fling with him. Join the crowd."

"No, I am *in love* with Nick." Elyse was quite proud of herself. This would keep them clucking for weeks, with no reason to discuss the embarrassing tax audit, her renovations on Andrew, or anything else.

Nick Salvatore was one-stop shopping.

"That's all of it?" Saban crossed her arms. "I think you're hiding something."

The woman was just plain annoying. There was something about Saban that seemed so wrong. In any case, Elyse needed a good story. This was Madeline's friend and protégé.

"You're right. He doesn't love me back. He doesn't want anything to do with me. We had our fling at the Sausalito Farmer's Market. Me. Him. In the back of a van full of . . ."

"In a van?" Saban gasped.

"In a van full of Argentinean freesias. The scent alone was like a thousand perfumes."

"Argentinean freesias," Madeline wailed. "They're the best. The very best. You must give me this flower person's name."

"Freshly harvested, cold shipped by air," Elyse added. The details always sold the story. Especially where Nick was concerned.

"I want a hundred. No two hundred," Madeline demanded. "Can you grow freesias here?"

"He made love to me like no man ever has. It was the best sex of my life." Elyse collapsed back into her chair, eyes closed. Only the farmer's market, the van, and the flowers were a fabrication. The rest of it was entirely true.

"Great, now I'm the only woman who hasn't been banged by Nick," Saban grouched. "I want my turn."

Elyse shot her a withering look. "Then you'll have to give up Andrew."

Saban glared back. "Okay, I'll take the plumber. For now."

Jackie eyed Elyse suspiciously. "You've had years to fall for him. Why now?"

It was a good question. Why would Elyse fall in love with him after all these years? "It's a cumulative effect. Like mercury."

"I've heard of that," Madeline joined in. "It's in fish. You eat it and eat it and it builds up in your body, and then you go insane."

"That's it exactly," Elyse agreed. "I'm insane because of my exposure to Nick."

"I want proof," Madeline demanded.

The effect of the martinis had taken hold. Bold, confident, Elyse got up from the chair. Her knees wobbled. What was in those drinks? Undeterred, she marched over to the bookshelf. "You want proof, I'll give you proof."

"Not the book?" Jackie whispered. "Really?"

Elyse swung the brass key around her finger, then plunged it into the lock. *The Big Red Book of Men* thunked to the floor. Elyse picked it up and carried it to the coffee table and wedged herself between Madeline and Saban. "It's all here."

"I never thought you'd share it," Jackie swooned.

"An intervention is all about sharing," Elyse said with

a shrug.

"Exactly." Madeline patted Elyse on the shoulder. "So what's this about?"

"A history of each man I've remodeled." Elyse opened the cover. On the first page was Rex Von Terrance, followed by each successive groom. "But I've been in love with Nick Salvatore since I first met him. I've based all my rebuilt men on him. They are all Nick clones."

"That's why I couldn't resist Cyril," Madeline whooped.

"Every one of them is another Nick. Nick, Nick, Nick. I am Nick-obsessed," Elyse said with her best soap opera voice. She didn't care anymore. They all knew. She'd turn Andrew over to Saban at the Charity Ball, collect her fee, and she'd be out of the Prince Charming business for good. This was the end of the line.

Saban turned a few pages. "That doesn't mean you're in love with him."

Elyse thumbed past more pages. It was pretty compelling. All six men she'd reformed were interspersed with Nick information. There were Nick's habits. Nick's charities. Nick's likes and dislikes. He was sprinkled through the pages like salt on corn on the cob. Everything was a reference to him. "Then how about this?"

She turned the book over and folded back the rear cover. The Nick files. Three long years of following every move he made in the public eye. And there had been a lot to follow. A scrapbook of Nick. A shrine of Salvatore.

The three women gasped in unison.

"Our little Elyse is a Nick stalker," Madeline trilled. "I'll get another book deal out of this."

Jackie nodded. "I didn't know you had it this bad."

"He's all I can think of." She emptied her martini glass. It wasn't a total lie. Through each day of sorting her filings and preparing for her meeting with Iris, Nick Salvatore had invaded her thoughts regularly. He'd been the most attentive, incredible lover she'd ever had. Perfect in every way, except for his inability to commit to any one woman.

Suddenly it occurred to her how little she knew about him. If he hadn't made everything up. Raised in New York. Parents in Italy. All very convenient and impossible to confirm.

Now, it didn't matter. Nick was out of her life forever. Pushing the sadness deep inside her, she'd never let anyone know that Nick Salvatore had stolen her heart.

Nick's Explorer ground along on the rutted gravel road. He hadn't intended to take a road trip north. It just sort of happened.

He'd been thinking for days about the 1,000th cheesecake. Something special. He'd compoted a hundred fruits and melted more chocolates than that. Nothing was right. Nothing was enough.

Maybe a drive to the beach would help. The beach didn't have the answers, so he headed inland. There were no solutions in Napa. He didn't know why he kept driving.

Winding through forested hills on a country highway, he saw a small sign pointing up a gravel road: SONOMA MONASTERY 23 MILES.

He remembered the name from Sun, the Buddhist monk he bought produce from at the Sausalito Farmer's Market. He'd tried everything else to come up with an idea for his cake. Why not Zen Buddhists?

Perched on the side of a mountain, the stark white walls and arched blue tile roof of the temple looked like a castle that should be in Japan or China, not Sonoma County. Nick pulled to a stop in front of a gated entrance. Next to the gate was a rope that led up to a bell.

Nick sweated as he paced to the rope. What was he going to say? He only knew the monks through buying berries and treating them to a meal here or there. The one he knew best, Sun, might not even be here. Still, what did he have to lose?

He rang the bell.

Nothing happened. He was tempted to ring it again, but didn't. It was loud. Surely someone had heard it. He could have waited in his SUV. He could have run the engine and sat in air-conditioned comfort. That didn't seem right, so Nick settled next to the gate, in the dirt. He leaned back against the wall and admired the view. Fir trees and untouched wilderness stretched before him as far as the eye could see.

He may have spent ten minutes or an hour staring at the nature before him. It was hard to tell. But just as his mind was beautifully blank, the gate clanked and swung open.

A young man wearing khaki shorts and a T-shirt looked at Nick. "You rang?"

Nick got to his feet. "Is Sun here?" he asked.

"Yeah, dude," the young man replied. "He's almost always here. Com'on."

Nick followed him inside and gawked at the buildings. They were simple, yet stunningly graceful. Dark wood timbers, white walls, long outdoor hallways under the gleaming blue roofs. "It's beautiful."

The young man glanced around. "Yeah, Master Sun says it's an exact replica of one built in Kyoto, Japan. You been to Japan?"

"No," Nick answered. He wanted to someday. He wanted a lot of things. Someday.

"Me, neither." The young man shrugged. "I like tofu, though."

They took off their shoes at the steps of the largest building, then walked the outside hallway to open paper doors. Inside, the entire floor was covered with woven mats and a dozen people in robes sat motionless. Sun, in his usual orange robe, paced between the seated people with a bamboo stick. When he saw Nick, he strolled over, held up a finger for silence, then waved for Nick to follow him.

Sun led Nick to a white gravel courtyard, empty except for a few big rocks. "What can I do for you, Nick?"

"I'm not sure," he admitted. He wasn't. "I wanted to make a special cheesecake. Something new. Nothing came to me, so I went for a drive and here I am. Pretty strange?"

Sun laughed a solid belly laugh. "Not here. Some people come to find peace of mind through meditation. Others seek answers to past problems. Everyone comes here for a different reason."

"Are you going to make me sit on the mats back there?"

"It depends on what you are looking for."

"I guess I need some answers."

"You want wisdom? Okay," Sun said seriously. "All suffering comes because we cling to things. Stop clinging."

"Easy to say."

"Hard to do. Practice," Sun advised. "Next, find your center. What is at your heart?"

"A woman," Nick admitted, "and cooking."

"Then those are the things you must let go. It's as simple as that."

"I have one more cheesecake to make, and I'll give it a try. Anything else?"

"I might have an answer for your cake," Sun nodded wisely. "We just finished making a syrup from wild hazelnuts. It's very potent."

Nick loved the chocolates the Belgians made with hazelnuts. It was a great combination. This might be his farewell dessert. "Hook me up, Sun."

Yesterday, Elyse had liked the martinis.
Unfortunately, martinis did not like her.

Her head throbbed as she carried the cardboard file box full of papers down an alleyway. For reasons unknown to her, Iris had asked to meet somewhere other than the Federal Building downtown.

The new location of her audit was a hamburger joint in Oakland.

In her arms, she held three years of her life. In the form of little scraps of paper. Each told a story of where she was and what she was doing. One restaurant receipt was where she taught Donnie about looking up while eating. He had a tendency to watch his food, not his date. Another, sunglasses for Cyril to celebrate his Lasik eye surgery. She had a lot of receipts for wine. Men were always more susceptible to change with a few drinks in them.

Funny that one box could hold so many experiences. So many successes.

Elyse stopped at the door of the Hamburger Hut. There was a good reason few people hiked down the side alley in downtown Oakland to the grease-smeared front door. For one thing, it had a grease-smeared front door. She opened it.

The restaurant, if three tables and a counter that could only seat six people was considered a restaurant, called to another era. The Depression.

Iris teetered on a cracked vinyl-covered stool at a battered wood table. Out of her usual business attire, she wore a mousy brown cardigan over jeans. Elyse assessed the situation. An untouched hamburger sat in front of Iris. Her eyes darted around the room nervously.

"Come here often?" Elyse hefted her box onto the table and sat down across from Iris.

"I wanted a place no one would see us," Iris answered.

This worried Elyse. Other than a little lonely and desperate, Iris seemed like a nice person. One who was helping her. "Do we have a secret?"

"We're going to," she confided.

Uh-oh. This sounded ominous at best. Something was up, and Elyse didn't like that one bit. She shifted around, wondering if they were being watched.

"Hey!" a burly man behind the counter shouted. "You wanna order or what?"

"I don't see a menu," Elyse shouted back. She was in no mood for pushy cooks.

"It's the Hamburger Hut. We got the hamburger, a cheeseburger, and a bacon cheeseburger."

"I'll have a bacon cheeseburger," Elyse replied loudly, even though they were the only customers. Maybe a top end order would shut the man up.

"We ain't got any bacon or cheese right now."

"Fine. A hamburger!"

"Comin' up!"

Elyse looked to Iris. "What do you mean we have a secret?"

"I was thinking," Iris started, "that I'm doing you a favor. You know, helping with the IRS and getting everything so you don't have to go to jail."

"What do you want?" Elyse felt panic rise in her chest. This wasn't going anywhere good.

The cook landed a lard-dripping burger in front of Elyse. "I think you're gonna like this. It's the specialty of the house."

"Thank you." Elyse pushed the burger aside.

"Aren't you gonna try it?" the cook asked, dismayed.

"In a minute," Elyse said sternly. "We're having a conversation."

"I'm just saying it's best when it's hot. The fat gets all jellied if you let it cool."

She couldn't believe this man. "Could we have a minute alone?"

"Fine. Eat a cold burger for all I care." The cook retreated behind the counter.

Iris nodded toward him. "That's the kind of man I attract."

"He's not exactly Prince Charming," Elyse agreed.

"He's not exactly Homo sapien." Iris smiled. "I want a man like you make."

"What?" She sat up straight.

"I'm helping you, you help me. Find me a man. He doesn't have to be able to do all the socialite things that you train men to do. Just a basic model. Like a Corolla."

Was she serious? She couldn't just whip up a man on short notice. "Or?"

Iris narrowed her eyes. "Or you're on your own."

"I'm not a man factory," Elyse objected. "I don't just stamp them out."

"I can't pay you, so I don't expect top of the line," Iris replied hopefully. "You must have some rejects that are still in running condition?"

Did she? Elyse thought about it. She'd met a lot of men. "How soon are you thinking?"

Iris smiled. "There's no hurry. How about next weekend?"

"I'm a little busy. I have to deliver a husband at the Charity Ball."

"That would be perfect!" Iris cheered. "Bring my man, too."

Chapter 11

Clenching two handfuls of soft Egyptian cotton, Elyse buried her face in the bed sheets and inhaled. *Nick.* Opening her eyes, the morning sun streamed in through the edges of the window blinds. After a fitful night of worrying, she'd slipped into an exhausted sleep and anxious dreams of Nick.

Nick in her house, in her bathtub, in her bed.

She should have stripped the bedding. Burned it. No. His male scent, and the sweaty-sweet aftermath of their union lingered on the sheets. Like a dog, he'd marked his territory.

She was his.

He was for sale.

What an idiot she'd been to call him. Still, that night had felt like pure magic. He'd taken his game to a whole new level. Intimacy.

Still sleepy, Elyse stretched. He might have tricked her into believing he wanted the happily-ever-after, but that was a ruse. A sexual master armed with a full-court emotional seduction, Nick Salvatore was a dangerous fantasy.

What she woke up to this morning was cold, hard reality.

Iris's demand for a man haunted her. It was bad enough she had to fix Andrew before the Charity Ball this weekend. But find another man, one with at least some potential, and deliver him to Iris? Impossible. Maybe Iris would take a rain check. Or she'd think of something or someone to appease Iris in the meantime.

Her top priority was to lay her hands on Saban's

$200,000 payment. It wouldn't solve all her problems, but she'd be on her way to figuring out whatever came next.

The night with Nick dodged through her thoughts again. Damn him. He'd unsettled her. Made her reflect.

What was the point of having an empty house? Were never-ending repairs and overdue mortgage payments the Tobin legacy? Why couldn't she find a good man? It didn't even have to be permanent. Marriage might be nice, but it wasn't a necessity. Children were. She wanted them. Her mother and grandmother and great-grandmother all found enough freedom from the house to procreate. But there had also been family then, too. Generations.

Now it was only Elyse.

Could she start the Tobin family again?

Where could she find a man who would understand and accept this?

The closest she had come was Nick. And that had been a disaster. Still, he was the ideal man. Witty, knowledgeable, capable. It thrilled her that he wasn't perfect. The man couldn't carry a tune to save his life. He might even be a touch tone-deaf. Somehow, that only made her want him more.

His voice, even off-key, echoed in her mind. Her Nick-less future felt bleak. She wanted him. The trouble was she wasn't willing to share him with the rest of the female world. She wanted Nick all to herself. Some charms were sacred. Like monogamy.

The sound of a truck rumbling up to the curb and cutting its engine rattled the single-pane windows. Elyse sat up and pulled the edge of a shade back.

Andrew was here.

She winced, knowing she'd overslept. Rolling out of bed, her bare feet met the hardwood floor, and she shimmied into a pair of jeans. Time to wake up and smell the coffee.

Andrew paid the coffee cart barista, then handed Elyse a paper cup. "I thought you only drank tea?"

They strolled the park walk along the Sausalito Marina. "There's a lot you don't know about me, Andrew." She huddled in her windbreaker.

He had started to worry. It began nagging at him in Modesto. Something was wrong. In two years, he'd watched Elyse train four husbands. The long, gradual process took months.

Suddenly, he was on the bullet train to the altar. What was that about?

Worse, Nick wasn't answering his phone, and he'd skipped last night's basketball game. They didn't have to forfeit, but it wasn't like Nick to bail on them. Add in the locker room rumors of Elyse's IRS audit, and Bishop Hegeland stewing in the bleachers, Andrew had a bad feeling.

"So what should I know about you?" he asked innocently. He had a pretty good idea she wasn't going to tell him.

"Just girl stuff." She sipped her triple-shot latte. "Nothing I can't handle. At least I have my perfect bath. Thank you again for installing the taps. They're beautiful."

"It's my job." He'd never seen Elyse look so tired and rumpled. "Is there anything I can help with?"

"I'd like to spend some time with you this week," she stated.

Andrew paced to a pedestal with coin-operated binoculars mounted on it and slipped in a pair of quarters. "Sounds good."

Elyse gazed out at the fog on the bay. "You're not going to see anything this morning. I've spent my whole life looking at this view."

Andrew wasn't sure how to deal with Elyse. He wanted her help. He just didn't know how to ask for it. His love of pipes, drains, and water pressure didn't couple well with dating. Or finding a wife. Elyse was his only hope. Maybe his last hope. He couldn't let on that her business wasn't exactly a secret among single men in and around San Francisco. He knew. Nick knew. All the guys on the basketball team knew, though they tried to keep it from Bishop Hegeland. Andrew was pretty sure the Bishop was clued in.

He turned the binoculars to look up the hillside away from the ocean. Ivy Loop and the row of Queen Annes stood out on the steep slope. "What you see depends on what you're looking for."

Elyse put her face to the glasses. "It's my house. It looks smaller than I imagined it."

"It's like plumbing," Andrew said, confidently. "You go into a basement that's underwater, it seems like there's no way to save anything. But once you turn the water off and get a sump pump going, well, it's usually just a little problem that got out of hand."

"That's a great way to look at things," Elyse admitted.

"I've been doing the same job, day in day out, for years. Fixing the little pipe and valve problems. Now I'm thinking outside the box. I want to try something new. Not for a job, but you know, social stuff."

She stared at him. "You're ready to leave your comfort zone? No questions asked?"

"I'm ready to try anything." He was. Anything to get a hookup to a good wife.

Elyse took a swig of her coffee. "What would you think about attending a black-tie ball?"

"Tux and tails?" Andrew scratched his head. "That's certainly out of my comfort zone."

She nodded. "This Saturday?"

He smiled. "I'd probably look like a giant penguin."

"A dancing plumber penguin," she added. "It might be fun."

He could tell she was waiting for his reaction. Was it

worth all this? Telling half-truths and watching every word was driving him batty. Still, it was only one week. "A guy like me is never going to be a Nick Salvatore."

Elyse put her hand on his arm. "Promise me you'll never try to be like Nick."

"Okay." Andrew nodded, though he'd give his left nut to be like Nick. But that would never happen. He was a happy blue-collar plumber now and would be one forever. He accepted that. He didn't have to be Nick. He just had to be an improved Andrew. "I'll need your help."

"I have all the time in the world," Elyse replied.

Andrew knew she was lying. They only had until Saturday. But at least there was hope. And a deadline. He could live with that.

Elyse couldn't help but smile. The weeklong intensive was underway, and Andrew was putty in her hands. Plumber's putty.

Monday was a trip to the bookstore in Corta Madera. It was a great place to talk about what Andrew should read, or pretend to have read. They walked the long aisles of books and paged through *GQ*, *Ode*, and *Newsweek* magazines. Afterwards, they had frappachinos and discussed world events. Andrew was a sponge, soaking up everything she put in front of him.

That night was a dinner lesson in an Italian Bistro. Not too fancy, but not hotdogs. Andrew liked saying *panini* and that it meant a grilled ham and cheese sandwich. Elyse had been honest, as much as possible, and open. She told him how to place the napkin on his lap, to dab his mouth with it when necessary, and not rub it around like polishing his truck. They even went over table settings.

Tuesday was even better. They took her car to Napa. After trying a few Cabernets from the wineries near the main highway, they had a lovely brunch, then sparkling wine and chocolates at the Chandon cellars. Food and desserts ushered in the beginnings of a new Andrew.

Strolling vineyard acres, Elyse tackled the way he walked. She had to say something, or he'd forever be the *Primate Plumber* in Saban's eyes.

"What's wrong with it?" he asked.

She couldn't help herself. "You look like you're always carrying a thousand pounds of pipe." She bent her knees and demonstrated the caveman stride.

"Well, I can't very well hop around like the Easter bunny," he objected.

"Maybe try this," she encouraged. She set a smooth pace of fluid steps between the rows of grapes. He followed. It took a mile or two, but by the time they returned to the car, Andrew was almost graceful.

Wednesday was a make or break day. In the morning, they toured the art museum. *Monet, Picasso, Renoir*. They raced through the basics. In the afternoon, they nibbled their way through the aisles of The Market, an organic grocery. He tried hummus and tapanade.

"These taste like beans and olives," he observed correctly.

The cheeses, *havarti, camembert, chevre,* served on little toothpicks, all went down smoothly with the exception of a stilton. She smiled at Andrew as he ate various bread samples. *Baquette, focacia, pugliese, ciabatta.* Even Elyse had to admit that they tasted a lot alike.

The crucial test, the San Francisco Symphony Orchestra. Luckily, it was Beethoven.

"I know this one," Andrew whispered to her as they played the 5th. "It's a classic. Is that why they call it classical music?"

They got shushed from the people behind them, but Elyse was relieved he didn't fall asleep or run screaming away. He even applauded in all the right places.

She decided to skip opera. Why push a good thing?

By the time Thursday rolled around, the inner groundwork was laid. It was time to polish the outside. In a whirlwind morning, Andrew happily turned himself, and his credit card, over to Elyse's control. $4,200 was not a lot of money, but it was plenty to work with at the Milpitas Outlet Mall.

Elyse learned early on that the rich judge everyone quite harshly, especially when it came to fashion. To be part of their crowd, she had to show at least some of the right labels. Steeply discounted quality clothing made the task easier.

Andrew checked his male ego at the automatic sliding doors of her favorite luxury department store discounter. He waited patiently as she pawed through the formal suits on a circular rack. "I love a tux, but how often can you wear one?" she asked.

"The Bishop Hegeland's Ball and my funeral?" Andrew quipped with a happy grin.

Elyse shook her head. "No one gets buried in a tux."

He rubbed his chin, thinking. "How about Fred Astaire?"

"Maybe." That reminded her, dancing. With the other husbands, she had months to work on it. Would a basic two-step and box step be enough? What if he didn't have any rhythm?

She'd book an hour at a dance studio later and go through the basics. This was cutting it close with the Charity Ball just two nights away.

She sent Andrew to the changing room with a black Hugo Boss tux. Wallets and belts took her attention while she waited. Even subconsciously, women measured men by their wallets and belts. A nylon wallet says, *Hello, I'm a plumber*. A quality leather wallet announces, *I'm doing well.*

Ditto for belts.

When Andrew exited the dressing room, her mouth dropped open.

"It's a little tight," he complained.

"In all the right places." The tux looked like it had been tailored for him. His broad shoulders stood square and tapered to his narrow waist. The pants hung perfectly snug without bunching. This was a showcase tux. His political views leaned to the right, and so did something else.

Andrew tugged at the price tag and choked. "Two thousand dollars!"

"That's a bargain."

"I'll be broke before I get new socks."

"Relax," Elyse said, calming him. "Everything else is easy."

After the Hugo Boss, she found two sport coats and several pair of pants. With a pre-faded polo shirt, Andrew would look good from a stroll on Fisherman's Wharf to a cozy dinner in Chinatown.

He even let her pick out new underwear. Gone were the tighty-whiteys. In their place, in a supporting role, were colored boxer briefs for day and silk boxers for night. Shoes were a temporary setback. She would have loved to see him in a pair of English oxfords, but at over a thousand dollars, they weren't in the budget. She compromised on a pair of black Ferragamo's. Then for a more casual look, loafers.

"You look great." She admired him.

He turned in front of her wearing a sport coat and chinos. "If I went to a plumbing convention, none of the other plumbers would know me."

Elyse paced the slate floor in the waiting lounge of the Oasis Day Spa. The final countdown was on. Andrew had one more important step left in his transformation. She checked the time on her cell phone before sliding it back into her purse.

"What's taking them so long?" She edged in next to Andrew by the fountain.

A waterfall trickled out its calming rhythm to an indoor pond surrounded by stone. Elyse regretted the morning caffeine rush that made her jittery. Nodding to a statue of Kwan Yin, the Goddess of Compassion, she tried to calm her nerves. She was beyond *compassion* at this point, she needed results.

"Did you see the fish?" Andrew pointed at several koi in the pond, swimming in lazy crisscrosses.

No pointing, she mouthed the words and wiggled an index finger at him. The key to successful man remodeling was repetition. Good habits replacing the bad.

Andrew's digit darted into his closed palm. "There's an orange and white one a foot long. You could make a dozen fillet o' fish sandwiches out of him."

Elyse drew a breath. "Some things are just to be admired for their beauty, not eaten. They're here to reflect upon. Nature." Before she could say more about Zen or meditation, a petite Asian woman dressed in a silk kimono emerged from behind a door.

The woman bowed deeply. "Mr. Young, this way."

The whole spa experience puzzled Elyse. Ylang Ylang incense, micro-derm peels, rainforest misting rooms, and hot stone massages, she didn't get it. If Grandma Tobin were alive, she'd have fits. Her beauty care rested next to the washbasin, a bar of Ivory soap and a jar of Vaseline.

"Are you sure Nick Salvatore does this?" Andrew froze. "It's pretty strange."

The woman giggled. "Nick is one of our regulars."

Of course he was. And the reason Elyse used the Oasis Spa for all her grooms. She stood and took Andrew by the hand, gently. Like breaking a horse, he was on the verge of becoming a world-class stallion. He'd be the seventh Nick-clone and her ticket out of the trouble with the IRS.

Elyse delivered Andrew's hand to the woman. "Give Mr. Young the Salvatore special."

"Of course," the woman enthused. She leaned to an intercom, punched a row of buttons that lit up like a string of Christmas lights and called, "Girls! Room Twelve! Full service!"

Andrew felt like an idiot. Shifting his gaze to a mirror, he was horrified. Was that even him? The man in the mirror wore a fluffy robe and had his face painted with a clay made with green sea algae. His hair, folded with strips of tin foil, stuck out at odd angles. A long strip of cotton edged his scalp. As one spa employee filed his fingernails, another scrubbed his feet with pumice stone.

"Andrew, no peeking." Sitting in the corner, Elyse peered up from a magazine.

A dark-haired woman in a white lab coat leaned him back and replaced cold slices of cucumber over his eyes.

"I'm packed in mud with *greens* on my face," he mumbled.

There, he'd used one of Elyse's fancy words. *Greens.* He couldn't swear to it, but even blinded by face-salad, he'd felt her smile.

"It's opening your pores," she replied smugly.

I want a wife, I want a wife, I want a wife he repeated silently. He tried to distract himself with the calming pitter-patter of rain that played over the sound system. Like a spring shower in hell.

The ring of Elyse's phone jolted him. His cucumbers fell away as he started to sit up, but the spa employee eased him back. She glared at Elyse and pointed to a sign on the wall: *All personal communication devices must be turned off or you will be asked to leave.*

"I'll be right back," Elyse apologized, then grabbed her bag and headed for the door.

The girl working on Andrew's calloused feet glanced up from her job. "Nice purse."

Elyse bristled as she fished her ringing phone from her bag. Her bright orange Hermes defined her, gave her status. Too bad there wasn't a grain of truth to be found in the leather folds. While she carried *the real thing* everywhere from Wedgeworth's to elegant spas like this one, the fraud was none other than the woman who brandished the show-stopping, Ostrich skin purse.

Perhaps it was time to trade her once-beloved bag in for something more practical, something reflecting the truth.

Her phone rang a final time as she hurried down one cork-papered hallway after another. This place was a labyrinth. She'd lost all sense of direction as one hall branched into another. Standing before a door that read, MEMBERS ONLY, she hesitated. She just needed somewhere to take her call in private.

She pushed the door open to a tiled passage leading past a series of smaller doors. The air was sweet-scented and humid. This would have to do. She clicked the call back button on her phone. "Iris?"

"I got you the deal," Iris answered.

Relief washed over her. "Thank you."

"There's good and bad news, though."

Elyse didn't need any more bad news. She took a deep breath. "Give me the good news."

The door at the end of the hallway started to open. Elyse couldn't risk another scowling employee cutting her off or evicting her. She hurried away down the hallway, listening intently to Iris.

"With your deductions, the settlement comes in at a hundred and ninety thousand."

For good news, it wasn't the best. That only left her $10,000 to start a new life. She'd deal with it. If that wasn't enough, she'd scour the house for anything left that might be sold at an auction. "What's the bad news?" she asked.

"They want it Monday morning, 10 a.m."

"Monday!" Panic rose in her throat. Impossible. Sure, she'd have her payment from Saban, but the bank didn't even open until ten.

"If not, they're taking your house."

"What?" Elyse stopped dead in her tracks as she came face to face with another spa employee rounding the corner in front of her.

The blonde pushing a nail station scowled. "No cell phones or . . ."

"I know, or I'll be asked to leave." Elyse rolled her eyes.

She couldn't afford to get thrown out or hang up on Iris, either. Stepping past the blonde, she bolted through one of the side doors. The room was filled with thick-scented steam. Citrus, and something else, maybe something a little woodsy.

Whatever it was, it smelled divine. Elyse inhaled deeply. At least she was alone. Finally. "Can I sign over Saban's check and get a refund?" she asked Iris.

"The IRS doesn't take second party checks."

She was so close, she'd figure out a way to make sure they got paid.

"More important," Iris continued. "Do you have someone lined up for me? I don't want to be demanding, but I'm desperate."

Great. She hoped Iris had forgotten about that crazy scheme. There was no way she could come up with a date for Iris on short notice. She already had enough problems just trying to get Andrew into shipshape before tomorrow. "Are you sure you can't wait a week or two?"

Feeling dizzy from the steam, Elyse staggered back a step and sat on a tiled ledge. Which was when she realized she wasn't alone. Her jaw went slack and she blinked, once, twice. Her eyes must be deceiving her, or maybe she'd just lost her mind and was seeing a mirage.

Sitting against the back wall of the steam room, wearing only a towel draped at his waist, Nick Salvatore glistened in the mist like a Greek god on his throne in Olympus. He was the answer to her prayers.

"No man, no deal." Iris laid out her threat.

"Fine, you'll have your man tomorrow night," Elyse answered, confident. She clicked off her phone, her gaze flickering over Nick's muscled chest and abdomen. Suddenly, everything seemed so simple.

"Aren't you a little overdressed?" Nick stood, arched an eyebrow, and stared into Elyse's familiar green eyes.

"Always trying to get my clothes off, aren't you?" Elyse volleyed back, taking a step toward him.

"I meant your shoes."

He missed her, but that was over. The woman he'd bared his heart to, made soul-searing love to, had rejected him. A man could only take so much. She'd gone off the deep end and hadn't even given him a chance to explain.

Yet she'd been on his mind all week.

Elyse glanced down at her feet. "Oh."

"No outside shoes allowed. Strict policy." With only 100 degrees of steam and a cotton towel between them, all he wanted to do was kiss her, touch her, be inside her. The question was, how long could he play it cool before he seriously embarrassed himself? Nick edged back to the tiled ledge and sat down.

She followed. "I've broken every spa rule so far, what's one more?"

"You don't want to get the employees angry at you," he replied.

"It's a little late for that. I need a favor." She undid the top button of her blouse.

He wanted to undo them all. "Favors come with a price."

Elyse moved in close to him. Her damp shirt grazed his chest. He could feel her nipples, taut against him. "I'll give you anything." Elyse undid another button. "And I mean *anything*."

Was she offering what he thought she was offering? As appealing as sweaty scx in the steam room might be, he knew he had to restrain himself. He'd heard disturbing information regarding Elyse's latest business associate. "What's the deal?"

"I need you at the Charity Ball tomorrow."

Few things surprised Nick. Elyse always did. "I'd be happy to be your escort."

"Not with me."

"We need to define the terms of this agreement," Nick said suspiciously. "I go to the ball with someone, I assume, of your choosing."

"Correct," she answered.

"And for said service, you will grant me any favor, be it reprehensible or vile, that I devise."

"*Anything.*" Elyse locked eyes with him. Her face glowed in the heat as clouds of steam billowed around them.

Nick steeled himself as longing coursed through him. It was all he could do not to take her into his arms and press his nakedness against her. "That's the deal?"

"Take it or leave it," she whispered in his ear, leaning into him harder.

Tight against him, he could deny her nothing. "Deal."

"Perfect. Be there when the doors open." She got up from the tiled bench, opened the steam room door, and left.

Nick wrestled with the needs fighting inside him. He wanted Elyse more than anything. He ached for her. He needed to be with her.

He needed a cold shower.

Chapter 12

Elyse opened her checkbook and prepared the final check. *Internal Revenue Service* she wrote in longhand on the Pay-to-the-order-of line. Proud of her elegant penmanship, each letter was perfectly proportioned, balanced against the dip or arc of the next. The last letter, an "e" ended with a controlled flourish. Just enough flair to give her cursive script an old-fashioned appearance.

There was something calming about writing out the words. Not so calming were the numbers that followed. One-nine-zero-zero-zero-zero-*dot*-zero-zero. One hundred and ninety-thousand dollars to Uncle Sam. A knot formed in her stomach.

Hunger? Well, that and anxiety.

Skipping dinner, she sat at her kitchen table wearing a black and white ankle-skimming silk gown and pushed away the calculator in front of her. In a few minutes, she'd climb into her car and head to the annual Charity Ball with its legendary buffet. Until then, bills.

Satisfied with Saban's promise to bring a cashier's check for two hundred grand, Elyse had taken control, tackling the stacks of mail and balancing her bank account. Why not get a head start?

Now, with the final check written, she breathed deep. *Done.* A pile of sealed envelopes listed toward the window. She added the one to the IRS, to be delivered first thing Monday morning, and felt warily joyous. With the exception of the mortgage, this was the first time in years she wouldn't owe her other creditors a dime.

She'd already made an appointment at the Sausalito Savings and Loan for Monday afternoon, right after she settled matters with Iris and went to lunch with Jackie to toast the end of the audit nightmare. At the bank, she'd discuss options for re-mortgaging, financial planning, and a savings account.

What the heck, why not open a savings account? Even if it only had a hundred dollars in it, the account would mark a new beginning. Tobin women had always been big believers in hiding money under the mattress, not that there'd been much to hide. The reality of her family's history of saving for a rainy day was spare change found between the sofa cushions.

A fresh start meant thinking long-term.

After Andrew's delivery to Saban and sending Nick off with Iris, she was giving up matchmaking. Forever.

She'd get a real job.

An income to count on.

The fluctuating paychecks were over. There'd be no more robbing-Peter-to-pay-Paul bill paying. She'd file her taxes on time, every year. With the house restored and the plumbing conquered, Elyse decided paying off her mortgage slowly with affordable monthly payments was the road to solvency.

If a new mortgage took 30 years to pay off, so be it. Elyse could not put her dreams on hold one moment longer. Not when her house, and her heart, needed to be filled with life. The grand old Queen Anne had been quiet too long.

Change was afoot. She felt it right down to her toes.

Of course, she'd still honor her commitment to Iris and find a nice guy to introduce her to. Nick was just a distraction. One that would save her house.

Satisfied with her efforts at the kitchen table, Elyse gathered a beaded black-and-white clutch hanging from the back of her chair. Her mother's clutch. She opened it and double-checked for her keys and wallet.

This morning, when she'd worked up the courage to go to her mother's bedroom on the third floor, she'd discovered the little French purse. Upstairs, fixtures and furniture had been caked with three years of dust. The loss and longing for her mom consumed her, but the overwhelming grief had vanished.

Necessity had led her to her mother's closet since the sequined Halston she planned to wear didn't zip. Not even close. Blame it on the cheesecake. Nick's cheesecake. The delicious mandarin confection had been too hard to resist.

Truth told, the responsibility was entirely hers. She'd greedily wolfed down every forkful of the sinful dessert. Too late to diet, she'd accepted the extra pounds and basked in her more womanly figure. Hadn't Nick expressed awe of her recent curves?

She wondered what he'd think of her mother's vintage gown. The plunging neckline and vertical stripes skimmed her curves in all the right places. Her lips twisted into a half smile.

She'd made a deal with Nick. *Anything.* Sexually, their bodies seemed in tune, a perfect chemistry. Assuming he wanted sex, sleeping with him one more time wasn't going to be a problem. As long as she kept her heart guarded, he could appreciate her rounded hips and breasts and anything else he pleased.

But only one more time.

The last time. Tonight she needed his help. He was the one man who she could count on to make everything right.

Limousines and luxury sedans jockeyed for position near the bright welcoming lights of the Westin St. Francis on Union Square. Elyse angled her Prius between the larger cars and handed her keys over to a uniformed valet. The gold buttons of his epaulets glinted in the last rays of sun.

Surrounded by gentlemen in tuxedoes and ladies in gowns, Elyse flowed with the crowd over the red-carpeted entry and into the hotel. Crossing the lobby to the bank of elevators, bellmen ushered partygoers into the lifts. The destination was the top floor of the tower. The Grand Ballroom.

At the entrance, she opened her clutch and produced a single ticket before stepping through the doors. Every year, the room filled Elyse with awe.

Displays of grandeur weren't normally her thing, but Bishop Hegeland's Charity Ball proved an exception. Chandeliers glittered while the floors and walls produced a stunning shimmer of refracted light that played out on sequined evening gowns. The overall effect was much like a thousand people landing together in the pot of gold at the end of a rainbow.

Especially if that pot of gold had a full orchestra, a buffet of the best finger foods money could buy, and a dance floor the size of a roller skating rink.

She couldn't wait to see Andrew's reaction. Not that he'd arrived yet. She'd told him to arrive at nine o'clock on the dot, even though the doors opened at eight.

"Welcome, Elyse," a familiar voice called.

"Bishop Hegeland," she greeted the host, dressed in his black suit and white collar. "Spectacular turnout."

"Up two hundred this year," he replied, almost giddy. "I think we're looking at a new roof for the church."

"Have you seen Madeline?" she asked.

Bishop Hegeland smiled. "No, but Nick's here. I think he's looking for you."

"I'll find him, I'm sure." She patted his arm. For once in her life, she was actually seeking Nick out, though she wasn't about to tell the Bishop that. "I think I'll check out the buffet."

Passing throngs of happy partiers, Elyse skirted the dance floor and closed in on the ice sculptures, platters of seafood, and bubbling champagne fountain. As she crossed in front of a row of potted palms that camouflaged the ladies' room entrance, there was a distinct hissing sound. Even over the orchestra, she heard it again.

"Elyse!" Iris called through the foliage. "I'm over here."

"Iris?" Elyse turned. Her belly lurched as Iris stepped away from the palms. *Dress* didn't describe what she was looking at. The cotton-candy pink gown screamed Easter. The puffed up sleeves were as big as watermelons, and the skirt billowed like a parachute. "What are you wearing?" she gasped.

"I'm sorry," Iris apologized and dove for cover behind the palms again. Eyes glassy, she'd been crying. "I just figured if I got a third wearing out of my high school prom dress, the cost averaging made the ticket to the ball almost affordable."

While no truer words had ever been spoken by an accountant, it was still a hideous outfit. "Where did you wear it the second time?"

"Bridesmaid at my sister's wedding." Iris raised her sleeve and wiped away tears. Mascara smeared across a shiny satin cuff. "All my sisters are married. Everyone except me."

"It's just a dress." Elyse did her best to soothe her. How was she going to fix this before Nick found them? Would he take one look at Iris and run the other way?

"Elyse," Iris hiccupped her name through a sob. "About our deal . . . you don't have to introduce me to anyone tonight. I'd just embarrass you."

"Maybe we can figure something out." Her heart went out to her.

Six bridesmaid stints, and every single gown she'd worn had been promptly donated to charity. The last one, the crinoline-couture-from-hell, dumped in a Salvation Army clothing bin on the way home from the wedding. That gave her an idea. Jackie carried a pair of scissors in her bag and maybe with a snip here and a deflated sleeve there, the dress might be salvaged. Something had to be done, she just didn't know what. She needed help.

"I'll still hold up my end of the bargain," Iris sniffled.

"Bargain?" came a voice behind her.

Nick. Elyse inhaled. His spicy scent, with a hint of citrus, made her knees weak. He smelled as divine as ever. Forcing herself to swivel and face him, she felt a thin bead of sweat rise on her collarbone as her eyes swept down his body and back up again.

Perfection in a tuxedo.

"What's this talk of a bargain?" Nick smiled.

"I'm afraid you're not needed here, Nick." Elyse stepped in front of him and blocked any glimpse beyond.

"Nick?" In the palms, Iris squealed. The leaves rustled, then parted. Iris peered out. "Remember me? We met at La Sals. I'm Iris."

"Iris," he repeated. "I never forget a pretty smile."

"Well, you should see this dress I'm wearing. You'd never forget that either."

Gracious as ever, Nick reached through the plant life and shook her hand. "Internal Revenue Service, right?"

Elyse squeezed her eyes shut and counted to ten. Then back again. "Can we talk privately?"

"Ask me anything."

She took his elbow, guided him a few steps to the side and leaned in close. "Iris is the one. I want you to *take care of her*."

Nick glanced back at Iris in the palms and raised an eyebrow. "I draw the line at rubbing her out."

"Not kill her. *Take care of her*. I want her to enjoy herself." She shivered, feeling his hot breath dance across her bare shoulders. Elyse desperately wanted to enjoy herself like she had a week ago, with him, in the worst way. Being in such close proximity to Nick was almost too much to bear.

"That's not much of a challenge."

"And sex. I want her to have lots of sex." She tried to act casual about it, but a twinge of jealousy surged through her. She didn't want to share Nick with anyone. As if fidelity was in a gigolo's vocabulary. Some fantasies were hopeless. He'd given her the best two nights of her entire life, but this was business. "Use everything you've got to make her happy."

"Your wish is my command," he said and bowed. "And you agree that for this favor you will do anything I ask?"

"Absolutely."

Nick turned, and in one fluid movement, took off his tux jacket. He carried it back to the palms and draped it over Iris's shoulders. Taking her hand, he looked deep into her eyes. "You're going to have to trust me, Iris."

Iris nodded.

As Nick led her out a side entrance, Elyse scanned the hundreds of gentlemen and ladies loading plates at the buffet, dancing on the grand floor, or chatting at banquet tables. She didn't know where Nick was taking Iris, but she was sure he knew what he was doing. This was Nick's territory.

She wished it was her snuggled into a borrowed tuxedo jacket, whisked away to a night of carnal pleasure. But she had work to do and a tulip heiress to marry off.

Where was everyone anyway?

"People like me don't belong at these fancy-schmancy shindigs." Iris sighed as the elevator plummeted downward. "I'll just go home."

"My assignment is to make you happy," Nick said calmly. "I intend to do just that."

"Really?" The shiny brass doors opened to the lobby. "You can make me happy?"

He would. As quickly as possible. Because all he could think about was Elyse, clueless about what was about to happen to her. He needed to get back to the ball pronto and whisk her out of enemy territory before it was too late. Nick rolled his watch toward him. Nothing would happen before Andrew made his entrance at 9 p.m. That gave him the better part of an hour with Iris.

On the main floor, Nick led Iris toward a row of shops housed in the hotel. Passing an upscale window, they stopped. A lacey white Chanel gown hung gracefully in the display.

"That's nice," Nick commented casually. "Let's try it on."

"I can't go in there," Iris protested.

"Why not?"

"I can't afford a pair of socks from a place like that."

"You don't have to." He linked arms with her and tugged her through the doors.

"May I help you?" a saleswoman greeted them.

"We need a ball gown. Fast," Nick announced, reclaiming his tuxedo jacket. "The one in the window would do."

The saleswoman smiled. "Everyone loves Chanel."

Iris shook her head sadly. "You can't just buy me a dress. I'm a Federal employee. We're not allowed to accept gifts."

"Am I under investigation?" Nick asked.

"No."

"Then this isn't business. I'm your friend," he argued. "How big a gift can one friend give another without it being a tax liability?"

"Ten thousand dollars."

Nick turned to the saleswoman. "Is the dress under ten thousand?"

"Forty-five hundred." She rifled through a rack and pulled out an identical white lace Chanel. "Size ten?"

Iris nodded, happily seizing the dress from the saleswoman, pressing it to herself and spinning in front of a three-way mirror.

Nick slid a credit card out of his wallet. "I'd say we're on the road to happy, Iris."

Clutching the dress, joy beamed from her eyes, brighter than a lighthouse. "If you're a gigolo, you're the worst one ever."

Finding her crowd hadn't been so hard after all. They'd been waiting for her. Camped out at a banquet table with her friends, Elyse's heart pounded like a jackhammer. They had a perfect view of the entrance.

So where was Andrew? She fidgeted with her cell phone. It was two minutes to nine. And where were Nick and Iris? A wave of frustration amped up her anxiety another notch. Forcing out her imaginings of just how good a time Iris was having right now, Elyse tried to stay focused on her work at hand.

Or elbow, technically.

Sitting beside her, Saban tapped her toe impatiently. "No groom, no check."

Elyse stared down at Saban's noisy, red Jimmy Choos. "Aren't those the same shoes you wore to Wedgeworth's, and the little Italian restaurant, and my house, too?"

That might have come off sounding a touch hostile, but she needed a distraction. Anything. Frankly, the sooner she unloaded the tulip heiress as a client, the better. What sort of socialite wears the same heels day in and day out?

"They're my signature shoe in my signature color," Saban snapped back. "I own fourteen identical pair. Size eleven-and-a-half wide. You try finding a decent pair of slingbacks to fit these dogs." She circled her ankle in the air.

"It's harder to find a signature shoe than a good man," Madeline chortled.

Jackie nodded along. "Which is why Elyse is such a blessing!"

Elyse couldn't drag her eyes away from Saban's scuffed leather and worn soles. Fourteen pair? Was she waiting until these shoes fell apart before she broke out the next pair? She'd heard the Dutch were notoriously thrifty, but this was ridiculous. Dressed head-to-toe in a black tent-like shift, Saban played with a long strand of pearls that appeared to have lost their luster. She couldn't put her finger on it, but something was wrong here.

Very wrong.

Saban sniffed. "We'll see if my little primate plumber even shows up."

"He'll be here," Elyse growled.

"Calm down," Madeline chided. "We know you do good work. Obvious as the nose on our faces. With the exception of Kinsey Adams. Her nose has been rebuilt so many times no one knows what it looked like a decade ago. Poor dear has to have her driver's license picture taken every year to match her surgeries. Her doctor is a whiz, though. Beautiful work, just like yours, Elyse."

The orchestra played the last bars of a waltz as a gold clock on the wall struck nine, on the dot. Everyone at the table looked to the entrance, expectantly. The doors to the Charity Ball openedStanding tall at the open doors, Andrew stepped into the light. He tugged the cuffs of his tuxedo, not in an uncomfortable way, but with confidence. He surveyed the ball like Columbus claiming the New World.

"Holy moly!" Saban clutched the edge of the table.

"That's the plumber?" Madeline and Jackie gasped in unison.

Elyse felt pride resonate through her being. She had

made him. He was beautiful. Every female eye in the room was on him.

It was true. Everyone loves a hunk in a well-cut suit.

"That's my plumber," she said.

Andrew stepped into the ballroom. The chandeliers gave his eyes a twinkle as the highlights in his perfectly coiffed hair shone. His skin was flawless, tanned and manly. The tux moved with him like a second skin as he paced through the crowd like a man above it all. Like a god.

"He's not yours anymore," Saban corrected Elyse. "That's *my* plumber. Come to momma!"

Necks craned and several women in the room swooned as Andrew walked by. The posture and presentation lessons had paid off. He sauntered to their table.

Elyse stood and greeted him. "Andrew! Look who joined us tonight." She swiveled to her right and placed a hand on the back of Saban's chair.

"Saban," Andrew said in a deep, smooth voice, drawing the attention of every female within earshot. He glanced toward the buffet and smiled. "Did you see those shrimp? They're as big as my fist."

Elyse felt her stomach drop. Terror pulsed through her. *Shrimp*, he wanted to talk *shrimp*? This was his future bride! She should have spent more time on conversation basics. Oh god, what if Saban refused him now?

"They're whoppers all right." Saban hopped to her feet and elbowed Elyse aside. "You look like a new man."

"Or at least a refurbished one," Jackie whispered under her breath.

Saban linked her arm in Andrew's. "No one minds if I take Andrew out for a test drive on the dance floor? Any objections? Speak now or forever hold your peace."

Elyse beamed with satisfaction. "Go right ahead."

Everything was going to be okay. Unless something went cataclysmically wrong, there was a 99.9 percent chance she'd just made another sale. A two hundred thousand dollar sale. *Ka-ching.* So why didn't she feel like celebrating? How come it felt like everybody else got to feast on their happiness while she only got a scrap here and there?

His arm linked in Iris's, Nick paused at the ballroom entrance. "Feel better?"

"Like a princess." She beamed, standing tall.

"And you're willing to trust me completely?"

"With my heart and soul," she replied.

Nick led the way to the middle of the room, swept Iris into his arms and glided across the dance floor. If only Elyse were as trusting as Iris. A dangerous situation awaited Elyse, and he was determined to pilot her to safety. Would she let him?

As Iris's heart beat against him like the fluttering wings of a baby bird, Nick skirted the edges of the waltzing couples. His eyes never strayed from Elyse sitting at her banquet table.

Andrew struggled to keep time to the music. *One, two, three. One, two, three.* On the dance floor, the woman in his arms felt strange, and not because he hadn't held a woman for a while. She wasn't soft like he had expected. *One, two, three. One, two, three.* If anything, dancing with her felt like the day he retired Elyse's old, rusted boiler and wrestled it up from the basement with a hand truck. *Are girls supposed to lead?*

"So how do you feel about all this?" Saban pivoted him to a corner near a fire door exit.

Shocked by her strength, he attempted to steer her back to the middle of the dance floor. "About what?"

"Elyse Tobin's been spiffing you up." Her voice took on a hard edge. "She's gonna *sell* your brawny ass to me!"

Andrew stepped on his own foot, stumbled and lost count. Sure, the brides footed the bill for improving the men, but were they supposed to talk about it? This wasn't what he expected at all. He stepped back into their box step rhythm. *One, two, three.* "I guess you're fine with it?"

"Me? Sure." Saban rolled her eyes. "You're the chump. I could be an axe murderer for all you know."

"Are you?" *One, two, three.*

"By the time you find out, it's too late." Saban drew her finger over Andrew's chin.

A shiver raced up his spine, and not a good shiver. The hair stood up on his neck. That meant danger. He looked into her beady eyes and swallowed hard. She was leading again. Toward the fire exit.

This wasn't love. This was torture. Andrew hoped that Elyse wasn't counting on the money, because if he made it to the exit, he was going to bolt. He just hoped he'd be fast enough to get away.

Nick assessed the situation as he wound his way between dancing couples. "I may need your help, Iris."

Trouble brewed on the sidelines. Watching Saban wrangle Andrew toward an emergency exit, Nick realized he had to do something. Quick.

"Anything," Iris purred.

"Do you like romance?" He tilted his head down to her and smiled.

She squeezed him tight. "I read a romance novel a week. Two on the weekends."

"I meant romance as in commitment, understanding and love."

Iris looked up to him. "I know this isn't real. Elyse put you up to it. Even if she hadn't tried, I wouldn't mess up her deal with the IRS."

Nick rolled her under his arm in a spin. "What deal?"

"Well . . ." She bit her lip. "I shouldn't say anything."

"I only have her best interests at heart," he confessed as he stepped back into time with the music, Iris in his arms. "I've been sweet on Elyse ever since I met her."

"I thought so. You've barely taken your eyes off her." She giggled, then turned more serious. "She has until Monday morning. The money for the match tonight will cover her settlement."

Nick nodded, pondering the words, then held her close as they two-stepped. "So romance for you is mostly in your novels?"

"It's only in my books." Iris slowed their pace. "Look at me. Even in this great dress, I'm tuna fish on Wonder Bread. You're pâté, Nick. I might hope for love, but I don't expect it. A girl like me is lucky to have pâté once in her life on a special occasion."

"Most people don't even like pâté." Nick scanned the dance floor, executed a series of turns, and aimed them toward Andrew and Saban, on course for the exit. "Iris, you need a man who'd be potato chips to your tuna fish."

"You find one, I'm game," Iris sighed happily.

"Remember you said that," Nick replied as they bashed into another couple.

"Watch it, buddy," Andrew grouched as another couple slammed into them, forcing Saban to release her death grip on him.

"Yeah," Saban sneered.

"Sorry," Nick apologized.

"Nick?" Saban's voice changed instantly, dripping with honey.

"Nick!" Andrew spun around, relieved to see a friendly face. Actually, two friendly faces. Nick's cute-as-a-button dance partner had a smile that could light up any room.

"Hope I didn't make you lose count there." Nick slapped Andrew on the shoulder.

"Were my lips moving?"

"Just a guess. Have you met my date tonight?" Nick waved a hand toward a blushing Iris. "Andrew, this is Iris."

"Uh, hi." He clenched his fists. Cute girls made him all tongue-tied. That's why he'd waited two years, hoping to be recruited by Elyse into her husband factory. He wished he was smooth like Nick and had clever things to say. *Uh, hi. Stupid.*

The confidence he'd felt when he'd walked into the ballroom had vanished, replaced with a desperate need to cut and run. Saban wasn't anything close to what he pictured as a wife. Nick had all the luck. All the great women. Like the one he had right now. Iris just seemed nice. A little shy, but wholesome. Why couldn't he find a woman like that?

Iris fidgeted with the sleeves of her dress, sneaking glances at him. "You look really nice, Andrew."

"Thanks, it's the tux," Andrew said, sheepish. "I bought it at the Milpitas Outlet Mall."

"I love that mall," Iris replied. "They have the best discounts."

"Jesus," Saban complained. "Are we gonna dance, or stand here yakking all night?"

Nick leaned close to Andrew and whispered, "I'm taking a bullet for you, buddy. Take care of Iris."

"You guys got some secrets I should know about?" Saban asked testily.

"None at all," Nick answered, then tapped Andrew on the shoulder. "As is the tradition, I request to cut in."

"Huh?" Andrew grunted. It was beyond him why anyone would want to give up a peach like Iris to dance with Saban. Oh! Nick was taking a bullet for him. "Sure."

"What?" Saban objected.

"It's the law of the dance floor." Nick took Saban in his arms and looked back at Iris. "Enjoy your potato chips."

If everything hadn't made any sense a minute ago, it made even less sense to Andrew now. As Saban and Nick disappeared into the crowd, he stood in the middle of a bunch of dancing couples staring at Iris.

"You wanna dance?" he asked.

Iris stepped up close to him. They looked in each other's eyes. "Do you like tuna fish?" she asked.

"Totally," he answered. "Who doesn't like tuna?"

"No one I know," Iris said and took his hand. "And I would love to dance with you."

"Don't tell me you're still on that crazy diet." Elyse eyed the seltzer in Jackie's glass as she sipped from a flute of champagne. "This is a time to celebrate."

"Never mind me." Jackie raised her drink in a toast. "Tonight is about love. To Elyse, Saban, and Prince Charming Number Seven!"

Elyse nodded toward Cyril and Donnie loading plates of hors d'oeuvres at the buffet. "To happily ever after for all of you." She clinked glasses with Jackie and Madeline, then scanned the dancers again. She'd lost track of Andrew and Saban. Ditto for Nick and Iris.

"And cheers to the wardrobe change for that little IRS auditor! She's a gem now. Speaking of gems, I didn't overdo, did I?" Madeline's ears, neck, and wrists were adorned with an entire mine's worth of flawless sparklers. "They're Canadian diamonds. No conflict stones for me. Speaking of conflict, Nick looked very comfortable with her."

"Nick is always comfortable," Elyse agreed.

"He certainly did a great job with Iris," Jackie marveled. "I almost didn't recognize her when she came back."

"Call it the Nick effect." Jealousy swept through Elyse.

It wasn't just Iris's beautiful white lace gown or that she was in Nick's arms. Iris was happy. How long had it been since Elyse had found that kind of joy?

"Why is Nick with her?" Madeline quizzed.

"He should be with you!" Jackie poked Elyse in the arm.

She tried to be adult about the deal she'd made. He'd never be hers, not exclusively. "If you love something, set it free."

"Whoever had the good sense to set Iris's pink monstrosity of a prom dress free should be awarded a Nobel Peace Prize." Jackie nodded along.

"It's like a fairy tale. Drab to fab," Madeline chortled. "But all cash and no flash makes a woman healthy, wealthy, and under accessorized. Coco must be rolling in her grave like a Hawaiian pig on a spit. That Chanel gown is just crying out for some sparkle. Even a ring would save her."

The real question was, would Saban save Elyse? She set down her glass and looked out to the dancing couples.

Still no sign of Andrew and Saban. Earlier, the undeniable tension between them had been clearly sexual. Like two dormant volcanoes, Andrew and Saban were a smoking duo of lust about to release a lava flow of pent up desire on each other. They better not have snuck out, not before she was paid for her services.

"Did Saban happen to mention a certain gift for me?" Elyse asked Madeline.

Madeline nodded, making her ten-carat teardrop earrings sway. "Oh my, yes. Though she was a little vague. I hate vague. It's so, well, vague. Quite inexact. That's why I like science. Question and answer. So to answer to your question, she said she had something special for you tonight that you will never forget."

"As far as I'm concerned, you deserve a bonus for Andrew's speed transformation." Jackie lowered her voice.

"How's it going with the audit?"

"Monday morning I pay the piper," she confessed.

"Everything?"

"Pretty much."

Jackie sympathetically held Elyse's hand. "At least you still have the house and *The Big Red Book of Men*."

"You're right." Elyse cheered, sitting up straight. She needed to be grateful for what she had. She had friends. True friends. And even if she had no idea who had turned her into the IRS, she'd been given a way out of trouble. Everything had a way of working out. As soon as she collected Saban's check, she'd go home, mail off her payments, and make a fresh start. She smiled as a sense of peace washed through her. "Everything will be okay."

"Absolutely the right attitude," Madeline concurred. "Silver linings, darkest before dawn, a stitch in time. I just have one little question. Why is Nick dancing with Sabby?"

Jackie gasped. "And why is Iris with your new Prince Charming?"

Elyse jumped up from her chair. *No, no, no*. This wasn't happening. Fear twisted in her gut. Everything depended on tonight's success. It was time to call in the cavalry. If only she had a cavalry to call.

Bishop Hegeland ambled up to the table with a plate stacked high with shrimp. "You look troubled, child," he said, munching one of the crustaceans.

"Man trouble," she confessed. "I could use some help from upstairs."

The Bishop swallowed. "God works in mysterious ways."

He was right. God did work in mysterious ways. Like having the Bishop show up at the exact moment she needed a man. Elyse grabbed his plate, set it down on the table, and whirled him into her arms.

"Hold on here," he sputtered a protest.

"Time to cut a rug, Bishop." She thrust out a foot and steered him toward the middle of the floor.

Andrew held Iris close. She felt good in his arms. She felt right. "Is my dancing okay? I'm trying not to look at my feet."

Iris glanced down. "It's okay. I keep stepping on them."

"Only a couple times," Andrew said shyly as they moved in tandem.

"Three times," Iris said with certainty.

"Who's counting?" Andrew smiled.

"I am," Iris confessed. Her face crumpled into a worried mask. "I'm an IRS auditor. I count absolutely everything. I can't help it."

"That's fine by me. I'm counting right now. One-two-three, one-two-three."

"I'm counting, too!"

"So how do you feel about plumbers?" Andrew asked nervously.

"I never think about them," Iris admitted. "Seems no one thinks about plumbers until they need one."

"Think you might need one now?" he asked with a goofy grin.

Iris giggled. "A girl shouldn't wait until the last minute."

Nick detested the woman he held in his arms. He was doing this for Elyse. A last ditch effort to save her from what was waiting outside the emergency exit.

"You dance well," Saban complimented him.

"I know," he replied. "Ten years of ballroom classes and three trophies. If I didn't dance well, I should sue someone."

"Aren't you a breath of fresh air?" She batted her eyelashes.

There was something disturbing about this woman, and

Nick knew what it was. "I couldn't help but notice that every word that comes out of your mouth is a lie."

He felt her weighing him. Her penciled-in eyebrows fell and her eyes narrowed. "Who are you, the ballroom police?"

"More like a detective," he replied. "Or at least someone who could hire one."

"Don't mess with me," Saban cautioned. "I have friends in high places."

Nick executed a fast series of turns ending in a dip. "And I have friends in the flower business. Funny that no one has ever heard of you."

She barely hung on. "Tulips are a hush-hush business. We have a lot of secrets."

"Stranger yet that a news reporter from the East Coast matching your exact description was fired for going too far to get her scoops. She applied at a local channel in the Bay Area, but was told there'd be no work unless she broke a major story." He straightened from the dip.

Saban leaned into him with force and led him back across the floor. "Someone like that should be avoided."

Nick flexed and took control again. Every minute he kept this woman away from Elyse was one more minute Elyse had to flee. Not that she knew the clock was ticking. "I haven't decided what I'm going to do yet. I'm just warning you that your charade isn't as secret as you think."

Her eyes shifted to the left as Elyse waltzed over in Bishop Hegeland arms. "Well you better decide fast, buddy."

"We need to talk!" Elyse shouted as the orchestra finished the number. Her voice echoed through the ballroom.

Nick Salvatore was ruining everything. Her future was at stake, and what was he doing? Dancing with Saban. Knowing her, she loved every second of cozying up to San Francisco's most notorious playboy. Elyse had seen the way

Saban devoured Nick with her squinty little eyes.

"If you'll excuse me, Bishop." Elyse tilted her head sweetly as the orchestra struck up a lively tango. She dropped his hands and stepped up to Saban and Nick on the dance floor.

Nick let go of Saban. "I was just about to ask the Bishop if I could cut in."

"And I was just leaving." Saban smirked and edged away.

"Permanently, I hope," Nick said under his breath.

Elyse grabbed Saban's elbow. "Wait, what about Andrew?"

She snorted. "Seems like he has his hands full." Saban swiveled and nodded to the far corner. Andrew and Iris fumbled through the tango, nuzzling and laughing with each awkward kick and turn.

This was all wrong. Totally wrong. Saban stomped away.

Elyse staggered back and glared at Nick. She needed Andrew with Saban. Nick with Iris. Without the $200,000 payment, she had nothing. "This is your fault, Nick. I trusted you. Now she's gone."

"I'm sure Nick was only doing what he thought was right," the Bishop interjected. "He's a good man with your best interests at heart."

Elyse couldn't believe her ears. Nick had everyone under his spell, including the church. He wasn't a good man; he was a traitor. She stared into his deep brown eyes, torn between wanting to slap him and desperately wanting to kiss him. Like a moth to his flame, he'd destroy her before the night was out.

"We need to get out of here." He held out his hand toward hers.

"No, she has something I need."

His eyes were soft, concerned. "Forget about Saban's

money."

"Money?" The Bishop lit up. "Maybe I could help?"

They both ignored the Bishop.

She fought back a torrent of tears. How did Nick know about the money? And how much did he know about her Prince Charming business? Panic ricocheted through her. Had he searched her house and found the book? Did Madeline or Jackie spill the beans? They wouldn't, would they? "I'm not going anywhere with you. My entire future is riding on tonight."

"I can offer you a better future, Elyse. Trust me." Nick slid his arm around her waist, resting his hand in the small of her back. "Come with me."

Pressed against him, she felt his heart pounding. She wanted nothing more than to leave, but without the payment, she'd be throwing away four generations of Tobin history. "Is this a trick?"

"Will you two stop bickering and go get a room?" Jackie tangoed past. She arched backward in Donnie's embrace. "Everyone knows you are both over the moon for each other. Give in."

Madeline and Cyril tangoed close on the other side. "If it looks like a lover's spat and smells like a lover's spat," Madeline trilled, "it most assuredly is a lover's spat."

The Bishop straightened his stiff collar. "Not that I condone premarital canoodling, but you and Nick could do a lot worse."

"We are not canoodling," Elyse protested loudly, twisting out of Nick's arms. "And I'm not going anywhere with him."

"Elyse, you promised me *anything*." He reached for her, and she pushed him away. "I'm asking you to walk out that door with me. Now."

Fury pounded her temples. He might have fooled her once, maybe twice, but not again. She would leave, but not with him. Maybe there was still a chance she could catch Saban in the lobby, convince her that she could fix things, make everything okay. Then again, the tulip ship might have sailed.

"You lied to me, Nick," Elyse exploded. "You let me believe you'd changed and that you cared for me. But it was all a lie. You've destroyed me."

"It's not like that," Nick pleaded. "You can trust me."

"Trust you? Not again. Not ever. Besides, how was Vicky?" Elyse forced her way through the dancers. She had to get out of here. Retreat before she burst into tears. But before she took another step, a bright red Jimmy Choo shoe landed in front of her. She raised her gaze.

Saban.

Followed by a man with a video camera and another man with a microphone on a stick.

"Too late." Nick buried his face in his hands.

Bright light flooded the ballroom. The couples dancing froze in the spotlight. The music faded as the objections of disgruntled gentlemen and ladies grew to a steady drone.

Saban stepped up next to Elyse. "This is Patricia Franklin of Channel 5 News. Tonight we're bringing you a shocking story of high society and government corruption. Live on Five!"

"What are you doing?" Elyse, dazed, squinted at the camera and lights.

"This woman is Elyse Tobin," Saban said confidently to the camera. "Better known as the Millionaire Madame of Sausalito. She is currently under the scrutiny of the IRS for tax evasion. Through our undercover investigation, we've discovered that many of our city's most famous socialites have used her service to buy men. Yes, human trafficking."

"Who called me the Millionaire Madame of Sausalito?" Elyse demanded. "I'm not a Madame!"

"I'm not on camera, am I?" Madeline whimpered

behind them.

Saban nodded to the cameraman to get a good shot of Madeline. "Madeline Whittlesworth-Rothburg, grand dame of San Francisco, is just one of the women accused of buying a brainwashed man and keeping him as a sex slave."

Madeline screamed and fainted into Cyril's arms.

Cyril looked at the camera. "I'm not a sex slave, I'm a cryptographer."

Saban nodded for the cameraman to get a closer shot. "How did the Millionaire Madame of Sausalito recruit you? Were you smuggled into the country?"

"I'm from Oxnard," Cyril argued weakly.

Elyse planted her fists on her hips. "Stop it, Saban. Stop filming. And stop calling me the Millionaire Madame of Sausalito!"

"That sounds like an admission of guilt to me." Saban turned next on Jackie and Donnie, who clutched each other tight. "And this was the first person to take one of Ms. Tobin's sex zombies. Is he a husband, or a lust-crazed servant? Only a full police probe will be able to tell."

Iris stepped into the lights followed by Andrew. "I know that voice, Elyse," Iris said. "That's the voice of the person that turned you in to the IRS."

Saban faced the camera operator and his lens. "It's true. I blew the whistle because I'm a true public servant. Not like this woman, Iris Buchwald, who is currently cavorting with one of Ms. Tobin's creations. Is she an upright civil servant, or a corrupt IRS auditor seeking sexual gratification in exchange for looking the other way?"

"I'm a good girl," Iris howled. "I've been saving myself for marriage. Thirty-two years old, and I'm still a virgin."

Andrew's eyebrows raised in surprise. "Really?"

Bishop Hegeland muscled to the front of the crowd. "I order you to halt this frivolousness right now, Saban. Andrew and Iris are nice people." He scowled at Elyse, who shrank from his glare. "And it's not too late for you to repent."

"There you have it," Saban stated proudly. "Lies and deceit from top to bottom. Government, church, and everyone in power. Some call this town San Francisco. I think not. I call it *Sin* Francisco!"

"I think we should sit down, Iris," Andrew said. He took her hand and led her to the banquet tables. Bishop Hegeland slunk after them.

Saban started to follow, but Elyse grabbed her shoulder and spun her around. "Your fight is with me."

"It sure is." Saban waved the camera guy over to continue her live exposé. "Elyse Tobin, for a price of two hundred thousand dollars, will target an unsuspecting man, erase who he is, and plant a program in his head, making him appear to be Prince Charming."

"It's not like that!" Elyse yelled.

"It's all true." Saban spat out the words.

Nick stepped up. "This woman has done nothing wrong. If anything, she's helped bring people together."

Saban wasn't about to let go. "Says Nick Salvatore, suspected accomplice in this whole sordid operation. Best selling author, gigolo, and the model that the Millionaire Madame of Sausalito builds her lobotomized husbands on."

Nick turned to Elyse. "Is that true?"

Elyse felt her face burn with shame.

"I've seen the book," Saban sniped. "You are the rotten core of everything she's done."

"There's a book?" Nick wrapped a protective arm around Elyse's shoulders. "You didn't mention anything about a book."

Saban turned proudly to the camera and smiled. "So there you have it, the scandal of the century. I am Patricia Franklin covering the Millionaire Madame of Sausalito, Live on Five. We're out."

Shell shocked, Elyse stood in the middle of the room.

The silence was quickly followed by whispers and murmurs. There would be no cavalry, no last-minute save. There would be no IRS settlement, and no house, either. She'd be lucky if she only spent the rest of her life in prison. Not that what Saban, or rather *Patricia,* had said was true. Not entirely.

In a matter of minutes, this chicken-legged, snake-in-the-grass reporter in her scuffed Jimmy Choos had undone more than a hundred years of Tobin history.

Destroyed, Elyse fled the ballroom.

Chapter 13

Elyse prayed that yesterday hadn't really happened, but she knew it had.

A lie can travel around the world before the truth can put its boots on. Elyse's mother always repeated that Oscar Wilde quote whenever unsavory gossip reared its head. There'd been plenty over the years. Tobins weathered storms, heads held high, even when the scandalmongers were right.

A house of strong women, generations of dyed-in-the-wool feminists, with a rotating cast of husbands, fathers, and boyfriends had spurred rumors for decades.

Elyse reclined in her tub.

The hot, lilac-scented steam rose from the water's surface as she steeled herself with family history. So what if her great-grandmother had been unconventional? Her granny had taken in male borders during the Great Depression, much to the dismay of neighbors. Even her own mother, a disco-era wild child, had had a string of lovers before taking up with Elyse's father a decade later.

Those had been hard times for her mom when her dad left. She remembered her mother crying for weeks on end. Having been only four years old at the time, with few memories of the mustached man who came to visit every weekend, Elyse blinked back tears now.

The bridge span basked in a street lamp glow. Her father and the bridge were linked in her mind, even though she had no idea why she connected the two. Only that people had talked about her family for years after he'd stopped coming to the house.

When Elyse was older, she'd asked about him. Her mother refused to discuss it. Now, there was no one to ask. Not about the past or for advice.

Elyse was alone.

Unplugging her phones and pulling the shades, she retreated into the house. The day had been a blur of sleeping and bathing. The only time she set foot outside the front door was to retrieve the Sunday paper from her step. The headline blared news of an alleged Madame in Sausalito, luring and brainwashing innocent blue-collar men into sexual servitude.

Lies traveling at the speed of light.

Her business was over. There was equity in the house, of course. But what legitimate banking institution would lend money to her now? The IRS wasn't likely to take an enlightened view of the headlines either.

Was it possible she'd somehow willed this upon herself?

Why had she ignored her gut feelings and risked everything on one potential husband remake? That was easy. She'd gotten greedy. Worse, she'd repeatedly offended the one man who had tried to save her from her mistakes. Nick.

Guilt churned through her. If Madeline, Jackie, Andrew, and Iris never spoke to her again, she wouldn't blame them. They'd been dragged into this nightmare, too. It was all her fault.

One evening at the Charity Ball and everything had changed. Every part of her life had fallen apart. Elyse drew a sponge across her chest and over her face, letting the water trickle down. There was nothing left to do except wait for a solution to come to her. Like her great-grandmother, her grandmother, and her mother, they'd survived. She'd come too far to lose her home and history. But she had to wonder, had her blind devotion to the house held her back and cost her everything?

Things were always better in the morning. Even on a Monday morning. Elyse knew it when she opened her eyes, felt it when she slid her feet into the fuzzy slippers by her bedside and shrugged on her cotton robe. She was done feeling sorry for herself, shrinking in the glare of negative headlines. With the morning light of the new day, she'd explore her options.

The first, a lawyer. Someone to defend her.

Then a publicist, an expert in damage control.

It was time for the truth to get its boots on.

After that she had no idea who she'd hire next. Or how to pay them. In the meantime, she'd get to work on a website, right after a cup of tea. If she did nothing else this morning, she'd sign up for a domain and begin to reclaim her good name.

Heading down the hall to the bathroom, she resolved that Saban, or *Patricia what's-her-name*, wasn't going to get away with this attack.

Thump!

Did that noise come from her front porch? She looked out a second-story window. Andrew's pickup sat parked at the curb.

Thump!

Elyse ran down the stairs three at a time. Rushing to the front door, she swung it open wide. Iris stood on her porch with a paper in one hand and a staple gun in the other. Andrew stood watch a couple feet behind her.

"What's going on?" Elyse gazed from one to the other, knowing from their guilt-ridden expressions something was wrong. Very wrong.

"I am so sorry," Iris answered. "They made me do it."

Elyse stepped outside and looked at a yellow notice stapled to her doorframe. "Seizure! You said we could work out a settlement."

"That was last week. I'm under review."

"You can't take away my house." She ripped down the notice and tore it into pieces.

Iris shrank back. "They said if I were willing to process your criminal case, it would show that we weren't in collusion. I might lose my job."

"You hate your job," Elyse protested.

"And I want to leave. Someday." Iris sighed. "Just not today. I wouldn't have any benefits. No health insurance. And Andrew doesn't have health insurance either."

"What does Andrew have to do with anything?"

He draped an arm over Iris's shoulder and puffed out his chest. "We got hitched."

Iris raised her left hand and sheepishly displayed a diamond ring. "Your friend Madeline loaned me a ring."

"What?" Elyse steadied herself on the porch rail. Scraps of yellow paper floated down the stone steps.

"After you left the Charity Ball, Bishop Hegeland declared last night the worst disaster in Episcopalian history and nothing could change the destruction of the church and all of civilization." Iris sighed. "Well, I got down on one knee and took Andrew's hand. He has really nice hands, you know."

"You asked him to marry you?" She sat down on the steps, stunned.

Iris swallowed, searching Elyse's face for approval. "It would be a shame to let the food, flowers, and orchestra go to waste, and on a government employee's salary, there's no way I could afford to have a fancy wedding."

Andrew grinned. "Bishop Hegeland performed the ceremony."

"It was a big hit." Iris nodded. "The Bishop got a bunch of checks for the church, too. Still, I don't think he's too fond of you right now, Elyse."

Elyse was having trouble taking this in. They were married and happy, positively glowing with bliss. Marital bliss. At least her work with Andrew hadn't gone to waste. Iris deserved a good man. But why didn't she feel thrilled for them? Instead, a deep ache settled in her chest. Everybody else got a happily ever after. Everybody but her. She was losing her house. She looked down at the last scrap of yellow paper in her palm.

Even the Bishop got his reward, raking in piles of cash, thanks to the last-minute nuptials. Iris had saved the day and gotten her man.

"We still need to file the paperwork," Andrew added. "My wife's a stickler for legalities."

"But as long as the ceremony was performed by a man of God, the Bishop said it was okay for us to, you know . . ." Iris blushed crimson red.

"Consummate our union." Andrew finished her sentence, then kissed his wife. Elyse saw the hunger, longing, and satisfaction in both of them.

When they stopped kissing, Iris turned to Elyse. "I should mention that the IRS isn't just taking your house. They're freezing all your assets, your bank accounts, your credit cards. You better grab some clothes and find a friend or someone to stay with."

"Now?" Elyse asked. This just got worse and worse.

Iris nodded sadly. "The Federal Marshals will be here any minute. I told Andrew we had to get here before they did so we could warn you."

It was a mad dash. Like a supermarket sweepstakes where the contestant has two minutes to grab as much as they can and stuff it into a shopping cart. Elyse grabbed a black plastic garbage bag from the kitchen.

First, she snagged all the old photos from her office. Luckily, they were all in a drawer. Two albums and some loose pictures of her great-grandmother, her mom before the cancer, Elyse as a little girl standing in front of the house by the then tiny Daphne bush. She didn't have time to be nostalgic.

Next, in her room, she changed into a shirt and jeans, then shoveled clothes into the garbage sack. A few skirts, some blouses, undies, bras, socks. She looped her orange Hermes bag over her shoulder and lugged the bulging plastic bag down the stairs to the kitchen.

What did she want? What did she need? Should she take her tea set? Or just the rooster teapot? The plaster bust of Woodrow Wilson, the one she meant to restore, was too big to bring along.

"Sorry, Woody," Elyse apologized.

A truck horn, Andrew's horn, tooted outside.

She was out of time. With one last glance into the dining room, she was ready to run. That's when she remembered *The Big Red Book of Men*.

It had ruined her. It had also given her purpose. Over the last three years, she had put six couples together. She made six marriages where there were only twelve lonely people before. She was proud of that. Jogging to the built-in bookshelves, Elyse jammed the key into the cubbyhole, opened the secret door, and tucked the book under her arm.

She dashed back to the kitchen, stopping to fling open the refrigerator door and latch onto the bottle of champagne. Her plan to toast the success of the house, free and clear, was never going to happen. Determined that some hired auctioneer wouldn't sell off her Bollinger Grand Annee for pennies on the dollar, she shoved the bottle into her handbag.

Sneaking out the backdoor, Elyse hauled the stuffed garbage bag, book, and purse to the carriage house and shoved it into the back of the Prius. She started the car, and then opened the garage door.

She stopped dead still and held her breath. Andrew's pickup waited across the street, but right in front of her house was a large, black American sedan. Exactly what Federal Marshals would drive. Two serious men in suits strode up the stone steps.

After being called the Millionaire Madame of Sausalito in the media, she didn't need to add a televised car chase to her besmirched reputation. How was she going to get away? She looked to Andrew and Iris in the pickup truck.

And they looked at her.

In an instant, the pickup engine roared, then the wheels spun and smoked. The men in suits turned as Andrew cookied his truck around in a circle, then raced up the hill, up to the dead end.

The men in suits ran to the street and stared uphill at Andrew revving his engine. Elyse had her big break. She eased the silent Prius out of the carriage house, into the street, and down the hill in the opposite direction. Glancing in her rearview mirror, her house grew smaller and smaller until she turned a corner and it disappeared from sight.

A tear slipped down her cheek.

She was officially a fugitive from the law. On the lam. Steering for the underpass tunnel that dipped beneath the 101 Freeway, she wound over to the state park beside the Golden Gate Bridge.

From the edge of the land, the bridge jutted out into the water like a fearless explorer. It had been a long time since Elyse felt fearless. She smiled weakly. There's a freedom in knowing you're totally screwed.

Her past had most definitely caught up with her. Her future, whatever it held, was uncertain at best. The house and its eternal debts no longer mattered. The house and over a hundred years of Tobin history had come to end. Though her ancestors had all been in dire financial straights at one time or another, not one of them had given up, placed a FOR

SALE sign in the front yard, or let the bank foreclose. They had banded together and won the day.

But not today.

Except for the buzz of traffic, it was peaceful on the bluff. Rolling green hills led to cliffs that dropped down into the ocean. She was alone. Almost. In the distance, a few joggers jogged, and some mothers pushed strollers along the paved paths. The only person within earshot was a transient woman who laid on a bench. Beside her, overstuffed, tattered garbage bags sat piled in a shopping cart. They rustled in the ocean breeze. Elyse winced. Was the bag in her trunk the start of this kind of life?

Grabbing the bottle of champagne, she walked to the bench. "Excuse me," she asked. "Would you like to have a glass of wine with me?"

The gray-haired woman sat up. "You're not supposed to drink alcoholic beverages in the park."

Elyse twisted around. There was no one watching. "I won't tell if you don't."

The woman scooted over. "Have a seat."

Elyse slid in beside her, took the foil wrapper off the bottle top, twisted off the wire safety net and popped the cork. It was a happy sound. "Do you have a couple glasses?"

"You betcha," the woman said, happily. She stood, bent over a garbage can near the bench and took out two used paper cups with hamburger logos. "Hang on a minute."

A few feet away there was a water spigot and a dog bowl station. The woman rinsed the cups and returned, handing one to Elyse.

Disgusting yes, but this was her life now. Besides, she hoped the alcohol would kill any germs. "Thank you."

The woman winked. "The trick to tasting a good champagne is a clean glass."

Elyse poured the Bollinger. "Do you mind if I make a toast?"

"It's your hooch."

Elyse raised her glass to the ocean. "To my mother's mother, her mother, and my mother. I never appreciated your sacrifices more than I do today."

"Skol!" the woman agreed, and took a drink. "That's good."

Elyse took a sip. Smooth, flavorful, rich in her mouth. It was a wine to savor. "I lost my house today," she confessed.

"Join the club," the woman said matter-of-factly and drank again.

"I'm going to have to live in my car." Maybe. If the IRS tracked her down, would they impound her car, too? Technically, it was an asset.

She couldn't count on her friends now, either. Chances were they'd avoid her like the plague. Why wouldn't they? Even if she cleared her name, found a job, and got back on track, she'd still be a social pariah. She'd always be connected to the scandal.

There'd be no lawyer, no publicist, no saving the day. Elyse realized she was alone in the world. Truly alone, except for the woman sitting next to her draining the last of the champagne from her cup.

"At least you got a car." The woman stared into her empty cup. "Be grateful for that."

Elyse raised the bottle and gave her a refill. "You're right. Maybe I have to let it all settle in."

"I been lettin' the crap in my life settle for five years. Tell the truth, it isn't gettin' any better."

They both drank. Maybe this was as good as the rest of Elyse's life was going to get. If it was, there was one more thing she wanted to remember.

Elyse pulled up to the unmarked awning, the entrance to La Sals, and stepped out of her car. The grand five-story building in downtown San Francisco was almost deserted. The lunchtime crowd had yet to arrive.

Funny how, for as many times as she'd come here, the finer architectural details of the brick building had escaped her notice. Perhaps she'd been too focused on the end result, the glorious cheesecake reward within, to appreciate the cornices and ironwork that trimmed the exterior. Atoning for this oversight, she stared up at the multiple stories. She admired the structure and flourishes that held together even through the Great Earthquake of 1906. It was a survivor.

"Ms. Tobin?" came a voice from the doorway.

Startled back to reality, Elyse faced Martine in the doorway. "How fast can I get an order of cheesecake to go?"

Martine, the maître d', huffed and held the door open wide. "Follow me. I think we need to speak."

At one time or another, Elyse had used that phrase on all the men she'd trained. *I think we need to speak.* A warning that something unpleasant was coming. The last thing she needed now was more unpleasantness, yet she followed him anyway. Into the darkened restaurant, winding through the elegant tables to the swinging doors that led to the kitchen.

Given her dire circumstances, chances were this was the last La Sals cheesecake she'd ever enjoy. Still, it was what she wanted most. She'd endure any amount of lecturing, finger wagging, or chastising necessary, just as long as she got her cake. "Can you make this speech quick?"

"I'm afraid not." Martine turned on his heel and blocked the entrance to the kitchen. He wasn't budging.

"Look, things haven't gone so well for me lately, and I just need to buy a cake and get out of here before anything else goes wrong." Aware that she came off sounding a bit desperate, like a depraved cheesecake junkie looking for one more hit before, well, she didn't want to think about what came next. Elyse used her best hopeful-puppy-dog-face. "Please, Martine."

Martine furrowed his brow.

"You'd throw a drowning man a life preserver, wouldn't you?"

"Yes," he answered warily.

"You'd give someone dying of thirst a drink of water?"

"Of course."

"All I want is a cheesecake," she pleaded.

Martine huffed again. "Madame is diner non grata. No cheesecake for you."

"Madame?" She bristled. "If this is about the news story, it's a complete fabrication. You can't deny someone cheesecake because of a news story." Elyse hated whining, but she couldn't help it.

"It is not about your infamy."

"You're upset that I threw water on Nick, aren't you? I'm sorry. I was angry. I know someone had to clean it up. I'll make it up to you. Please give me the cheesecake."

"First you must answer a question." He placed his hands on his hips.

"Anything," she moaned. "Just promise me a slice. One slice of cheesecake."

"Why don't you like Nick Salvatore?"

"What?" Elyse straightened. *Nick? What did he have to do with her getting what might be her last-ever taste of a La Sals' cheesecake?*

"You heard me," Martine stated. "Why do you not like Nick?"

She paused. Explanations might take a while. To summarize three years of her love-hate non-relationship with Nick defied logic. "It's complicated."

"It's complicated?" Martine snorted. "That's a box you click on your profile for a social website."

"It's hard to explain."

"Start explaining. No explanation, no cheesecake."

Elyse recoiled. The man wasn't kidding. She needed to come up with something. Right now, she'd say just about anything to get her hands on a slice of heaven. But did she need to lie? *No.*

She'd come clean. The whole sordid history laid out bare. What did she have left to lose? Taking a deep breath, she told Martine everything. From the very beginning. The crazy night of raw, emotional sex three years ago when she'd shamelessly used Nick to exorcise every ounce of sadness, longing, and loneliness from her psyche.

The years of avoidance in between, when she denied any attraction to Nick. She told him about the bath and the cheesecake and the slap in the face after discovering he was seeing someone named Vicky that night.

She even confessed to the deal she'd made with him in the spa. And how, at the Charity Ball, Nick had tried to save her from herself. To leave before her world came crashing down. And crashing down it had. The IRS had seized everything. Her house, her possessions. She was officially homeless.

"I was too stubborn to listen to him, to trust him." Tears rolled down her cheeks.

Martine pulled out a chair for her to sit down, and she did. He sat across from her and patted her hand, sympathetically. "But why don't you like Nick?"

She hiccupped a sob and wiped her eyes with a cloth napkin. The answer was obvious. Right in front of her nose and she'd never seen it before this second. "Because I love him," she blurted.

The galley doors to the kitchen creaked open. "You have a strange way of showing it."

Elyse raised her head and stared at Nick. In his chef's whites, he smiled sadly. "I heard everything."

"You work here?" she asked.

Martine shook his head. "He is La Sal."

"Short for Salvatore." He looked down at his feet shyly. "Guess all our secrets are out now."

"You make the La Sals' cheesecakes?" Her mind spun, thinking of all the cheesecake she'd consumed over three years. *Cheesecakes of seduction*, her mind reeled back to the text message she'd read. No wonder the restaurant was never advertised and there were no signs out front. This wasn't really a restaurant at all.

It was a front for a top-secret love laboratory.

"Martine." He sidled up to the maître d'. "Bring Elyse her cheesecake."

Through the galley doors, Martine disappeared into the kitchen as Nick sat down. "I made all of the cheesecakes."

"1,000 cheesecakes, 1,000 women?" If she hadn't had proof before, she had it now. Disappointment settled in her bones. She'd been his 999th seduction and just another recipe in his next book. "All I am is a mandarin cheesecake to you!"

"No," he shook his head, serious. "One thousand cheesecakes, one woman."

She bit her lip, not believing what she heard. "There's no damn way I've eaten one thousand cheesecakes."

"Nine hundred and ninety-nine so far." The smile crept back on his lips.

"Impossible."

"Three years ago, La Sals provided the cheesecake dessert for the Bishop's Charity Ball. Where we met. You went back for seconds, and then a third helping. By the time you went back for a fourth serving, I knew I had to introduce myself. Find out who this woman was who loved my cheesecake so much. And one thing led to another."

Elyse blushed. Not so much at the memory of their night together, but that Nick remembered she'd had four servings of cheesecake. She thought she'd been discreet.

He continued. "After that night, I knew I'd met the woman I wanted to spend the rest of my life with. But you wouldn't have anything to do with me, wouldn't take my calls. So I started courting you the only way I knew how, the only way I knew you wouldn't reject me. I made cheesecakes for you, Elyse. One thousand cheesecakes."

She did the math in her head. "That's like 333.3 cheesecakes a year."

"More or less. Some days you had two different slices in one visit." Nick went to the kitchen and brought out a huge spiral notebook. "I kept a log of every recipe and what each one meant. You've had at least a slice of every one."

Her pulse climbed steadily. Thinking about it, the numbers didn't lie. The scale didn't lie either. She'd put on a few pounds, and, come to think of it, of all the cheesecake she'd put on her revolving account at La Sals, she hadn't received a single invoice. She'd eaten a lot of cheesecake, delighting in every divine forkful. "Let me get this straight. You're *La Sal,* and you baked all those cheesecakes for me?"

"Yes."

"What about all the rumors about the owner?"

"There's only one that's true," he confessed. "The one about the broken-hearted East Coast chef whose wife took their restaurant in the divorce."

"And he lived on the Bay in a sailboat and started La Sals," she said completing her favorite story.

"That's me. I have my boat docked at the wharf. You're welcome to stay there."

The rumor she loved most was true. Her mind spun with hope and despair and sadness, too. If she'd known this three years ago, or even last week, everything might have turned out differently. But there was still one more question that burned inside, demanding an answer.

Yet she couldn't bring herself to ask about the woman who'd sent the text message. This Vicky clearly felt entitled to more of Nick than just his confections. Was it worth asking? Worth ruining this perfect, tiny moment of joy?

Elyse bowed her head. She loved this man, flaws and all. She could turn a blind eye to his past if he'd promise her a monogamous future. She could even imagine spending the rest of her life in his arms. But she wouldn't drag Nick into the front-page headlines, the lies, and the scandal. Never.

A woman had destroyed him once, and he'd started over in a new city. She wouldn't let him throw away everything he'd worked for because of her. Because he'd been foolish enough to love her.

Her battle was hers alone. And she was done fighting.

If she wound up pushing a shopping cart of beat-up trash bags through Golden Gate Park, at least she'd have her memories of Nick Salvatore. She'd cleave to the knowledge that once a man had loved her so much, he'd spent three years baking cheesecakes just for her.

Martine returned, carrying a large white box tied with a gold cord. Written across the top, *#1000*. "Your cake." He settled the box in front of her and left.

Elyse ran a hand over the number. "This is the last one."

Nick nodded. "It's yours. What are you going to do now?"

"I'm done running. I'm beaten. I rolled craps. Game over."

"That isn't the Elyse I know."

"This is the Elyse that's left."

Nick furrowed an eyebrow. "You are not a runner. You're a fighter."

"What's the point?" Elyse lifted the cheesecake box off the table.

"The point is that you always do what's right. You're proud of your house and your matchmaking. Saban took it all away from you."

"She did," Elyse agreed. "But if it hadn't been a reporter spinning the truth into a sordid news story, then it would have been something else. The Tobin women have been battling to keep the house for over a hundred years, and it's a war I'm not sure I can win anymore."

"I'll fight alongside you, Elyse. We can come up with a plan, hire lawyers. We'll beat them and take back your house. Just say the word." Nick stepped to her, arms open.

"You don't want me. You're a kind man and the best lover a girl could ever have, but I couldn't live with myself if I ruined you, too. I've done enough damage." Tears stung her eyes as she turned and walked away. "I'll never forget you, Nick Salvatore."

Driving up and down the hills of San Francisco, Elyse contemplated her fate and took inventory. She had a sack of clothes, a few photos, a cheesecake, and her orange Hermes bag on the passenger seat. On the minus side of life's ledger, she had no home, no family, no friends.

In the distance, the Golden Gate Bridge peeked out between buildings. She loved that bridge. Even as a little girl awake past her bedtime, she'd sneak into the attic. Sitting in the dim light that crept under the door, she'd stare for hours, hypnotized by the galaxy of pretty lights that spanned the bay. For her, each twinkling light was a star she would wish upon.

Now, all those wishes were used up.

She tried to remember the advice of her mother, grandmother and great-grandma Tobin. Nothing was of any use. *A penny saved is a penny earned.* She was out of pennies. *Every cloud has a silver lining.* The clouds today were all thunderstorms.

She wasn't thinking about where she was going as she angled into the lanes over the Golden Gate Bridge. It was like the car just decided to go there, and she was along for the ride.

Moving through traffic helped clear her mind.

Everything was simple. She had nothing. Her life was nothing. She'd gambled and lost everything Tobin women had struggled to build. She'd failed, finally and completely, and there was no one left to pick up the pieces. Elyse pulled her Prius against the outside curb, braked hard, and put on the flashers.

Car horns blared as she turned her handbag upside down and emptied her wallet, keys, and a lipstick onto the passenger seat. She cradled her orange Hermes bag in her arms. The purse had been with her through everything, all her problems. It had given her purpose and an entrée to high society. It was always loyal, always there for her.

But she was done pretending. She didn't belong in San Francisco's elite social circles, just like her handbag didn't belong at a church jumble sale. Undervalued oddities that didn't fit their surroundings.

There was only one thing left to do. She wouldn't be held back any longer.

Elyse jumped out of the car with her Hermes and hurried onto the sidewalk. Staring out at the water, the bay called to her. The only thing between her and the endless ocean was the heavy chain-link fence that ran the length of the bridge. It towered up for ten feet of public protection. Only the most determined and athletic jumpers flung themselves from this bridge.

It would take some effort to clear the top.

If she was serious about this choice, she didn't have long. The bridge patrol, in their heavy-duty trucks, were probably already on alert. Soon they'd be on their way with their flashing lights.

Once you hit bottom, the only way to go is up. She remembered her mother saying that. It was good advice. She wound the fingers of her right hand into the cold wire of the fence. Hundreds of feet below, the choppy surface of the water reflected silvery flashes of light. *What does up look like?*

If her former friends knew what she was doing, they'd have her committed to one of Madeline's *recovery* institutions for the rich and deranged. If they even cared.

Maybe she was crazy. It didn't matter anymore. Nothing mattered. For a while, she'd thought she had found her calling in life. She had enriched the lives of others and tended the family home. But that was gone. Now, she had become an object of ridicule to the world.

None of the good she had done counted toward anything in the final tally. She'd been a light without purpose. Even the house had let her down. Stepping back to the curb, she scanned the full height of the confining safety fence.

It was time to be free.

With one fluid swoop of motion, she fearlessly flung her Hermes bag high. The brass lock of the handbag caught a glint of sun as the purse cleared the top of the fence and hurdled down to its watery grave.

An old Chinese saying went something like, *if you seek revenge, you should bake two cheesecakes*. That's what Elyse thought as she carried the pristine box tied with gold cord through the lobby of the Channel Five news station. Too bad she only had one cheesecake.

"Excuse me," a security guard behind a reception desk called. "I need to see inside any packages. Who's this for?"

Elyse set the box on the desk and opened it. What was the name Saban used at the Charity Ball? "Patricia Franklin. I just wanted to congratulate her."

The guard eyed the hazelnut cheesecake. "Hope she shares," he said with a bit of drool at the corner of his mouth.

Elyse closed the box and headed to the elevators. "She was on floor three?"

The guard glanced at the clock. "Fourth floor, studio

two. She should be on air."

"Perfect." Elyse hopped in the first elevator to open.

If you're accused of something, and it happens to be true, own it. Elyse marched into the studio with a new mission, a new confidence. Letting go of the handbag had released something in her. She didn't care anymore.

Sure, the allegations were sensational. And so was the story. The real story. It was true that she'd trained regular men and sold them off as husbands. Just not sex slaves. And the lonely women who'd paid her to deliver their spouses were all happily married.

It wasn't a crime. Not technically. Though she supposed that morally she'd crossed a few lines since the men had no clue they were being sold off.

So why not set the record straight?

The set of the show was exactly what she had watched a thousand times on TV. Two anchors sat at a desk and Saban stood in front of a green screen. One of the anchors said, "And now the weather with our newest reporter, Patricia Franklin."

There were two crews that swiveled a pair of cameras from the anchors to Saban.

She waved at the camera. "Welcome to the weather on Channel Five Live! As you know, a low pressure system is perched off the Pacific, and we'll be in for a turbulent night . . ."

"I would definitely agree with that." Elyse marched onto the set. She turned to the surprised cameramen. "I'm Elyse Tobin, or as you may know me, the Millionaire Madame of Sausalito."

The cameramen shrugged at each other, confused. Saban looked off stage to a man in a suit at the back of the studio. "Keep rolling!" he said in a hushed voice.

"Yes." Saban faced the cameras. "The Millionaire Madame of Sausalito, here on Live at Five!"

"I just wanted to thank you," Elyse continued.

"Thank me?"

"You freed me. I was stuck where I didn't belong. Completely and utterly stuck. Granted, you freed me by lying, conniving, and duping some of the wealthiest people in the city. And let's not forget all those slanderous statements you made. But I'm sure the TV company has great insurance and lots of lawyers."

"It was all *kind of* true," Saban sputtered.

"Am I a matchmaker or a madame?" she demanded.

"What's the difference?"

"The end result." Elyse shook her head. "A madam sells sex. A matchmaker puts together marriages. In the latter department, I was six for six."

"Fine." Saban shrugged. "I retract my previous statement. You are the Millionaire Matchmaker of Sausalito."

"I'm not a millionaire."

Saban huffed. "Whatever. The Matchmaker of Sausalito."

Elyse enjoyed this. Though she was far from having her life back in order, it felt good to stand up for herself. "I lost the house. I don't live in Sausalito anymore."

"Okay, you're just the Matchmaker."

"Out of the business."

Saban glared. "You don't matter anyway. I got the job. I'm on TV."

The man in the suit stepped forward. He had a cell phone to his ear. "It's for you, Patricia." He handed the phone to her and pointed to a soundman at the back of the studio.

Madeline's voice came over the speakers. "Hello, Saban. Or should I say, Patricia?"

"Madeline?" she squeaked.

"A rose is a rose is a rose, isn't it? What a naughty little reporter you've been," Madeline continued.

"It was just a job," Saban snipped.

"I just wanted you to know that you have definitely caught the eye of corporate."

Saban stood tall and smirked at Elyse.

Elyse crossed her arms over her chest. What the hell was going on?

Madeline spoke again. "As the chairman of the board of this broadcasting company, we are very interested in you."

"You own this company?" This was the first time that Elyse had ever heard Saban sound afraid. "You're firing me, aren't you?"

"Of course not. Contracts are contracts, and you signed a five-year contract this morning. We always honor our obligations whether it be to friends, our marriage, or in business. We just never said you'd be employed in San Francisco."

Saban bit her lip and stared into the camera lens. "But I belong here, Madeline."

"Home is where the heart is. Chin up. Your job is safe. You can be a celebrity. Everything is peachy. We're simply loaning you to our affiliate station in Latvia."

"Latvia?" Saban snorted. "Do they even have TVs?"

Madeline's voice came back on. "I love saying Latvia, don't you? Lat-vee-yah. It sounds so exotic. I bet they grow freesias there. Have fun. Tah-tah."

A dial tone sounded over the speakers.

Saban stared at the phone in her hand.

"You should have done a little more research." Elyse felt a glow of satisfaction. If misery loved company, so did being ruined. "Everyone knows that Madeline owns a dozen major corporations."

"I don't want to move to freakin' Latvia!" Saban howled.

"And I didn't want to lose my house. One more thing .

. ." Elyse hefted the cheesecake. It must have weighed five pounds. With more than a little satisfaction, she shoved it into Saban's face. "Consider this a snack for the trip."

Saban cleared eyeholes with her fingers. "I hate you!" she shouted, cheesecake sputtering out of her mouth.

Elyse scraped cake off one of Saban's ears and shouted, "Bon voyage!"

Saban howled once more and stomped off-stage, dripping splotches of cheesecake.

The news anchors clapped.

Elyse bowed to them, then turned to the cameras. "To wrap this up, I would like to say that I am so sorry to anyone who got hurt. Please don't let my mistakes break up your marriages. Everyone hopes that fate will bring two people together. Six glorious times, I was fate. You're together because you love each other. Never forget that. How you met, well, that's just a story you tell on your anniversaries. At least you'll have a good one."

She took a deep breath and raised herself to her full height. There'd be no more evasions, no more lies. She wasn't a socialite and never had been. She was done pretending. "I'm going home now. I'm going to fight anyone who comes between me and my house. That includes the IRS. You want me? You know where to find me."

Looking at the cheesecake smeared in her fingers, she licked the sweet confection off her hand. It was incredible. Nick Salvatore had outdone himself this time. Sweet and nutty. Intense hazelnuts. And something else.

Victory.

Cheesecake #1,000 tasted like victory.

Chapter 14

As Elyse turned onto Ivy Loop, she was surprised by the number of cars parked along the curb. There was Andrew's pickup, Jackie's Prius, and Madeline's Bentley. Pulling up to the carriage house garage, she took a sharp breath. A mob waited for her on the front porch. There was Madeline and Cyril, Jackie and Donnie, Andrew and Iris, Nick and a woman with long, blond hair whom Elyse didn't know.

Elyse turned off the engine of her car, pulled out her garbage bag of belongings, and marched up the thirty-two stone steps that led to her door. Her eyes met Nick's, and neither of them said anything.

"Elyse!" Jackie ran up to her and hugged her. "We've been so worried."

"Why are you all here?" Elyse asked while Jackie continued to hold onto her.

Madeline stepped up and gave Elyse and Jackie a light, group hug. "Nick called Andrew and me, Andrew got Iris, then I told Jackie. This is just like a spy novel. We should have used Morse code. Dots and dashes."

"Why didn't you tell us what was happening?" Jackie chastised Elyse.

"It's my screw-up," she admitted.

Jackie hugged her harder. "Well, we can't have the godmother of my daughter in debtors' prison."

"You're pregnant?" Elyse was floored.

Donnie held a finger to his lips. "We're only in our first trimester, so it's a secret."

Nick laughed. "Good luck with secrets around here."

Elyse flashed him a smile. She'd keep his, forever, if necessary. But it still didn't change anything between them. Dragging him into the tabloids and the IRS fiasco would only put him at risk. He deserved better.

Madeline strutted to the front door. "Can we talk about this somewhere not so public?"

Elyse looked at the new notice of seizure stapled to the side of the door. "I'm not sure we're supposed to go in."

Iris ripped the notice down. "Everything's fine."

Madeline opened the front door. "Just like a dot and a dash, we all dashed downtown and paid off that little debt thing."

Elyse shook her head. "You can't just pay off my debt."

Madeline exhaled a long breath. "Of course we can, dear, we're rich. That's the whole point of it. It certainly isn't about chasing your gardeners around. Did you know that I have beds full of chrysanthemums? For the world, I thought they were dahlias!"

Elyse looked down, embarrassed. "I'll pay you back every penny. Somehow."

"Of course you will." Madeline marched into Elyse's house and held up her giant bucket bag. The silver cocktail shakers spilled out the top. "But in the meantime, I brought supplies."

Everyone followed Madeline into the living room and settled on the overstuffed chairs and sofa. Cyril fished out a bottle of gin, the shakers, and glasses.

"Make mine a virgin," Jackie said, grinning from ear to ear.

"I'll get the ice," Andrew offered, and left with Iris on his heels.

"Is this another intervention?" Elyse objected.

"Would you expect anything less?" Madeline quipped. "I love a good intervention. I wrote the book on it, you know. Don't you just love the feel of a book in your hand? They have weight. Not that any of us need to think about our weight. I love that about being in a solid relationship."

"Absolutely, sweetness." Cyril lined up glasses.

"But enough about us. Shall we get started, Elyse?"

Andrew and Iris returned with the ice. Cyril filled the shaker, mixed the martinis, and poured. Donnie made sure everyone had a drink.

"Can you make a toast at an intervention," Andrew asked and held up his glass.

"I don't see why not." Madeline nodded. "There aren't any hard and fast rules."

"Like not bringing a date to an intervention?" Elyse eyed the blond woman sitting next to Nick. It galled her that he'd moved on so quickly. Mere hours after he'd offered to let her live on his boat with him A twinge of jealousy shot through her.

"She isn't *with* Nick," Madeline squealed.

"My partner Tawna would kill me if I took up with the likes of Nick." The blond woman rolled her eyes.

"She's our literary agent, Victoria Barnsdale." Madeline slapped her knee.

Victoria stood and shook hands with Elyse. "Call me Vicky. I was hoping to convince your boyfriend, Nick, to donate his sperm to my partner so we could have a child together. Could you put in a good word for us?"

Oh god. Elyse's heart pounded. Nick had been telling the truth all along.

Vicky continued. "And I couldn't wait to see your book."

Elyse wasn't sure what to say, but the truth had been working pretty well lately. "I have to set the record straight. Nick and I aren't an item, and I don't have a book."

"What's that sticking out of the top of your trash bag?" Jackie leaned over, plucked *The Big Red Book of Men* out, and placed it on the coffee table.

"That isn't *a* book," Madeline howled. "That is *the* book."

"And it's private," Elyse said, sternly.

Jackie giggled. "Says the Millionaire Madame of Sausalito."

Madeline shook a finger at Elyse. "I'm afraid you don't have any secrets left, dear."

"Including why you don't like me." Nick looked at her with that twinkle of confidence in his eye.

"I don't like you because you are far too cocky," Elyse snapped back.

"And you love me."

Elyse felt her cheeks flush. She couldn't just announce that in front of everyone, could she?

Jackie opened the book. "You do love him! He's on every page."

Vicky huddled beside Jackie and flipped the pages. "This is fabulous. With the press from the Madame of Sausalito thing, I could sell this for a million bucks."

"How much?" Elyse was stunned.

"I have a better offer for you." Nick took a long sip of his martini. "We open a finishing school for men, Prince Charming, Incorporated. You recruit and teach the guys, and I might have an in at a certain restaurant where we could practice manners."

"Does the offer include cheesecake?" She winked.

"For you, Elyse, *anything,*" he replied.

Holding her drink in one hand, she rested her head on Nick's shoulder. Suddenly, her world was opening up with possibilities. She had friends. Real friends. Ones who stood by her through thick and thin.

Like family.

"Hey," Andrew called. "What about my toast?"

"Go ahead," Madeline commanded.

"Rose are red, violets are blue, you got all of us together, whoo-hoo." Andrew clinked glasses with Iris, and they kissed. Madeline and Cyril kissed. Jackie and Donnie kissed.

Nick nudged Elyse. "There seems to be a lot of kissing going on."

Elyse smiled and tilted her head up to his. Maybe, just maybe, she could have her cake and eat it, too. Their lips met, softly. The intensity built as a deep satisfaction swept through her.

"I know a lot of the story, but did Nick ever get the favor you promised him?" Vicky inquired.

Elyse pulled back. "I don't owe him a favor. He didn't sleep with Iris."

"You told me to make her happy and be sure she got plenty of sex." Nick turned to Iris. "Did you getting plenty of sex, Iris?"

"Oh yeah," Iris nodded enthusiastically as Andrew blushed.

"Fine. You want a favor?" Elyse grinned. "You can have a favor."

Nick put his arm around her. "No matter how reprehensible or vile?"

"Anything."

Nick reached into his pocket and took out a ring. "I love you, Elyse Tobin. Marry me."

Her mouth dropped open. What should she do? If she said *yes,* her life would be chaos. Every holiday would be a big production of food. Turkeys at Thanksgivings and hams at Christmas. The peace and quiet of her house would be lost forever.

Gloriously, wonderfully lost.

She and Nick would fill the rooms of her rambling four-story Queen Anne with life and love. She looked in his expectant eyes and remembered his hot breath and the things he had done to her body. She longed for his touch. His embrace. He was the whole package.

Nick dropped to one knee and held out the ring. Before her was Prince Charming in the flesh. He had all the charms.

Elyse inhaled until her lungs were full, then held it until her chest ached. All the joy and happiness bottled up inside her pounded to be released. She let it all out in one word. "Yes!"

CPSIA information can be obtained at www.ICGtesting.com
Printed in the USA
BVOW081638010812

296815BV00006B/2/P